CARRIE

A Novel By

Bette Jennings

To: Sarah

My very best wishes
to you. May you enjoy.

Bette Jennings

03-27-08

CARRIE'S FARM

Copyright © 2007 by Bette Lou Jennings

Carrie's Farm a fiction novel

Cover drawn by: Jan Cicle

Cover design by: Trinity Davis, Trinity Graphix

Misty Peak Publishing
Box AL
Filer, Idaho 83328

www.mistypeak.com

ISBN 978-0-9746794-0-2

Acknowledgments

A Big thank you goes to those who have helped me with my first novel, first my family and friends who have stood by me and believed in me. EDIT 911 who told me I should go forward with my story.

Cliff Johnson with Misty Peak Publishing in Filer, Idaho who published my book. My heartfelt thanks goes out to you for all your help and knowledge. Thank you for making my life long dream come true.

Jan Cicle of Twin Falls, Idaho for her outstanding and wonderful artwork. Thank you so much.

A special thank you to Trinity Davis, Trinity Graphix for your help with the cover design.

The encouragement from my special friend Louie, he has definitely given me the push I needed to finish my novel and move ahead to get it published.

Bette Lou Jennings
God Bless You All.

Love doesn't make the world go around; love is what makes the ride worth-while.

By: Franklin P. Jones

AUTHOR'S NOTE

Carrie's Farm is fictional, but the setting of the farm is not. I lived with my grandparents on most vacations and weekends. My home was in Albany, Oregon, with my parents until 1947; that's when my father walked out on us.

I remember my grandfather coming to pack us up and we moved to the farm, my special safe place. I hope some of the farm that I remember brings you some good reading and that you experience some of the adventures and hardships that I remember and that my characters lived.

The buildings on the farm are as I remembered them. However, the original farmhouse burned down. I returned to the farm twice while writing this novel and found that the same people who bought the farm in 1958 still own it. The big barn and milk house, as well as the sheep barn, are still there. However, the silo is gone. So are many of the trees, most of the old oaks. The same corner drug store, Taylor's, is now a museum in Independence, Oregon. My grandfather brought me ice cream sodas from Taylor's on Saturday nights.

I vaguely remember some of the things about the first farm. I remember I fell into a well. My grandfather was forced to move off the first family farm at Airlie. During World War II, the government came and moved us off our land and used it for an Army base, Camp Adair. This base was located between Corvallis and Airlie, outside of Albany. I was only 4 or 5 when this happened.

The field fire really did happen, as did the storm. There was a pond and a sheep barn. And I really did churn the butter. I took care of the baby lambs by the wood stove in the kitchen. I also rang the dinner bell.

My novel is titled after my grandmother Carrie Ellen Dunn Banta Withrow. I did have a name for my grandfather (Bepo). My memories of my grandmother and grandfather are true through Carrie's eyes.

This is my first novel. It has been fun, even though hard work at times, and rewarding for me. I have thought a great deal about the book and how to bring some things to light about my childhood. It occurred to me that, once we grow up and start getting older, we assume we know all there is about our family members. Unfortunately, I wish I knew more. I sincerely hope that my children and grand-children will go back in time with me and enjoy the story inspired by my family and childhood.

The future is always exciting and new, but the past is gone forever. Let us remember the good, happy days. Happy reading!

Bette Lou Jennings

PROLOGUE

Carrie Roundtree stepped into the barn silo and pushed her long black hair from her face. She stood still looking around the cold empty room, then turned as the door slammed shut with a bang. Carrie leaned her tall slim body up against the door and shoved with her shoulder pushing on the door, but to no avail it wouldn't budge.

As she moved away from the door and observed the empty circular darkened room, Carrie thought: What do I do now? I have to get out of here. She looked up at the whirling vents, hearing their screeching sounds. Shadows moved round and round the room. Carrie was overwhelmed with these strange feeling of lightheadedness; she slipped on the icy floor, the silo wall catching her fall. Letting her body slide down, she sat on the wet floor feeling the dampness through her gabardine slacks. Carrie sat still, shaking her head. She told herself: Come on girl, get it together.

It didn't take her long to figure out she was very much alone except for the dog on the other side of the door. No one knew where she was. She stood up and pushed again on the door thinking it had to open, but it seemed to be jammed.

Carrie heard the dog pawing on the other side of the door, whining and panting and then barking very loud. He lay down as if waiting for Carrie to appear.

"Go for help! Blackie, do you hear me? Please go for help," her voice echoed about the room as she leaned her head against the door.

A cold chill ran through her body. She sat down close to the door and pulled her wool jacket up around her to keep warm. Tears stung the corners of her eyes and then ran down her face. She was cold and her eyelids were heavy.

Carrie put her head between her knees and remembered the walk with Blackie moments earlier.

Carrie couldn't help but to think about the old weathered red barn with its tall silo standing in the middle of a hundred-year-old-oak grove. The stone milk house had been built close to the entrance of the barn. Tall oak trees hovered over the farm dirt road that led down to the old pond. Memories of her childhood came drifting into her mind as she got up and moved around the silo room trying to keep warm. A hot summer day, a young girl hanging onto a rope, swinging out over the pond, letting go and falling down towards the water below. Looking up towards the light blue sky with its fluffy clouds, she saw the ducks returning from flight as if to be coming home. Watching as the birds landed on the water with ease.

Winter was coming to an end and the farm looked so bleak and unsightly. The old leafless oak trees with their branches blowing in the breeze, the fence rows leaning with broken brush, the fields with no sign of life. She thought about the farm and the good times when everyone was busy doing the chores, feeding the cows and chickens, and time outs to ride Old Spot, the horse Bepo brought back from Canada.

The farm held such wonderful memories, like the day grandfather was shearing the sheep, a ram butted him and he fell right on his rump. Carrie heard her first swear words that day.

Grandmother was a small petite woman. Always smiling and busy like the time she would bring in the bummer lambs on a cold night. She would put them in a box beside the wood stove in the kitchen to keep warm. Sometimes the sheep would abandon their babies. Carrie always thought that was just awful as the baby lambs were so darling and cuddly.

The animals were all gone now; there was a sense of being all alone on the farm. Those thoughts of her grandmother came into her head again. She could see her in the kitchen pouring fresh cream into the butter churn then handing the handle to Carrie. It would take several hours to make the butter; the golden nuggets would appear and Carrie thought it was magic.

Childhood is a true gift from God. Carrie felt so blessed and then another chill ran through her body. She was so cold she could hardly move.

Carrie closed her eyes; she could see the old man that was so special to her. Hank Roundtree was a tall man and stood straight, with his broad shoulders, and his snow-white hair, even his big ears stuck out. Bepo was her pet name for him; she had called him that since she was very small. Her Bepo would take big long steps and a small child like Carrie had to run to catch up with him. She remembered his walks with that red-checkered hanky falling out of his bib overalls.

"Wait Bepo! Wait Bepo," she would yell stumbling behind him.

The farm, my special home, and now look at it. No one cares and it is so rundown. I wonder if I will ever see it come back to life. I feel so sleepy, why did I come here three days ago? What for? I feel so funny and so very cold, if only.

"Is someone there?" she called.

Again she thought she heard someone or maybe a dog barking, footsteps. Someone is coming to rescue me, I just know it.

"Please!"

Carrie sat very still in the cold. But who? No one knows where I am. Carrie settled down against the silo wall, pulling her knees up to her and resting her head. Waiting in the cold.

Chapter One

February 17, 1967 was a typical winter day in Oregon. The United 727 jet circled Portland's International Airport and finally landed with a jolt on runway Number 5.

The late plane taxied to the terminal. It was a long seven-hour flight for Carrie Roundtree and she wasn't happy about the bumpy landing; however she was very pleased to be on the ground.

While Carrie was waiting for the plane to come to a full stop she looked out the window and watched the snow blow over the runway. The passengers were starting to move forward to the front of the plane, and she would soon be able to reach for her bag.

Waiting, she sat thinking: here I am back in the city of Portland doing the same thing that devastated me five years ago. What she had to do today would tax her strength to the breaking point. She knew she would have to be strong. The tragic images of the past revolved in her mind until she had no choice but to remember that unbearable day five years ago.

Carrie was sitting at her desk in her Boston office when the phone rang. She heard a strange voice on the other end of the line, a person telling her the horrible news: both of her parents had been killed in a car accident. A drunk driver had rear-ended them and caused a roll over.

Carrie's parents had both been schoolteachers in Salem, Oregon. Her father was very serious about his teaching and was known as one of the toughest teachers on campus. Her mother, on the other hand, was a caring person and some-what timid, and her caring nature and beauty made her a favorite. Since Carrie was the only child, she meant the world to her parents and she was the most important person in her mother's life. Their love was very strong.

"Ladies and gentleman, you may proceed to leave the aircraft," the stewardess announced. Her thoughts inter-rupted, the announcement brought her back to the present. People were standing in the isle moving forward. She could now reach her overhead bag.

A young man pushed up behind Carrie, a guitar on one shoulder and a satchel on the other. He was wearing a floppy hat with long uncombed hair falling onto his shoul-ders. Carrie noticed the flowers around his neck and sat back in her seat to let him pass. Carrie wondered if he was one of the flower people she had heard folks talk about, a war protester. Carrie thought about the Decade of Peace, love and harmony. There were peace movements and demonstrations against the Vietnam War all over the coun-try.

Carrie got up again and walked to the front of the plane. As she walked into the terminal she noticed there were many other passengers inside as well. There must have been at least a dozen other flights delayed or canceled due to the winter storm. She was glad to have been on an early flight out of the East.

Carrie moved slowly among the passengers with her bag on her shoulder. Walking by a newsstand she read – "United States' troop strength in Vietnam now reaching 475,000." She stood looking at the headline thinking she was lucky not to have a brother in the war.

Standing in line with every one else Carrie waited for her luggage. Giving the clerk her claim ticket, she picked up her large bag and unhurriedly moved towards the car rental booth. After waiting about an hour she signed for a car and made her way to the vehicle pick-up. A young man drove up and put Carrie's luggage in the trunk of the car. He then handed her the keys and opened the driver's door for her.

"There you go, Miss. Have a good day and drive careful. The weather is acting up today," the young man pleasantly remarked.

"Thank you, I'll try," Carrie smiled at him. She took the keys and slid behind the wheel of the car. What a relief it was going to be to get away from the confusion of a busy airport, she said to herself.

As she was driving out of the airport and looking for the turn-off to go south on Highway 99, she couldn't help but think of Bepo. *"I will be with you soon, dear man,"* she thought.

Hank Roundtree was a tall man with broad shoulders, a happy man and always smiling. The community of Oak Valley loved him very much. He was there to help the needy and the homeless and if you were sick he would be the first to help with chores. Carrie remembered her grandfather as a strong and healthy man and couldn't understand why his health had failed so very fast and why hadn't she been notified of his illness. She wanted answers.

Oak Valley was known for its volcanic soil. The talk was that people from California were buying up the land to put in vineyards. The small farming community's population was around seven hundred, Oak Valley proper was a small township, with a bank, one motel, a country store, café, gas station, a home-owned flower Shoppe, and a popular beer hall with pool tables and the best hamburgers around. It also had a sheriff's office, one doctor, a veterinarian, and a hardware store where all the old timers would gather to chat. There was the church her grandfather founded and a two-story school house. The country Christian church had been built in the early 1900s by her grandfather. It sat on a knoll in an oak grove with the cemetery behind the church.

Carrie was settled in on Highway 99 and moving along with the traffic when the sleet started to turn into snow. The pavement was still dry and she knew she had only a few more miles till the turn-off to the coast highway which would lead her to the Oak Valley turnoff. She hoped she would arrive while it was still light. Making the turn off at 3:30 P.M. she slowed down considerably: only a few more miles to go. She drove over a covered bridge, reaching for her headlights as the snow was really starting to come down and it was sticking to the ground. The country road wound around the small hills and switchbacks and then as she came around a curve she could see the small valley. What a welcoming sight, Carrie felt as she took a deep breath of relief.

Carrie drove slowly down the road, made a left turn onto 3rd street, and stopped in front of Baker's Mortuary, where a wooden sign hanging on the picket fence was blowing in the wind. She pulled on her gloves and put on her wide-brimmed wool hat, pulling it down for warmth. She opened her door and made her way through the gate and to the mortuary. She opened the entrance door and was startled by the jingling of a small bell. She stepped inside, closing the door. Carrie stood for a moment waiting for someone to come out of the office.

"Carrie, it's so nice to see you. I wish it were under different circumstances," said Mr. Baker as he reached for her hand...

"Hello, Mr. Baker. I'm sorry if I'm late… the storm and all."

"I'm sure you want to see your grandfather. Come this way, Carrie, he is here in the large room." Mr. Baker led the way. The two of them entered and Carrie saw several caskets in the middle, one with the lid open, and Mr. Baker stopped and turned to Carrie.

"Will you wait here for a moment?" he asked. Carrie stood looking around the dimly lit room, watching Mr. Baker bending over her grandfather's casket, and then he turned and motioned her forward.

"Would you like me to stay with you, Carrie?" he asked.

"No. I need to see my grandfather alone, thank you." Mr. Baker left the room, waiting just outside the door. Carrie moved slowly toward her grandfather and looked into the casket. Here lay her beloved Bepo. "Oh Bepo, I'M so very sorry I wasn't here for you. I didn't know you were so ill and I can't understand why you didn't call me. You always told me you were well and things were going so well at the farm. Why?" The tears ran down her cheeks and she wiped them with her gloved hand. She felt odd and she started to tremble: her legs were weak. She brought her hand to her lips and kissed it and then touched it to her grandfather's lips. "I love you so much Bepo and I am so alone now. What do I do? And how can I do it without you? Goodbye my, dear one."

She stood there looking at this kind man, the last time she would ever see him, took a deep breath and turned and walked out of the room. Mr. Baker took her hand and helped her into his office and motioned for her to take a seat. He then gave her some water and sat down behind his desk.

Carrie sat for a moment and then thanked him. "I feel better now. This is such a shock to me, I didn't know my grandfather was so ill," she said, taking a sip of water.

"What do we do now, Mr. Baker?" she asked

"Your grandfather took care of everything way before he passed on. However, he did ask me to ask you if you would pick out the flowers. He knew you would like to do that."

"Well, yes I will."

"The church ladies will be fixing a lunch after the service, and Hank requested that no one go to the grave but you, my dear. That was one of his wishes. He wanted to be put next to your grandmother."

"I see," Said Carrie calmly.

"You know, your grandfather knew how sick he was. He also knew you would be upset with him for not telling you. He told me he couldn't bear seeing you hurt. After all, it was not long ago since your parents... well, you know what I mean. He wanted to save you the hurt, my dear," Mr. Baker said sympathetically.

"Yes that does sound like my Bepo; he was a special kind-hearted man, always thinking of others first. What time is the service, Mr. Baker?"

"It's at two tomorrow afternoon."

"Will you sit with me? I'm rather alone now."

"Why yes, my dear. My wife and I will be happy to."

"I guess I better go now." Carrie said.

"I'll see you at the church tomorrow, my dear." Mr. Baker got up out of his chair and walked towards the door. They shook hands and Mr. Baker opened the door and Carrie stepped out into the heavy falling snow and made her way to her car.

Fumbling for the car keys she opened the door, sat down behind the wheel of the car, and asked "Why? Why," while resting her head on the steering wheel.

Snow had built up on the windshield, and she sat till the wipers cleared off the snow before she drove back to Main Street, pulled into the motel's parking lot, and parked the car. Carrie, looking in the rear view mirror, she could see that her makeup was spoiled from the tears. Wiping her face the best she could she pushed the door open and made her way to the motel office.

Carrie stepped inside to find an older man sitting behind the desk reading; he looked up as she entered.

"Yes, may I help you?"

"I need a room for one night," Carrie said as she removed her gloves, laying them on the counter.

"I sure don't have a problem with that here in this town, and on a night like this. I have a room right by the office and it's nice and warm." He handed Carrie the key with a number on it as she paid him.

"Let me get your bags for you, while you sign the register."

Carrie signed the register and turned and followed the man to the car. She handed him the keys and waited for him to remove her bags. She then opened the door to the room and waited for the man to set her bags down.

"Thank you that will do.," she said as he turned to leave.

"Now if there is anything you need please feel free to come to the office. We may be a little farm town, but we are friendly and take care of our guests," he stated as he left.

Carrie stood for a moment looking around the room, small but nice and warm. The gas heater was going full blast. The room was dark, so she reached for the lamp on the table and then opened up the blind on the window. Taking her coat off she reached for the lock on the door. She had better unpack and hang up her dress for the service tomorrow. Carrie unpacked then sat on the bed thinking.

The farm…what in the world will I do with it? Tomorrow I'll go there and stay and meet with Bepo's lawyer and maybe he can give me some advice.

Carrie looked at her watch. If she called Mrs. Foster, maybe she would be able to fix the flowers for the service. She reached for the phone book which sat next to a Gideon Bible on the desk. She ran her fingers over the leather cover and smiled.

The phone rang several times before a soft women's voice answered.

"Hello,"

"Is this Mrs. Foster in Home Flower Shoppe?"

"Yes," replied the voice.

"Mrs. Foster, this is Carrie Roundtree. Do you remember me?"

"Why of course I do, Carrie. I'm so very sorry about your grandfather Hank, such a loss for you and all of Oak Valley. He was so loved by all and a friend to everyone," Mrs. Foster paused and cleared her throat.

"How can I help you, my dear?" Mrs. Foster asked sadly.

"I think I would like white roses if you can get them? For the casket you know."

"No problem I have a late shipment coming in, so many flowers have been ordered for the service. Now don't you worry. I will fix them personally and you can stop by anytime, Carrie."

"I will be by day after tomorrow to pay for them. I will be staying at the farm after today. I have so many things to think about." Carrie thanked Mrs. Foster and said goodbye and hung up the phone.

Thinking about food, she was all of a sudden very hungry. She hadn't eaten much but a snack on the plane. She looked out the window and could see the café with its neon lights blinking. Well, that will have to do she thought. Pulling down the blind and then slipping on her coat, she reached for her purse and opened the door onto a wet snow-covered sidewalk.

As she walked the short distance to the café, she noticed how bright the snow made everything look even as darkness was setting in. The fir trees rustled in the blowing wind; there was the sound of a car, its tires crunching on the road. She turned and noticed that it had also pulled into the entrance of the motel. It was a very expensive car, a BMW, she couldn't help but notice. She kept walking, reaching the café door, stomped her feet to remove the wet snow and entered. She took a seat at the counter, removing her gloves and then reached for a menu.

"Hello, can I help you?" Ida the waitress said.

"Yes, I guess I will have the roast beef dinner please," Carrie said, rubbing her hands together trying to warm up from the cold.

"Hey," aren't you Carrie Roundtree?" Ida asked with a smile.

"Yes," I am, do I know you?" Carrie looked at her with a surprised look on her face.

"I'm Ida Hansen. We went to school together. Remember?"

Carrie studied her face a moment and then said; "Yes, I guess we did. How are you, Ida?"

"I'm still in this one-horse town. Hey, I'm so sorry about your grandfather. Hank was one of my best customers. He always came in here for breakfast on Sunday mornings before church. He liked to read the paper, sat over there in that booth by the window."

The door of the café opened and a tall man entered and took a seat in the booth her grandfather always sat in.

Carrie looked into the mirror in front of her and could see the man. He was wearing a dark wool coat with a bright red turtle neck sweater underneath. She watched as Ida gave him a menu and a glass of water.

Ida went on about her work and then brought Carrie her dinner.

"Carrie," she said "Tell me where you have been all these years?" Ida asked.

"I left after college and moved east. I work for a newspaper in Boston." Carrie couldn't help observe the man in the booth. He was staring at her. She wondered if he was the man who drove up in the BMW. He got up as if to come over to her, but stopped and picked up a newspaper instead.

"Boston! Wow, Carrie, you must be doing real well for yourself. Who would have thought Carrie Roundtree would ever leave the farm." Ida said, placing the man's order down in front of him, then returning behind the counter still talking.

"I know. I have missed the farm and now I wished I would have returned more often," she said, looking down at her empty plate and placing her napkin on the counter.

"Thank you, Ida. I hope to see you again before I leave Oak Valley," Carrie said as she stood up to leave.

"Me too," Ida called out as Carrie opened the door and stepped out into the winter weather.

Brad sat still, watching this slim young woman move towards the door. He had heard her name, and he wanted to say something, but he couldn't bring himself to do so. He looked out the fogged-up window and could see Carrie tugging at her coat, bringing it up close to her for warmth, as she huddled herself against the wind.

As Carrie moved along the street, she listened to see if anyone was walking behind her. Looking up at the sky she could see nothing but big snow flakes falling. *What weather for Bepo's service. It couldn't be worse,* she thought.

She hurried to reach the motel door, searching through her purse for the room key. Carrie pushed the door open and closed it and turned the lock. The blinds closed tightly, a good hot shower and then to try to get some sleep was what she wanted. As she stepped into the shower, she felt the warm water running down her stressed body. She took the bar soap in her hands and gently made a lather. She rubbed the soap over her body and then let the water rinse it away. She just stood in the shower taking it all in. Carrie stepped out of the shower; toweling off, she walked over to the bed. She put on her nightclothes and then laid out her clothes for the service. Her mother's pearls, the black dress and then a sweater, her felt hat and wool coat would have to do. As cold as it was she needed to keep warm.

Sitting on the bed brushing her hair she was thinking about the day ahead — the service for Bepo and then her trip to the farm. What would she find? A T.V. sat on a table near the window. Carrie reached over and turned it on. *Gun Smoke* was on.

Funny, she thought. It was Bepo's favorite program, he loved Miss Kitty. Carrie smiled, then turned the T.V. off. She set the alarm clock and pulled back the blankets and crawled into the bed, pulling the blankets up close to her and then reached for the light. The room was very dark. Suddenly she heard a door shut. *Must be the man in the BMW,* she thought. *I have to go see Mr. Temple in the morning before the service, he always took care of things for the family, oh please, God, help me make it through another nightmare so I can leave this place behind me and go home.* Carrie drifted off into a sound sleep.

As Carrie lay in bed half asleep, she curled up in the covers. For a moment she thought she was in Boston, and then, thinking a train whistle blew, she woke up startled and realized it was the alarm clock and she was still in Oak Valley. She looked at the clock. It was nine thirty and she knew she had to call Jo. She had promised. She lay under the covers reaching for the phone and dialed the number.

"Hello, Jo Hamilton's desk," a woman's voice answered.

"Hi Jo, it's me, Carrie."

"Well girlfriend, I was beginning to worry about you. How are you doing honey?"

"I'm here in Oak Valley. There was a snow storm and still is, I guess. I haven't looked out yet; I'm still in bed being lazy. My plane was late and then I had to rent a car and drive through the messy weather. I got in here about three thirty."

"Have you seen him yet?" Jo asked with a break in her voice.

"Yes, Jo. It wasn't easy, but he looked so peaceful just like he was sleeping." Carrie thought about Bepo in the casket.

"I knew I should have come out there with you. I hate you being alone and all," Jo said.

"I'll be all right as soon as this day is over. So how is work? Am I missed?"

"Oh yeah, Alex misses you, complains about doing your work and keeps asking now how long is she going to be out West," Jo said with a chuckle.

"I guess I should talk to him, but Jo, I just don't feel up to it right now, so tell him I will call him tomorrow okay?" Carrie got out of bed and started to walk around the room.

"That's up to you, kiddo. I will stall him as much as possible. Really, all is well here. It has slowed down a little," Jo remarked.

"I am going to the farm today after the service, but first I'm to see the family lawyer."

"Good, maybe he'll have some good news, Carrie."

"I'll call in a few days, Jo; if you want to reach me you know the number at the farm okay?"

"Sure enough, honey. Take care now, I wish I was with you, know that. "I really am okay, so "bye for now," said Jo as she hung up the phone and sat back in her chair choking the tears back.

Carrie knew how fortunate she was to have a friend like Jo. They had attended college together. Jo was the sister Carrie never had. Alex, well he was a sort of boyfriend, dinner now and then and a movie or play but not the man she would want to be the father of her children. Something about Alex worried her. There was definitely something missing in their relationship. Carrie knew she had to do a lot of thinking about Alex and their friendship at this time. It was going no where.

Carrie got dressed and stood in front of the mirror thinking. *I hate black.* She ran her fingers over her mother's pearls that hung around her neck and fell onto the black dress with its pleated skirt. The pearls, with their beauty, were to be admired.

Carrie pinned her hair up and placed the felt hat gently on her head, put on her coat looked around the room to make sure hadn't left anything behind, picked up her bag and opened the door.

As she drove down the road, she noticed that the snow had stopped falling and it felt warmer. The snow was melting and the road was covered with slush. Carrie drove to Mr. Temple's office which was in his home; she parked and made her way to the door. She remembered Mr. Temple to be a small man, sort of frail. She rang the bell.

Mr. Temple opened the door, not surprised to see Carrie.

"Miss Roundtree, my, my, it has been a while."

"Yes it has, Mr. Temple; I thought I should come see you since you are the family lawyer" Carrie said as she moved into the room.

"Please come on into my office, Carrie. We can talk better in here," he said.

"Thank you." Carrie followed Mr. Temple to a room at the back of the house; he motioned for her to take a seat.

"Now let's see what I have here for you." The elderly man picked up a large envelope.

Carrie sat quiet, waiting for the lawyer to say something about the will.

"You see my dear I have your grandfather's will here, but first I must tell you how sorry I am about Hank, he was one of my best friends." Mr. Temple took out a handkerchief and wiped his eyes.

"I have a copy of my grandfather's will unless he made recent changes," Carrie stated.

"Oh no, no changes were made, my dear; you will need to go by the bank and sign some papers on the accounts, the deed to the farm, well it's all in here for you" he said.

"I am so confused, Mr. Temple. About the farm? What do I do with it?" Carrie said reaching for the envelope, her hand shaking.

"I understand that you know that your grandfather and I talked about the farm. He wanted you or was hoping you might stay and run the farm since it has been in the family for so many years, and then again he knew in his heart that you have a new life back East."

"I know the farm should stay in the family, but how can I do that?"

"Well, dear, I think you just need some time to think this all over and I'm sure you will do your best in regards to the property and we can talk about this again." Mr. Temple stood up. "You go over the will and the papers, and if you have any questions please come back and see me I will help in whatever capacity I can." Mr. Temple was having a hard time talking about the Roundtree Estate and Carrie felt this. She knew then that Mr. Temple was grieving her grandfather also.

Carrie left Mr. Temple's office and decided to drive around the best she could under the conditions of the roads. She wanted to look at the small village, the old school she had attended. She drove looking at the rundown weathered buildings, some falling apart, some rather new. She found herself parked in front of the Country Christian Church. Carrie sat in the car. Looking out the window she noticed some children playing in the snow, building a snowman.

Then she saw the florist's van pull up in front of the church, saw flowers being removed and taken inside, and saw several cars parked next to the community hall-- ladies with boxes of food. Carrie thought to herself. *This is it the day I never wanted to come true. Wasn't one five years ago enough? Now again; only it's my Bepo this time.* Carrie's flashbacks came and went, in the same place only on a spring day and five years earlier, and two loved ones to say farewell to. She shook her head to come back to now, this day.

People started to arrive and then she saw him, the man with the BMW. He drove up, parked across the street, got out, then walked up the church steps and went inside. She wondered why. Who was he? And how did he know her grandfather?

Mr. and Mrs. Baker drove up and Carrie got out of the car and met them at the front steps. Mr. Baker reached out and gave Carrie a hug, then Mrs. Baker took Carrie by the hand and they walked to the front of the church and sat in the first Pew.

People filled the church and some were standing along the walls, flowers and plants covered the altar, the white roses spread over the casket with a ribbon, letters spelling out "Grandfather."

Carrie sat looking about and listening to the soft music she knew the words ("He walks with me and He talks with me"). *What am I doing here? I would rather be on a warm beach, on vacation, but no I'm here to say goodbye to my loved one, and* *all these people I don't even remember most of them. I know they loved Bepo, and they will miss him, but so will I, oh hurry and say what you have to say I want to run, just to leave, but I know I can't do that, I have to be here for him, they say funerals are for the ones left behind, but I do not want this, oh please hurry...*Carrie closed her eyes. Then a hand was on her shoulder and she looked up.

"Miss Roundtree, will you follow me please." Carrie stood up and looked towards the entrance of the church. All the people had left and she was alone with the Bakers; she took his arm and let him lead her out of the church. People were standing around. It seemed as if they were all watching her. The man helped her to the community hall, and Carrie and the Bakers sat together at a round table. Food was served and Carrie must have seen several hundred people offering their condolences. It soon was a blur to her: everyone looked alike. Finally they started to leave and the room was empty.

"Would you like me to go with you to the grave site?" asked Mr. Baker

"No. I need to do this alone." Carrie stated.

Carrie thanked Mr. and Mrs. Baker and then walked to her car. She drove up the knoll and stopped where the workers were just finishing up. She got out of the car and made her way to the grave. There was a stand of oak and you could see the family plots. Carrie first went to her parents' graves, bent down, and shoveled the snow off with her hand. Then she stood up and said, "Hello Mom and Daddy, I'm here to bring you grandfather. I know he will be here with you and grandmother. I just don't know what to say, WHY..."

The tears started to run down Carrie's face and she bent over, picked up some frozen sand and dropped it on Bepo's casket and said, "Goodbye, my dear one." She turned and walked as fast as she could to the car, got in and started to cry. She thought *at least no one can see me, I must move on to the farm and leave this day behind me.* Carrie turned the key and started the car, followed the sanded trail to the street and drove to Oak Valley Road.

Brad stood by a large oak so Carrie wouldn't see him. He was thinking how beautiful she was. *I should go to her and tell her who I am, she is so alone, she needs someone to hold her and comfort her. Where is her family and why is she by herself? I'm such a fool, she is so lovely. This has to be so very hard for her, it's not fair. But I can't tell her just yet. Someday I will. I hope you can forgive me, Carrie Roundtree. The day will come soon.*

Brad waited until Carrie was out of sight, then he walked out from behind the tree and made his way to the grave site. While he stood in front of Hank Roundtree's grave, he saw three other headstones, thinking this is a family plot. He stood in shock as he read the headstone— "Carol Ellen Roundtree," it read, "June 2, 1918, to May 21, 1962." *How can this be, it must not be true, but it is, here is the proof.* Brad bent down to his knees, took his gloved hand and touched the headstone.

Chapter Two

The well-traveled country road was covered with snow and ice. Carrie was trying to keep the car under control following the rutted path of slush. The snow had let up some and she could see better. The day had been so unbearable, the cold and all and she was ready to put it all behind her, at least most of the day was behind her and how hard could it be from now on? The farm, her real home from the past, lay in front of her. Carrie took a deep breath, trying to relax, but not yet, just another mile maybe. Five years hadn't changed the valley too much, but the snow covered fields and fence rows made things look out of place.

Maybe she should have had Jo come with her, but then again she really needed her at work. She kept on driving, holding the steering wheel with both hands, concentrating on the road.

Carrie was trying to stay alert: she hated this driving and darkness was starting to set in. *Where is that darn turn and the big oak?* This thought kept running through her head.

Looking in the review mirror she could see lights moving up behind her rather fast. The vehicle seemed to be right on her bumper. *Why don't you pass?* Carrie thought to herself. Carrie slowed down to a crawl, grasping the wheel. Then the truck passed her, the slush from its wheels splashing over her windshield, the wipers barely clearing it off.

"Thank goodness," Carrie said out loud.

Passing over a small bridge she could see the frozen water. A covey of quail was startled as they rushed over the ice. The fields all white, the fence posts with their white caps on. A Christmas card look for sure. Carrie thought.

She kept looking for the big oak and the sign Bepo nailed up, saying the "Roundtree Farm." Then, all of a sudden, the big oak was right in front of her. She stopped and noticed the lane was pretty much covered with snow. Perhaps a car had been over the lane the day before as some ruts were noticeable under the snow.

Carrie made the turn, her tires spinning on the icy slush, but she was able to steer the car down the middle of the lane. She looked ahead to see the farmhouse, straining her neck to look though the foggy windshield. It looked eerie, the house in among the large oak trees and the darkness settling in. The house seemed black and even a little ghostly. Carrie shuddered at the thought. *Don't be so silly, girl, it's home, remember.*

Driving around the circular driveway, she stopped in front of the house. She took a deep breath, rested her head on the steering wheel, closed her eyes and said a little prayer.

Carrie had remembered the house being two stories. The discolored stone sidewalk was covered with snow and ice. She could see footprints: someone had been here recently. *I wonder who was here.* Carrie thought. As she walked closer to the house she could hear the crunching under her feet from the snow. She observed the old house with its tall chimney and the loose shutters around the windows. The house was very run down and weathered.

Carrie stood on the stone porch, setting her bag down and reaching into her purse to find the key that her grandfather had given her so many years ago. As she opened the door, a musty smell hit her in the face; along with a fireplace smell as if wood had been burning recently, and a feeling of incredible cold. She moved into the house, closed the door, and reached for a light on the desk. All the blinds were pulled down so she moved quickly to open them so that at least some light would filter into the living room. Carrie picked up her bag and took it to the rear of the house and opened the bedroom door where Bepo had slept, put her bag on the bed, and then removed her gloves, coat and hat.

Hank Roundtree had helped his father build the old farm house in the early 1900s and Hank had grown up on the farm as did Carrie's father. The two-story house had two bedrooms with a large closet between them on the upper floor. As you came into the house you walked into the living room. On the first floor were one bedroom, a bath, a dining room, and a kitchen. Adjoining the kitchen was a large back porch covered to keep wood for the fireplace and wood burner which sat next to the old electric range and a makeshift pantry with a very large tub. At the far end of the dining room was a steep stairway leading to the second floor.

Moving around the house, Carrie entered the living room and saw the wood box by the fireplace. It was full of dry oak wood and a small pile of kindling beside it. Someone had gotten a fire ready for her. Carrie reached up inside the fireplace and opened the damper. Reaching to the mantel she found the matches and lit the paper; she could feel the warmth almost at once and the smell of the oak was comforting. She placed the fireplace screen in front of the fire and then stood taking in the room. The old lumpy sofa and the piano were still there. She walked up to the piano and ran her fingers over the keys. It was still out of tune. Everything was the same as she remembered it, nothing; nothing at all had been done to the house. Even Bepo's chair and his pillow still sat in front of the fire.

Carrie wandered into the dining room. The buffet still had her grandmother's bowl and picture on it and under it sat a handcrafted linen runner, one that she no doubt had made.

In the kitchen the wood burner stood out in its ugliness, but it would keep the kitchen warm on winter mornings. She saw the bright yellow flowers on the curtain under the kitchen sink, with a drawstring holding the curtain in place. At the far end of the room was a chrome table and chairs. The same salt and pepper shakers sat on the table under the window as if they had never been moved. Carrie ran her fingers over the soiled tablecloth and realized the chrome chairs had the same gray plastic on them. Nothing had changed: it was as if she had never been away.

Walking back into the living room she could see that the fire was burning nicely. She stood in front of it for a moment and then went into the bedroom, got her purse and brought it back to the desk, took the large envelope out of it, and sat it down. I'll look at it later, she thought. She picked up the phone to see if it worked.

Carrie was startled when she heard a shutter bang against the side of the house. When the wind had picked up, she bent over and looked out the window; the limbs on the trees were blowing and several had broken off and lay on the ground. Carrie reached for the door and turned the lock.

In the bedroom, changing into a house dress, she noticed that Bepo had put in a new bathroom and a small shower stall. As she unpacked she felt the quiet around her, the stillness, and then a shutter pounding on the side of the house, perhaps a little frightening for a city girl, but she was not afraid since she knew the house was locked up.

A small chest of drawers sat near the bed. Carrie opened the top drawer and saw a small box. All of Bepo's clothes were gone, so Mr. Temple must have had someone come in. That explained the foot prints. Carrie opened the box and found some rings, her Grandmother's and Bepo's wedding rings and a wrist watch and a gold pocket watch with a bob on it. Carrie slipped her grandmother's ring on her right hand, replaced the box, and unpacked her things.

Back in the kitchen, Carrie opened the ice-box; it was well stocked with milk and eggs, even bacon. Someone did a good job replenishing the kitchen. Carrie turned on the kitchen lights and made herself a sandwich and poured a glass of milk. Then she made her way back to the living room and sat down on the lumpy sofa listening to the fire. It made sounds as if talking to her — *crake, pop, crake* a spark or two hitting the fire screen.

Sitting and thinking, *I'm really here at the farm the day is about behind me.* She looked at her watch it was six thirty. She pulled the quilt from the back of the sofa and tucked it around herself and leaned back watching the fire, looking at the empty chair where he used to sit. It must have been very lonely for Bepo after grandmother passed away, she thought

Memories came to Carrie as she rested – popping corn over the fire, Grandmother would say, "Carrie be careful now, that handle gets very hot, now shake it fast." Carrie thought about the times Grandmother would make her sleep upstairs and then would shut the stairway door, but then Carrie would sneak down the stairs and wait till Bepo and she were in bed, and then wake them up and beg to sleep on the lumpy sofa: it always worked.

A shutter banged up against the house again." Need to get that fixed." She said out loud. Carrie pulled the quilt up closer and settled down in the sofa, watching the fire and drifting off into a sound sleep.

Mary stood at her kitchen window to see if any lights had come on at Hank's. She was told that Miss Carrie would be arriving to take care of the farm business. *I wonder, will she keep the farm? What would a young city woman do with a run-down place such as it is?* She reached and pushed back her long stringy gray hair from her face and strained her eyes to see if any light came from across the field. Then she saw it come on, the light was there. "Blackie, now you can go home," She said reaching for the large black lab standing by her.

Mary hurried to the closet and reached for her coat, her red hat, mittens and boots, and went out the door, calling her two hounds. Blackie raced ahead, the hounds at his heels. Mary shuffled along in the snow. It was just a short walk across the field; she and Hank had worn a path so it was easy to follow. The wind was at her back and as she came close to the farm house her hat went blowing in the wind. Blackie retrieved it for her. Mary was always astounded at this dog of Hanks—he was half human for sure.

Blackie raced to the front of the house. Mary could see the smoke from the fireplace and smell the oak burning. It was so good to see life in the old house. The dog pawed at the door. Mary made it to the porch and knocked on the door. No one came and Blackie was really barking and wanting in. *Poor dog, he thinks Hank is at home, she* thought. Mary reached down and petted the dog." It's going to be just fine, boy. You have a new master now; here move aside." Mary knocked louder this time.

Carrie woke up with a start, hearing the dog and the banging on the front door. Pushing the quilt aside she got up and made her way to the door. Carrie moved the blind aside and saw this figure with a floppy hat bright red. It looked like a woman all bundled up from the cold. Carrie opened the door and the dog raced around her, almost knocking her over, and disappeared into the house.

"May I help you? Carrie asked. "You best come in and get your dog."

Mary pushed the door open and stepped into the house, taking off her coat and throwing it on the floor.

"May I ask who you are?

"Yes My name is Mary." I'm your neighbor, you know, over there, pointing towards the kitchen. I've brought your grandfather's dog home. He has gone wild looking for Hank; he has missed him so very much." "You mean this was my grandfather's dog?" Carrie asked, pushing Blackie away from her.

Mary walked in front of Carrie and headed for the kitchen. She pulled the coffee pot out of the cupboard and made coffee. Then she stood on her tip toes to get two coffee cups, and set them on the table.

"There, you see it's better now. We can have a cup of coffee and talk over things." Carrie stood dumbfounded thinking. *Wow, what a friend! What did my Bepo do to have a lady friend like this? Some neighbor!* She thought to herself.

Carrie sat down at the table and let Mary proceed with the conversation because she didn't know what to think of this person. Blackie kept licking Carrie's hand, and she kept pushing him away.

"No need to do that, missy, I think he knows who you are. Animals sense things, you know. Why my two hounds, they always told me when Hank was near, even before I could see him in the field making his way to the house."

"How well did you know my grandfather, Mary?"

"My, that coffee sure smells good; here let me get you some, Missy." Mary poured the coffee and then sat down across from Carrie.

"Well, I guess I better tell you about myself, huh? I live on the next farm over. I've known your grandfather, Hank that is, for several years. My husband, George, and I bought the Walker place, they moved on, but then my George he passed away about three years ago, and your Hank was such a nice neighbor. He helped me a lot with my chores and such, and we became good friends. You know I cooked for him at times and watched over him too." Mary took a sip of her coffee.

"And the dog, Mary?"

"You see that was your grandfather's best friend. He loved this here dog so much, why he even let him sleep on the bed. He made me promise to take care of him till you arrived, then I was to take him home here. I saw Hank every day till, well."

"Mary, I didn't see you at the service."

"No, I just couldn't go. I said my farewell the day before he..."

Mary eyes started to fill up with tears. And she wiped them away with her hand.

"I'm sorry, Mary, I can see you were very close, and I'm happy to know that Bepo had a good friend."

"Bepo, he said you called him that since you were so little."

"Yes I did. I am going to miss him ever so much." Blackie put his paw on Carrie's lap," What do I do with you, dog?" Carrie asked, petting his head.

"You can keep him."

"Oh no, what can I do with a dog, Mary? I live in a city."

"Well, I tell you what, keep him here for tonight and then we can try to find him a home, but I will warn you he will want to stay and you will want to keep him." Mary smiled.

They finished their coffee and visited, talking about the farm and Carrie's Grandfather; he had been sick for a long time. Cancer was not a kind illness, but Mary was there for him every day and took Blackie to see him every time she could. The neighbors had planted the last crops for Hank and did the harvest. Mary told Carrie how much Hank wanted her to keep the farm. It was a dream of his to keep it in the family.

"Well I best be getting home now, before it gets any colder out," Mary said, reaching for her coat and then her boots.

"Thank you for coming tonight, Mary. I was a little bewildered being here alone, and now, with Blackie here, I'm not. I hope we can get along okay." Carrie reached down and gave the dog a pat.

"Okay, you will be fine, and you, dog, be good to this young lady if you want to stay here?" Mary said as she went out into the night just as she had come, her two hounds walking at her side. Carrie stood there watching the woman walking in the ankle deep wet snow. She stepped inside and closed the door. She looked down at this dog named Blackie. He sat looking up at her, his tail wagging and dusting the floor, and he whined as to say now what do we do?

"So you were Bepo's friend, Blackie," Carrie bent down on one knee, bringing the dog's head towards her and

petting him. "I bet you're hungry. Shall we go find something for you to eat?

The two of them made their way to the kitchen, Blackie
went right to the back door, pawed on it, and waited for
Carrie to open it. The dog made his way to an old green
painted cabinet, pawed at the door, and dragged out a bag
of dog food. He made his way to the kitchen with it where,
by the wood stove, sat two empty dishes. Carrie just stood
watching this amazing dog. Carrie filled his dish and then
filled the other one with water. She then made her way back
to the living room. She sat in Bepo's chair, taking the pillow
and holding it close to her, then bringing it up to her face to
see if she could smell her grandfather's scent. Yes it was
there. Carrie could feel her eyes fill, the tears came rushing
through. Blackie could sense this and came and sat next to
the chair, putting his head in her lap and looking at her with
his big black eyes.

"Well dog, it's just you and me for tonight. You must
have been so dear to Bepo, and I am so happy he had you to
be with him. You must miss him too." She sat petting the
dog.

"Maybe I better call Mary and make sure she didn't fall
or something." Carrie got up moved towards the desk
looking for a phone list. She found Mary's number right by
the phone pad.

"Yes, who is it?"

It's me, Mary, Carrie. We were just checking in on you, making sure you're safe at home and out of the weather."

"Oh, my missy, I'm just fine, thank you for calling." The line went dead.

"Strange woman, Blackie, but I'm sure I will get to know her better." Carrie shook her head.

The phone rang and Jo turned on a light and reached for it. She thought it might be Carrie, but not this late.

"Hello" Jo said.

"Jo, Oh, I'm so sorry. I forgot about the time change."

"That's okay, honey, I've been waiting for your call. So tell me, how did the day go?

"Well, I'm here now at the farm, and I have a new friend."

"Really? You had time to make friends already?"

"My Grandfather had this black lab, and a strange woman who is a neighbor brought him to me and said here, take him he is yours."

"Wow, what a neighbor," Jo remarked.

"Yes she is something. She wasn't at the service."

"How did that go, Carrie?" Jo asked.

"It was very nice, over 200 people." Carrie went on and told Jo everything that had happened, even about the man and his BMW and how weird he acted and that she sure wished she knew who he was. The two friends must have talked for an hour. Blackie lay at Carrie's feet sleeping.

Hanging up the phone Carrie said, looking at her watch, "I think it must be bedtime and I bet you must go out and do your thing." She walked to the door and called Blackie. She opened the door and the dog went out, running in the snow. Carrie closed the door and lifted the blind until she saw the dog do his business and then let him back in.

The wind was still doing its thing and the shutters now and then would hit the house. Carrie turned off the lights and put more logs on the fire and made her way to the bedroom, the dog on her heels, Carrie put on her night clothes and as she turned the dog leaped onto the bed. "Oh, no you don't, Blackie, not on the bed while I'm in it." She made him get down. The dog lay on the rug at the foot of the bed staring at Carrie.

Because the night was so cold, Carrie put an extra blanket on the bed, pulled the covers back, climbed into the welcome comfort, and turned the lamp off. She settled in and listened to the trees blowing in the wind. The house was dark, but she could hear the dog that lay at the foot of the bed. The day had been very stressful and coming to an end a new day to think about and she was ready. She felt something warm by her back. She felt the dog against her and gave in to sleep.

Carrie woke with Blackie's eyes looking into hers; she was startled at first, then smiled at him, and asked, "Do you want to go out?" The dog jumped out of the bed and ran to the front of the house. Carrie slipped into her robe and followed him to the door.

Returning to the bedroom, Carrie turned the water on in the shower, and then she stocked up the fireplace. The house was rather cool; the weather had let up some, she saw as she looked out the bedroom window. Removing her clothes she stepped into the warm shower. The warmth of the water felt so relaxing as it ran down her back and over the front of her body. A tranquil feeling came over her: some of the sadness was gone and today was a new day. She wanted to look about the farm, as well as the house, and she thought the daylight would make a difference. After getting dressed, she made her way to the kitchen, put on some coffee, and then heard a pounding at the front door. She moved quickly and opened the door, and there stood Mary with a pan in her hand.

"Good morning, missy, I made some hot buns for you. I hope you have the coffee on?"

"Why, yes I do, Mary. Won't you come in?" The two women sat at the table with coffee and buns, talking about the snowstorm and Mary told her of some trees down. They talked about the dog. Carrie didn't tell her that Blackie got his way and slept on the bed. The sadness of Hank's not being at the farm was hard on both of them Mary told several stories about her and Hank. Mary kept asking Carrie if she were going to stay and work the farm. Carrie told Mary she was going to see Mr. Temple again and see what she might do, but she felt her place was back East.

Mary seemed disappointed at this and kept trying to change Carrie's mind. After all, Hank wanted her to stay here in Oak Valley. Time would tell if Blackie would win her over; that might change things. And then she left as she arrived, in a hurry. The smell of Mary's cinnamon buns lingered in the kitchen and Carrie was grateful to have met this strange person who was so kind and a new friend.

Returning to the living room Carrie stood in front of the desk. *Well this is as good a time as any. I might as well look this over.* She picked up the envelope and sat in Bepo's chair; she took a deep breath and opened it. There were several papers—the deed to the farm, a bank book, some old pictures of the house, and a sealed letter. The front said, "For Carrie."

Carrie opened the letter. It read:

"Dear Carrie,

I wanted to leave you this letter: maybe I can explain to you and help you to understand why I didn't let you know how ill I was. When I found out I had cancer the Doctors told me it would be a slow death and waiting as you know is not one of my best virtues, anyway I just didn't have the heart to tell you, you had been through so very much and I was very ill. The loss was so great for all of us when your parents were killed I just couldn't do that to you again. I hope you will forgive me. Mr. Temple has taken care of everything you should not have to be concerned about anything. The farm hasn't been worked very much but it did produce an income."

Carrie rubbed her eyes, trying to read through the tears. She read on.

"I know this old house is run down but that can be fixed. But the land, it's good Carrie and if you take care of it, it will be good to you and you can reap the harvest. If you don't want the farm, I've been told that there are people coming in from California who are buying our land here in the valley to put in vineyards. This may be an out for you. Mr. Temple knows of several large corporations who have an interest in the land. I do hope you will give some thought about the farm you know I've always said, you would have it someday and run it. Now I have a friend his name is Jake Thompson, he has his own vineyard and he knows the business well, I think you might like him Carrie, he is a good man and you can trust him. If you have any questions please give him a call.

I also have another good friend her name is Mary, I know you will fall in love with her, she is kind and caring. Some think she is touched in the head some but not really she is special, believe me she will be there for you whenever she can. Oh, one more thing my dear now I have the best of friends and his name is Blackie, I love that dog and he is very smart, he never left my side except when I was getting worse, anyway I want you to have him, he will give you so much love and will look after you, he knows your name I told him all about you.'"

Carrie dropped the letter and took a deep breath. She picked it up and read on.

"I want you to know how much you meant to me child, I will miss you I'm sorry to leave you Carrie but I know you will do fine in what ever you decide to do. I will be watching over you from above.... You're Bepo

"You wonderful man, I will miss you so." Carrie took the letter and held it to her breast and just sat still.

The barking of the dog interrupted her thoughts. She got up and looked out the door window; Blackie was playing in the snow romping about.

Carrie put on a sweater and then her wool coat, her high top shoes, and grabbed for her hat and out the door she went. She whistled for Blackie and he came around the corner of the house. "Hey dog, you want to go exploring with me." The dog was jumping all over and ran ahead of Carrie towards the garage.

Carrie picked up a stick and threw it for Blackie. He brought it right back. She walked to the garage door and pulled on the latch. The door opened with a bang. "The spring must be broken Blackie." She said as she entered the garage. "What a mess, Blackie, look at this place," she said, looking over the inside of the building. Carrie noticed the pick-up truck. It was rather new. She looked inside and there were the keys. Old tools were lying on the work bench, some old tires leaning against the wall, and a lawn-mower... She stepped through the side door of the garage that led to the barnyard.

There it was - the old red barn with its silo standing beside it. She walked slowly towards the building, Blackie at her heels. She wandered down the dirt-rutted road, passing the barn, and found herself standing by the ice-covered pond. The snow was melting.

"We better not go any farther, Blackie, the snow is deeper here." She called the dog and made her way back to the barn. The old stone milk house door was standing open so she took a look inside. Then she and the dog entered the barn. Carrie heard strange noises coming from the silo. Blackie ran off chasing a mouse into the grain bin. The noises were getting to her, so she thought she should investigate. She stepped into the open silo and stood up looking at the moving vents.

Chapter Three

Jake sat at his desk in the sheriff's office leaning back in his chair. He took off his hat, sat it down on the floor, and then ran his hand through his dark brown hair; the gray at the temples gave him a handsome look. He looked out the window, hoping this was the last of the snow. Several trees were down and Mr. Cooper's barn roof had fallen in. Thank goodness no animals were about.

Jake stood up and stretched. He was wearing jeans and a blue wool shirt and had kept his summer tan. Working in the vineyard and being outdoors were advantages for him; he was a very good looking man. Jake had never found the right woman, but he was looking for that special person he would want children with. He had been dating Ida from the café; she was fun but not quite what he wanted in a woman. He smiled and thought; *I do believe I am the only available bachelor around; yes, I am proud of myself. This year I will have my first crop and be able to move into my new home that I built with my own two hands. And then Pop will be here soon. My life is about the best it could be.* Jake sat back down daydreaming when the phone rang.

"Hello, Thompson here; can I help you?

"Hi, Jake, it's me Temple. I need a favor."

"Sure thing, Temple. What can I do for you?

"You know that Miss Roundtree arrived on Tuesday for Hank's service. Well, she is staying out at the farm. I had Mrs. Woodburn go out there. She did some cleaning, removed Hank's things, and replenished the kitchen. But I would like someone to go out there and make sure she is settled in. You know, the storm and all. I have to go over to Amity or I would go myself."

"No problem. I'll be happy to go over there, but it will have to wait till the sheriff gets back from lunch."

"That's great, Jake. Thank you; I owe you a beer." Temple said.

"Hey, you got that, old man," Jake said laughing.

Jake leaned back in his chair again. *Oh, yes. I want to meet this lady.* What he saw of her at Hank's service was not enough. He thought about Hank and how special and kind the old man was, a true friend. Always a smile on his face and he'd go out of his way to speak to you even if you were a stranger in town. After all, that's how they had met. He remembered all the times when he and Hank would sit at the café. Carrie's name always came into the conversation. He knew things about her that most boyfriends knew, like her favorite flowers and her favorite color and that she loved horses and she liked to write. And her laugh was special.

The farm was also a topic. Hank knew his land was rich—prime land for a vineyard—but he wouldn't sell. No way—it had to be for his granddaughter Carrie. Jake wondered what would happen to the farm. It was only a mile from his property as the crow flew.

Jake mulled over some paper work at his desk and hung around waiting for the sheriff. The door opened and he walked in. "Boy, I sure had good soup over at the café. Jake, you better go try it."

"No, not now. I guess I'll skip lunch. I need to do an errand for Temple."

"Did you get all your paper work done?"

"Sure did, boss. I best get going. Need to stop over at the boarding house first, then I'm headed to the Roundtree farm," Jake said as he placed his hat on his head and reached for his coat. "Hey, sheriff, are you a betting man?

"Why? What are you up to, Jake?

"Well, are you betting on the first Super Bowl," Jake asked.

"Gee, I never thought about it, but hey, you're on, Jake. I'll take Green Bay. That leaves you Kansas," the sheriff said.

Jake left the office and got into his truck. He had been living at Mrs. Jenkins' boarding house for the past three years. His new log home he had built was about ready for him to move in and he needed to tell Mrs. Jenkins that he would be leaving in a few days.

As soon as he was moved in, his pop would be coming to the valley from Napa, California. Jake was getting excited about having his father with him. His pop was known to be one of the best winemakers in Napa Valley and he had taught Jake just about everything you could know about grapes.

There were five vineyards and one winery in Oak Valley; Napa Valley vintners had made substantial investments in the valley and wanted more land. The valley was known for its perfect slopes, undulating hillsides, and fertile soil. Along with the marine breezes coming in from the coastal mountain range and the long summer hours of sunshine, this could open the door to bring the valley back to life.

Jake was happy to be on the ground floor. His dream was to build a winery and have Pop run it. Making their wine would surely be a challenge.

Jake drove up to the front of the boarding house, got out, and walked up the stairs to the front door. "Mrs. Jenkins." Jake called as he entered the house.

"Out here, Jake. I'm in the sewing room doing some mending."

"That is very nice of you, Mrs. J. What am I going to do without you to take care of me?"

"Well, I hope you're not leaving too soon, Jake."

"I best tell you now, I guess. I will be out of here the first of the month; my house is finished and I can move anytime now," Jake said, patting her on the shoulder.

"Do you want some lunch, Jake?" she said as she wiped a tear from her eye.

"No, I'm going to go out to the Roundtree farm. Mr. Temple wants me to check on the pretty miss."

"Oh, Jake, she is a lovely girl. I guess I should say young woman now. She followed her grandfather everywhere and spent all her summers and vacations at the farm. I really didn't know her very well, seeing her at the service for Hank. She is a very beautiful woman, you know," she said smiling at Jake.

"Oh, yes, Mrs. J, I know." Jake smiled.

"Now, Jake, don't you make eyes at her. I thought you had a thing for Ida?"

"Now, Mrs. J, don't you think I would tell you if I had any ideas?" Jake said moving towards the door. "I best get going. I'm running a little late. See you later," Jake called as he went out the door.

Jake drove through the township and turned on Valley Road, which would take him to the farm, thinking about what he might say to Miss Carrie Roundtree. He looked at his watch; it was twelve thirty.

As he crossed the bridge, he noticed that the snow had melted; however, he could still see the fields in their white blanket. He made the turn onto Roundtree Lane and looked towards the big old farm house. Jake thought about the work. Poor Hank just couldn't do it anymore. *I wonder if Carrie will keep the farm. Probably not. She doesn't know a thing about farming.* Jake stopped the truck and got out. Normally Blackie would run to meet him, but the dog was not in sight.

Jake knocked on the door and listened. No answer. He stepped inside and called out, "Anyone at home?" Still no answer. He walked into the kitchen and saw the coffee cups on the table and noticed there were two. *She must have a visitor.* He turned and went back to the front of the house, called out again, then made his way to the truck. Jake thought he might as well whistle for the dog; he knew if he were at all close by he would come to him.

Blackie was sitting in front of the silo door; his paws were red with blood. He had pawed the door so much he even had splinters in his toes. His ears went up at the sound of the whistle and he crawled towards the barn door and made his way slowly to the barn road, which led to the garage.

Jake was getting in his truck when he looked down the road and saw this thing on its belly crawling towards him. *My God! It's Blackie!* Jake ran to the dog and bent down.

"Boy, what on earth has happened to you." He started to pick him up and the dog growled at him. "Okay, Blackie, easy now. I just want to help you." The dog turned and started towards the barn. Jake could see how much his front feet hurt, but he wouldn't give up.

Jake followed the dog; he wanted to solve this mystery and maybe find Miss Roundtree. They entered the barn and Blackie led Jake to the silo door. Blackie barked and barked as Jake pulled on the silo door; the latch had locked some-how.

Carrie was so cold. Maybe she did hear something! The dog and a voice. Was it—could it be? Carrie stood up and put her weight to the door. "Blackie, are you there?" Just then the door opened and Carrie fell into Jake's arms. She looked up at this wonderful handsome man and said, "Are you an angel? Am I alive?"

He took his coat off and wrapped it around Carrie. Then he swept her into his arms and called Blackie. "Come, boy; you can make it." With long steps, Jake walked as fast as he could. He could see by the look on Carrie's face that she had been in the silo too long. He was worried about hypother-mia. He just didn't know how long she had been in the silo. Blackie limped slowly behind Jake towards the farm house.

Carrie was asking Jake all kinds of things. "Who are you? Put me down, please; I can walk. Why won't you talk to me?" Then she felt herself being laid on the sofa in the house. Jake turned and put more logs on the fire and then wrapped Carrie in the quilt. He then just left.

Carrie was all mixed up. Was she safe with this man? Who was he? And where was her dog? "Blackie, Blackie?" she called. The dog made his way towards the sofa and put his head in Carrie's hand. "You poor dog! Your feet! Oh, Blackie, you did try to save me and you stayed with me like I asked, you dear animal."

"He did save you, Carrie." She looked up to see this tall man with a cup in his hand. "If he hadn't come to me when he did, I would have drove off. Here. Take this cup and drink it all down," Jake said.

"What is it and what are you doing, sir?"

"Just drink. I'm going to remove your wet shoes and stockings. We need to get some blood circulating in your feet. Now drink up."

"But this is awful! What is it, sir?" Carrie said making a face.

"It's brandy and milk; it will warm you up."

"Where did you find this?"

"Your grandfather and I were friends; we were known to have a nip now and then." Slap, slap.

"Ouch! Do you have to do that?" she said in a loud voice.

"You want to be better, don't you? I think I see some pink coming back into your toes." Jake got up, reached for the poker, put it into the fire, and moved the logs around. The room was becoming warm and Carrie was getting some color in her cheeks.

"How long were you in the silo?" Jake asked. Carrie looked at her watch.

"Since about ten thirty, I guess. Blackie and I were checking out the farm and I heard this weird noise in the barn. I guess it was the silo vents turning. Anyway, I stepped in and the door slammed shut and you know the rest." Carrie's eyes were filling with tears. "If you hadn't come along, I wouldn't. . ." He stopped her.

"Let's not go there, Carrie; you are going to be just fine. I'm more worried about your dog here. Look at his paws. He must have tried to dig you out of there. I'll have to get some help for him, but first I'm going to clean him up. You rest here and keep warm. Are you feeling better now?"

"Yes, I can feel my toes now." She looked up at him and smiled. "What is your name?"

"You can call me Jake." He picked up Blackie and took him into the kitchen.

Jake. I know that name. Grandfather said he had a friend named Jake and that he was a nice man. Carrie lay thinking about the morning in the cold and then closed her eyes, pulling the quilt up around her tightly.

Jake washed Blackie's feet and pulled the splinters out; he knew he would have to take him in to see Doc Gene. Maybe he could go get some medicine for him and wrap his feet. Jake came back into the living room and found Carrie fast asleep. He picked up Blackie and laid him on the floor in front of the fire and then tiptoed to the door. He could go to Doc Gene's and be back in an hour; he would let Carrie rest.

Carrie woke, looking about the room. The warmth of the fire filled the living room. Carrie noticed Blackie by the fire, and then she looked around for the man who was there. *Jake was his name.* He wasn't about. She got up. She was sweating. That brandy had made her warm all over and she must have slept for over an hour. Just then she heard Jake's truck drive up. Blackie let out a bark, his tail wagging. The front door opened and Jake walked in. "I see you're feeling better, Carrie. I went in to see Doc Gene; he is our vet. I have some medicine for Blackie's feet."

"Thank you, ah, Jake; you're so kind to help us out here." Carrie stood up, pulling the quilt up around herself.

"I might suggest you take a hot shower, you know, the silo smell." He looked at her with a funny face.

"Oh, my! Of course, I will. Will you stay awhile? I would like to talk some more."

"Sure, I need to work on Blackie's feet anyway."

Carrie entered the bathroom, stripped off her clothes, and reached for the faucet in the shower. She was embarrassed because of what he had said about the smell; she just hadn't realized.

Jake took Blackie to the kitchen, cleared off the kitchen table, took a clean kitchen towel, tore it into strips, and then put medicine on Blackie's paws. The dog looked at him and whined as Jake wrapped each paw with the cotton strips. He tied them the best he could and gave the dog fair warning not to chew on his feet. Blackie just moved his head from side to side like he would really mind Jake. Strangely enough, the dog seemed to know that Jake was helping him.

Carrie returned to the living room to see Blackie and Jake sitting in front of the fire. Carrie had combed her long wet hair and it fell on her shoulders. She had put on a clean pair of slacks and a light purple turtleneck sweater. She sat down by the fire, Blackie between them, fingering her hair to let it dry.

"Blackie will be all right. Doc Gene said to keep the bandages on his paws, if we can, for a day or two; then he wants to see him," Jake said, petting the dog sympathetically.

"You seem to care for my grandfather's dog," Carrie said, reaching for Blackie and fluffing his hair.

"Oh, yeah. We're friends. I was with Hank when he got him; he's about two now. I just never thought he was so smart, but Hank always said he was his wonder dog. Now I believe it."

"Jake, we want to thank you for all your help. My grandfather left me a letter. He mentioned you and said you were a man I could count on."

"He did, did he? He was a good man. I will miss him." Jake sat looking at Carrie. "Do you feel okay now, Carrie? I hope you don't mind if I call you Carrie."

"Only if I can call you Jake." She smiled at him. Carrie moved over to the sofa and Jake got up and sat in Hank's chair. Blackie lay soaking in the heat from the fire. "I think Blackie is tired after going through this ordeal," Jake said.

Carrie got a good look at Jake; he was truly a very good looking man, with a kind face, and he was concerned about them. "Tell me about yourself, Jake."

"I live just down the road or will in a few days." Jake told Carrie about his log home, that his father would be here soon, and that he was going to have his first crop this year from his vineyard. "I hope within the next few years I will be able to drop my position as a U.S. Marshal. I work out of the sheriff's office. This keeps me pretty busy," Jake said, running his hand through his hair.

"Really? I have always wanted to know what a marshal did." Carrie said.

"Well, for instance, last night I had to deliver a subpoena just down the road from your farm. I had just a few minutes to get there; the guy had run out on me before, so sometimes it can be difficult, but I got my man." Jake smiled.

"Did you pass a car on the road not far from the big oak?"

"I did. No way? Was that you?"

"Yes, it was and I just about ran off the road. I couldn't see through my windshield; your truck splashed slush all over the car, and I have to say I was a little unhappy with you."

"Wow," Jake got up and paced back and forth. "I'm really sorry, Carrie; I should have been more careful, being a marshal and all. I promise I will never do that again. That's what happens when someone is in a hurry."

"Since you helped save my life, I guess I can forgive you." Carrie motioned for Jake to sit down in the chair.

Chapter Four

Carrie sat looking at Jake, wondering how this day seemed to him: this silly girl who gets locked in a silo and then this good looking man comes along and saves her.

"What are you thinking so hard about, Carrie?"

"Oh, I just was thinking to myself this is sure a funny way to meet a neighbor." They both laughed.

"My, you have a nice laugh and it's so good to hear because you have gone through a lot today, little lady. It's really something and I'm happy I came along when I did and for that dog. He surely is Hank's."

"Well, Jake, we are indebted to you. Isn't that right, boy," reaching for Blackie and petting him.

"Let's see. Can you cook, little lady?" Jake asked.

"I've been known to fix a good table. That's it! Blackie and I will have you out for dinner and you'll see," Carrie said. Then she stood up. Carrie moved over by the fire, holding her hands out to warm them. "But I'll be leaving for the East next week, so we better invite you out soon. Not to change the subject, but do you know Mary?"

"Yes, sure do. Old Mary, she's a neat person and has a heart of gold. You know Hank and her were the talk of the valley. Real close friends." Jake moved up to the fire and stood beside Carrie. This made Carrie nervous. She moved and sat again over by Blackie on the sofa.

"No kidding! She brought me Blackie last night; I guess you knew." She hugged the dog. "I just don't know what to do now. I just can't part with him and I believe he wouldn't fit in the city with all the cars and people."

"You're right. It would be a shame to take him out of the country."

"He really did save me, didn't he?"

"Yes, he did, little lady; he sure did." Jake moved over and sat on the floor by the dog, reaching out to him, checking his bandages.

"I'm worried about his feet. Do you think we should take him in to see the vet?"

"Doc Gene wants me to bring him in by noon tomorrow," Jake said.

"I have to come into the village anyway on some business. Where is the vet located?" Carrie asked.

"He works out of the back of the hardware store; he has a small office there. Gee, it's getting late. I best head back to the office; need to check in." Jake got up and made his way to the door; Carrie moved along behind him. "If it's all right with you, I would like to meet you at Doc Gene's."

"Sure, that would be just fine, Jake," Carrie said with her hands in her pockets.

Jake turned. "You know, I feel that you might just need a big hug. We folks out here in the country always hug people when they leave or say goodbye. Do you mind?" Jake took Carrie in his arms and hugged her. Carrie could feel his heart beating. *How did he know this was well needed?* "I'm really glad you're feeling better, so until tomorrow." Jake opened the door and went straight for his truck. Carrie stood in the doorway and watched him get in. He tipped his hat and then left.

Carrie closed the door and started to think. *I like this man; I wonder if he is taken. He's older than I, but by how much? Oh, damn, I wish he wasn't so good looking and kind. Bepo knew him and said in his letter that he thought I would like him. I wonder!*

Carrie helped Blackie onto the bed. "Let's get a good rest for the both of us. Okay, Blackie?" The dog knew things would be different for him from now on. After all, he was up on the bed. Carrie drifted off into a sound sleep.

Startled by a banging shutter, Carrie looked at her watch; she had slept for an hour. She rose from the bed, leaving the dog curled up. She sat on the edge of the bed then moved to the dresser looking in the mirror. She didn't need much makeup; her skin was so clear and her cheeks had their color back in them. She reached for the lip gloss and then tied up her hair. Carrie slipped into her penny loafers and put on a sweater. *I can't remember a day in my life being like this and filled with such surprises.*

The phone ran unexpectedly. She made her way rather quickly to the desk and picked up the phone. "Hello." Carrie said.

"Hello, it's Mr. Temple. I wanted to come see you today, Carrie, but I was called over to Amity. I just wanted to see if there was anything you might need."

"Everything is fine now, Mr. Temple; I want to thank you for sending Mr. Thompson out here. He literally saved my life today!"

"My, my, how so?" Carrie began to tell Mr. Temple the story of the day and filled him in on everything, even Mary's visit.

"Damn, I'm glad I sent him. Are you sure you're okay? Do you need to see a doctor?"

"Oh, no. I'm fine now; I just had a nap. And thank you for the food. The house is fine. I even have the dog here so I'm not alone."

"Now you come by anytime, if you need to talk."

"Thank you, and I'll see you soon." Carrie sat the phone back in its cradle.

Carrie thought while she was at the desk she might just as well call Alex, a dreaded phone call, but she knew she best do it. The phone rang several times; then he picked up. "Hello."

"It's me," Carrie said. "I thought I would call and check in with you."

"You sure took your time. Why didn't you call when you got into Portland? I have really worried about you," he said firmly.

"Alex, I know that Jo told you I had called her; she said she saw you at work."

"Well, I just would have liked to have heard it from you," he said.

"It hasn't been easy, Alex. I arrived in Portland in a storm and then the service and all and then coming to the farm. You knew I hadn't been here for four years."

"Yeah, I guess so. So when are you leaving the farm country and coming home?"

"Let's see, perhaps towards the end of next week."

"What? Why do you have to stay that long? The service is over."

"I know but I have to make arrangements for the farm and now I have this wonderful dog of my grandfather's," she said softly.

"A dog! What in the hell are you going to do with a dog? You know you can't bring him here."

"Alex, don't talk like that. He saved my life," Carrie said.

"Sure he did. How?"

"He did. I got locked in a silo, and a farmer and Blackie found me."

"Well, thank God for old farmers and dogs, I guess."

Carrie smiled to herself. *If you only knew who the old farmer was.* She laughed.

"What's so funny?"

"Oh, nothing."

"So, how are you, Carrie? I sure miss you, you know what I mean."

"Alex, please. I'll keep in touch. I better go now. Okay?"

"I guess so. Call me when you're on your way and I'll meet you at the airport. We'll celebrate your home coming."

Alex grinned to himself, thinking erotic thoughts. Then he hung up the phone.

Carrie went into the kitchen looked in the icebox and found an apple, cheese, and some crackers. She set them out on a plate and turned when Blackie started to bark.

"What is it, Blackie?" she called. She heard a noise and went to the door, pulling back the blind to look outside, and saw Jake's truck pull up. Her heart skipped; she was actually happy he was coming back so soon.

Jake got out of his truck and Carrie opened the door. "My, that was a fast trip. Did you forget something?"

"Yes, I ran into Doc. He said I should look at Blackie's paws, so on my way home I thought I would stop by. I hope that's okay."

"Sure, anytime; come on in."

Jake made his way to the sofa and bent down where Blackie sat; he somehow had gotten off the bed and one of his bandages was showing some blood spots. "We had better dress this one again. Can you help me take him into the kitchen?"

They both carried the dog into the kitchen. Jake asked Carrie to clear the table off and put a towel down; then he gently laid the dog down on the table. She watched him; he was so tender with the dog and seemed to be very concerned. He gently removed the cloth and washed the wounds and then put on more medicine and wrapped the paw.

"I'm very grateful, Jake, you know, for coming back out here and all." Carrie smiled up at him.

"I told you it was on my way home. Besides, I really wanted to check on you. Did you get any rest?"

"Yes, we had a nap. I was about to have a snack. Do you want to join me?"

"Sure, why not? But let's see, what goes with apples and cheese? Good bottle of wine maybe? You do drink wine, don't you?"

"I have been known to. If I remember, Bepo always had a few bottles of wine up in the top cupboard." Carrie stood on her tiptoes, reaching as far as she could. Jake was taking it all in, watching her slim body stretch as Carrie pulled the back of her sweater down. Then he reached over her head and took a bottle of Chardonnay off the top shelf. Carrie smiled and then got down two wine glasses and set them on the table. Jake pulled open the silverware drawer and took out a cork screw. "You seem to know your way around this kitchen," she said.

"Remember, little lady, I told you that your...ah...Hank and I used to get together. I even played cards with him once or twice. Besides, this is wine country," telling her as he opened the wine.

Jake poured a glass and tasted it. He then poured Carrie a glass and pulled a chair out so she could take a seat.

The two of them sat for a moment, sipping the wine. "This is a very nice Chardonnay. My pop and four generations before him all came from the old country."

"Really? Tell me more about your family, Jake," she asked.

"Well, Pop was from the wine growing region of Wurzburg, Germany, and came over to the States as a young man with his parents and lived in the Napa Valley. You know, in California. Pop met my mom there; I guess I was born to have my own vineyard someday." Jake refilled the glasses and took some cheese.

"That's very interesting, so how long have you been in Oak Valley?"

"I came here about four years ago, found the land I wanted, and then I moved in with Mrs. Jenkins; she has a boarding house."

"Gee, is that Martha Jenkins?" she asked.

"Yes, do you know her?"

"Sure do. She is a very nice lady and a friend of my family. So, is your vineyard coming along?"

"Well, I should get a fair crop this year, but it will be better next year. My pop will be coming out soon; he's going to live with me in my new log home. I hope to move in at the end of the week."

"I've never seen a log home. Did you have it built?"

"No, I built most of it myself. I guess that's why it has taken so darn long."

Carrie looked at Jake as he talked and they both stopped and suddenly found that they were staring into each other's eyes. "Ah...hmmm...so tell me, are there many of these kinds of houses around? They call them something special, don't they?"

"Yes, the word is *chalet*. They build them here in Oregon by Salem. All the logs are cut and placed, and then they take them apart and build them on your land."

"Wow, I sure hope you will let me see your home before I leave." Jake got up and took the wine bottle in one hand and helped Carrie up. "Let's go in by the fire, okay?" Jake moved behind Carrie, with Blackie limping along after them.

They sat in front of the fire, sipping their wine, talking about the farm, Jake's vineyard, and Carrie's work back

East. The conversation always came back to Hank and how much he meant to Carrie. Jake listened and felt it was a good way for Carrie to grieve and to get things out in the open; her feelings were mending and it seemed to make her happy to talk about her parents, especially her mother whom she missed very much.

Jake felt bad for Carrie; she had lost so very much—her parents and grandparents—and had no brothers or sisters.

Carrie went on with her stories. When she was about seven, her grandmother would bundle her up in old blankets. She'd sit Carrie on the front seat of the old farm truck, and then her grandfather and she would go all day through the cold, delivering milk and then picking up grain, sometimes in heavy rain and fog. It was nice to come back to the farm and stand in front of the fireplace to get warmed up.

"Those are good memories, Carrie; you must never forget them." Jake took her hand in his. Carrie started to laugh. "What's so funny, little lady?

"Oh, I was thinking about a time after we came in from the cold. I would run up to this very same fireplace and I would raise my dress up and back up my backside to the fire and then I'd wiggle. Bepo always said I was going to burn my bum." They both laughed.

"Funny, huh," Jake said as he looked at Carrie. "You have a beautiful laugh and smile; you know that, don't you?"

"Yes, I've been told that once or twice." She looked down at her wine glass. Jake took his finger and raised her chin and looked at her. "I could stay here and look at your pretty face all night. You're very beautiful, Carrie."

"Gee, Jake, you make me blush."

"Let me tell you something. Pop and I feel we're on the ground floor of something big so to speak. This valley has a future and I just know people will be buying up the land for vineyards."

"Do you have good land, Jake?"

"Sure do, some of the best around. Hank and I talked about this often. He was just too ill to get a vineyard started, I guess."

"You are so lucky to have your dad; I miss mine so much, but there were times when I wasn't close to him. He was a serious man and into his work so much. I guess that's why I was so close to Bepo; he always found time for me." Carrie looked away; she could feel the tears coming.

Jake pulled her close to him and just held her. Carrie began to sob. "There now, let it all out, little lady. You will feel better, believe me." Carrie moved backwards and looked into Jake's eyes.

"Why do you call me that? Little lady?"

"I don't know; it just seems to fit you. Do you mind?"

"No, I guess not," she smiled. "Do you think I could sell this land? You know, is it good for grapes?"

"Sure is and, if you decide to sell, it will move very quickly. Why, they will be standing in line; you can bet on that." Jake stood up, put another log on the fire, and then took the poker and moved it around in the coals.

"Maybe it's too valuable to sell, Jake." Carrie's glass was empty.

"I would think so; it's been in your family for a long time," Jake said as he filled her glass. "You have been through a lot these past days. I might suggest that you give it some time and think about the farm. I want to be your friend and I want you to know that I am here for you, Carrie. I promised Hank."

"You did? I was thinking along those lines."

"Well, one thing is for sure, I am here and if you need anything…" Carrie reached out for his hand.

"I think I understand." Jake took his hand and moved it around her waist and pulled her close to him, looking into her dark eyes. He wanted to take her in his arms and kiss her ever so tenderly, but instead he kissed her on the forehead.

"You will always be able to count on me, little lady." Jake reached out and held her face in his hands. His movement brought her body to his and he kissed her gently. "I'm so sorry. I guess I shouldn't have done that, Carrie." He moved away and then stood up. Carrie reached out her hand and let Jake help her up and smiled at him.

"Jake, do you have anyone special in your life, like a wife or girlfriend?"

"Heck, no. Well, I see Ida once in a while, but nothing serious."

"I see," said Carrie, as she moved slowly away from him. "I have kind of a boyfriend too; his name is Alex and I work with him."

Jake's eyebrows went up and then he looked at her. "I don't know what this is, Carrie; something seems to draw me to you."

"I know; me too." Jake cleared his throat and moved about the room, making his way to the piano. "Do you play?" she asked.

"Years ago."

"Come with me; I think there may be something you might like to see." Carrie took Jake's hand and led him upstairs to the far bedroom. "I haven't been up her yet, so

I'm not sure it's still here, but I hope so." The old victrola sat in a corner all covered up. Carrie removed the cloth.

"My goodness, I can't believe this! Does it work?"

"It did years ago. Here. Put this on." Carrie handed him a record, one of Nat King Cole's. Jake took the side handle and wound it up and then set the needle on the record. The room filled with music and Nat's voice; the song drew them close and Jake was holding Carrie in his arms, moving around the room. When the record stopped, they were still holding on to each other. Jake looked down at this young woman and then he moved away.

"You're a good dancer, Jake," she said.

"Uh, we better get downstairs. It's getting late and I better get going."

Carrie thought she had done something wrong. "Okay," she said. Jake followed Carrie down the steep stairway, watching her every move, which just made things worse. He knew he had to get out of here and fast. Carrie Roundtree was too much woman for any man to resist.

Standing by the front door, Carrie asked, "Is something wrong?"

"No, little lady. I just best get going." His face was flushed. Jake opened the door, hugged Carrie, and left.

Carrie was in some sort of shock. *This man,* she thought. She had no idea what she had done to Jake Thompson. She sure had butterflies in her stomach and such a good warm feeling about this man she had just met a few hours ago.

Carrie watched him walk away. He was so tall and such a nice man and handsome too. *Why couldn't I have met him in Boston? Was this what Bepo wanted? He seems to have been so close to him. Had Bepo planned all this or was it fate that Jake Thompson just happened by to save my life on a cold winter day in Oregon?* She closed the door and stood there with her nose on the glass, watching the truck disappear. Her heart was beating fast and she was excited. She felt like singing; she called Blackie and bent down and hugged him. "Let's hope he hurries back soon."

As Jake drove down Roundtree Lane, he thought to himself; *Man, she's the one I've been waiting for. A gift has come my way; I need to be real careful. I know she is very fragile, and am I too old for her? Damn, I wonder how old she is. Mid twenties, I think; that just puts us about twelve years apart. I just never have felt like this before—never—about any woman.* He adjusted his hat and laughed to himself. He had just driven right straight through town and past his office.

Chapter Five

Jake couldn't help thinking about Carrie and daydreaming about her, wondering why he felt like a school boy falling in love at first sight. *She is beautiful, smart, and younger than I am. So what?* His memory of the past few hours overpowered him. Carrie's sparkling black eyes, her rueful sweet smile, her humor, and the way she walked and held herself. He knew she was the person he had been waiting for. Jake felt this strange tug at his heart and he was very happy all of a sudden. Damn, she is getting to me. It's no wonder I drove right past the office, he said out loud.

He parked his truck and made his way to his desk. Picked up the phone and checked in with Temple. He wanted to get back to the boarding house before Mrs. Jenkins left; it was her church night. He opened the front door, threw his coat on the chair, and sat down. His head was spinning; he couldn't get Carrie out of his head. He went up to his room and sat on the edge of the bed. Soon he started to think again. *I wonder what she would look like lying on the bed next to me with her hair falling on the pillow. What is the matter with me? Get a hold of yourself, man. You just met this woman. Oh, God in Heaven, she is so special. If only she would keep the farm and stay here in the valley. Together we could build a dynasty.*

Jake washed up then went down the stairs. Mrs. Jenkins had left him a plate in the oven. A note was on the bulletin board:

Please help yourself, Jake. Will be home about ten.

Mrs. J

Jake ate his supper, then read for a while, and decided to turn in. He undressed to his shorts and crawled into bed. He started to think again. *Carrie's smile. It really reaches out to me. Tomorrow I'll see her at Doc Gene's. I know I have to do something special and think up a romantic day for this little lady.*

Carrie woke up to the sound of birds outside her window. She smiled and then stretched her arms over her head. Blackie was lying on the bed beside her; he knew where his place was. "You know, Blackie, you are the first dog ever to sleep with me. Do you know how special you are? You do, huh." Blackie's tail beat on the blankets. Carrie gave the dog a big hug. She thought about the silo and how this wonderful dog had saved her life.

It was time to get up. She slipped on a clean pair of wool slacks, put on a dickey, then pulled her sweater over it. She adjusted her collar and put on a cross necklace and gold hoop earrings. Then she brushed her hair back into a pony tail and slipped on her loafers. Blackie was at the door waiting to go outside. Carrie opened the door and let him out and then stood on the porch. She looked around the yard. There were broken tree limbs on the ground and most of the snow was gone.

Carrie shut the door and then sat at the desk; she called Jo.

"Hello," Jo said.

"Hi, it's me. You sound kind of strange?"

"Yeah, well, I stubbed my toe getting to the phone," Jo remarked.

"I've told you not to go barefoot, girlfriend."

"I know, mother," Jo joked. "So, how is it going in Oregon?"

"If you have half a day, I can tell you all about it, but it's better." Carrie went on to tell Jo everything, and then she came to Jake. "Jo, he is wonderful. I get butterflies when I think of his name. Never have I felt like this. He is so gentle and caring…"

"Wait a minute, girl. You sound like the love bug has taken a bite right out of you."

"I really don't know him. He has his own vineyard. The best thing is he knew my grandfather very well, and Bepo even mentioned him in my letter; he wrote that I could trust him and that I should go to him and ask him anything I wanted to about the farm."

"Gee, Carrie, he lives there and you live here in the East. Now that doesn't match up for a relationship"

"I know, Jo. What do I do?"

"I really wish I knew what to say. Give it some time though."

"I will, Jo. I'm meeting him in about an hour at the vet's office. I need to take Blackie in, so whatever happens today, I'll let you know."

"You take it slow, Carrie; your worth a lot of money and now with the farm too...do you hear me?"

"Yes, I will; I'll call in a few days, girl. Talk to you later." Carrie hung up thinking about what Jo had said about going slow. *That may be difficult, but isn't it time for me to find some happiness?* She had to admit this man she had just met already meant something to her. There was a connection for sure.

Carrie knew she had a full day ahead of her: a fast stop at Mrs. Foster's, then Blackie to the vet, and then to the bank. The phone rang. Carrie reached for it, "Hello."

"How are you this morning?" asked Jake.

Carrie smiled and felt her heart beating fast. "I feel good, thank you. Blackie and I were just leaving for the village."

"Well, that's why I'm calling. I was wondering if you might be interested in seeing some of the valley after we see Doc."

"Yes, that will be just fine. I have a few errands to do, but I should have them done before ten-thirty. Will that be okay?"

"Sure will, little lady; see you then." Carrie said good-bye and hung up. His voice was so strong, and she felt that funny, excited feeling.

Carrie called Blackie and they made their way to the pickup. She thought it would be better than the rental car for the dog. She lowered the tail gate and helped him in, and then she started the truck and headed towards the village. On the way, she remembered that Bepo had been behind the same wheel not long ago. In a way, it made her feel close to him.

The road was clear now, and the sun was trying to make its way through the clouds. Carrie drove straight to Mrs. Foster's, so she could pay for Bepo's flowers. Mrs. Foster saw her through the window so she opened the door for her. "Carrie, how are you this morning?"

"I'm better now, Mrs. Foster."

"Well, some rest will make a person feel a lot better; I must say that service was the nicest I have ever been to.

Your grandfather would have been so proud. All his friends from all around came."

"I know. So many folks I didn't recognize, but it was special. Mrs. Foster, can I ask you a question?"

"Why yes, dear, what is it?"

"I met this Mr. Jake Thompson; he helped me out at the farm."

"Oh, Jake is so nice. You don't have to worry about him, Carrie. You know he's the most sought after bachelor in this county,"

"Is that so? Doesn't he have a girlfriend?"

"Yes, I think he does. The girl at the café; Ida I think is her name. Anyway, they have been seen together."

"Well, here is the money for the flowers." Carrie said goodbye and then left. She made her way to the bank. *Girlfriend, was Jake telling me the truth about Ida? Was she just an on and off again friend? Someone to be with? Or was it more? Maybe Jo is right. I better take this slowly.*

She entered the bank and looked around; she couldn't help but notice several people looking at her. Carrie stepped up to a desk that said *Manager* on it. A lady came out from behind a filing cabinet and greeted her. "I'm Mrs. Winthrop. May I help you?"

"Yes, I'm Carrie Roundtree. I think we have some business to take care of. Hank Roundtree accounts? I need to see them and then sign some papers."

"Oh, just a moment. I will get the file." Carrie sat looking around the bank. Old paintings of the village hung on the walls. She stared at one in particular; it was her grandfather in front of the church when it was being built. Carrie felt a chill then turned, and Mrs. Winthrop was sitting down behind the desk with a large file.

"Here we go. There are several bank books here, savings and a checking account; and you will need to sign for both of them. The other papers are certificates and some bonds."

"Thank you. Can I sign now on the accounts?" Carrie asked.

"Oh, yes, you may." Carried signed the papers and then picked up the file and left.

The hardware store was just about a block from the bank. Carrie looked at her watch; she was on time. She seemed to be a little nervous but was a little bit excited too. She pulled into a parking place. As she took the keys out of the ignition, Jake stepped out in front of the store; his tall body and handsome look moved Carrie. She could feel her heart beat. Carrie opened the door and stepped out, closing the door behind her. Blackie was jumping all over the truck bed — his bandages all off by now — he was so happy to see Jake.

Jake walked up to the truck, opened the tail gate, and let the dog out. "Good morning! Again," he said, smiling at Carrie.

"Hi, I guess I'm on time."

"You sure are. Here. Let's go on in. Come on, Blackie," he called out.

Jake took his arm and put it behind Carrie, guiding her into the store. She felt like she was an exhibit; all the farmers turned and one of them gave Jake a "thumbs up" sign. They entered the back office where Doc Gene met them.

"Hey, Doc, here we are and may I introduce you to Carrie Roundtree."

"Hello," she said, reaching out to shake his hand.

"My goodness, you are exactly what your grandfather said you were. It's nice to meet you, Carrie." She felt a little bit of a blush as she looked at Jake.

The doctor and Jake lifted Blackie up and sat him on the examination table where the doctor washed his paws. "It seems like the medicine is working. My, he sure did dig at something," he remarked. Jake and Carrie filled Doc Gene in on the silo incident.

After Blackie had a shot and was treated, Jake and Carrie walked to the front of the store and stepped out on the sidewalk. Jake took a look across the street at the café. Carrie wondered if Ida saw them standing there. "Well, shall we go? I have some things you should see."

"Okay," Carrie said. Jake walked around the front of his truck and helped Carrie inside. "Will it be all right to leave Bepo's truck here while we're gone?"

"Sure, it will be fine. They're never that busy here," Jake said climbing into the cab.

"Will Blackie be all right in the back as cold as it is?"

"Sure, he did okay when you came to the village, didn't he?"

"Yes, I guess so."

"Is there something wrong, Carrie? You seem a little tense."

"I guess I feel like everyone is looking at me, you know, the granddaughter from the East and never coming back here. I guess I'm a little guilty maybe."

"Hey, that's a normal feeling. Don't let it worry you. Most of these people are into everyone and their business. You know, a small village like this is," Jake said as he reached for Carrie's hand. "The important thing is that you are here now, and I'm hoping to get that smile back on your face." He winked at her

Jake drove to the Coast Highway turnoff. "Do you remember this road?"

"Yes, I do. We took this way to the beach and would end up at Seaside."

"Well, let's see where these wheels will take us. Maybe I can drum up a surprise for you."

"Really, I guess I'm game; you're the driver and it's been years since I have been up here on the coast highway." Carrie pulled her hand from Jake's.

He drove ahead on the mountain road; the road was clear, but there was about a foot of roadway snow. He must have driven about five miles and then, when he saw a clearing and a road turn off, he pulled in slowly and stopped the truck.

"Get out and come see," Jake said; he got out and helped Carrie with her door and then moved to the edge of the road. "Look," he said, taking Carrie by the hand and leading her. He stood behind her and pointed to the valley below.

Carrie was overwhelmed at the sight; she was speechless. She had not known what the valley would look like from this far up the mountain. "It looks like a map, Jake; all the farms and vineyards, the fence rows."

"Yes, it is a great sight all right. Look, you can see the village too; look over this way." He wrapped his arms around her; she could feel the warmth of his body. Jake pointed out his farm and then Carrie's.

"I thought you might be interested in your valley and what has been going on around your farm. It's the future, Carrie, all here waiting to be taken. See all the vineyards? That's the long rows, one after the other." Jake pointed out the rolling grain fields where the spring crop would be planted. "If you look over here, you can see the silo where you were trapped. "See?" He held on to her tightly. Then he turned her around, pulling her to him, looking into her eyes, touching her cheek with his finger, "Oh, Carrie, I need to do this." He kissed her softly and then again. This time Carrie responded; she could not help herself.

"Well, Mr. Thompson, was this one of the surprises you told me about?" Carrie said as she moved away from Jake with a little smile on her face.

"Not exactly, Carrie, that just happened. I'm so sorry if I offended you."

Carrie turned back to Jake. "How I can be offended by you, Jake. You saved my life, remember?" Carrie reached up and then stood on her tiptoes and kissed him quickly. "I think we better move on, okay?"

As they drove up the pass, Jake asked, "Do you believe in love at first sight?"

"Jake, that's only in fairy tales, don't you think?" They both laughed. Carrie was enjoying the ride. She couldn't help but enjoy the snow covered trees with the sunlight trying to come through. Suddenly, a deer ran right in front of them. "Wow that is the biggest buck I have ever seen. At least a four pointer," Jake said. "That was great! Wasn't he wonderful?"

Jake kept driving till he saw the sign on the right: *KELLY'S CHALET* carved in wood with a wine bottle. He slowed down and then finally came to a stop. Blackie jumped out of the truck and headed off into the woods.

"Jake, where is that dog going? Shouldn't he be with us?"

"He's fine. This is like a second home to him. He loves it up here. Hank used to bring him up here a lot, and he loves to hunt rabbits," Jake said getting out of the truck.

"Where are we, Jake?"

"This is Kelly's, friends of mine. Come on; let me introduce them to you." They walked happily to the door arm in arm, opened it, and stepped inside. Carrie froze, standing there trying to take it all in. The room was so cheerful with a roaring fire. The whole dining area looked as if she had stepped right into Italy: small, round wooden tables for two were set with red-checkered tablecloths with matching napkins tucked into dark red wine glasses. There were homemade breadsticks in a basket on each table. A candle was in a wine bottle with wax drippings running down the side of it. As she looked up to the exposed ceiling beams, she could see the artificial grapes hanging everywhere in outstanding colors. She smelled the oak burning in the stone fireplace. Then Carrie noticed the basket by the fire: a big yellow tiger cat was curled up sleeping.

"Jake, you are incredible. Tell me this is one of your surprises," Carrie said, turning to look at the room.

"Kind of, I guess, but I wanted you to meet my friends, Fred and Kelly." With that he called out. "Hey, where are you two anyway?"

The double doors that led into the kitchen opened and a man in a red apron and chef's hat came storming through. "Jake, it's about time. We haven't seen you for some time now." Fred made his way to Jake and gave him a big bear hug.

"Where's my favorite girl, Fred?" Jake asked.

"Kelly, come out here!" Fred called. Kelly came walking through the swinging door, wiping her hands on her apron. "There she is," said Fred.

"Jake, it's so good to see you," Kelly said, reaching for him.

"Ah, this is someone you know," said Jake, "only by what you have been told. Fred, Kelly, this is Carrie, Hank's granddaughter."

"Ohhhh…so this is Carrie. My dear, your grandfather was so special to us. We only knew him a short time, but he became part of our family and you too because he told us so much about you." Kelly hugged Carrie. "Please let's all sit down. Fred, drag another table over, but first turn that sign around. We are closed for the rest of the day."

Carrie sat down looking at Jake; he reached out for her hand, as if to say she was among family. Carrie was fighting back the tears when Fred came and sat next to her.

"You know, Carrie, my wife makes the best Italian sausage and cheese pie. That's what she was doing when you came in. Jake, you know where the wine is. Go get it while I fill this little woman in on you." Jake went to the wine cabinet and picked out a nice red wine.

"You see, Jake and I go way back. We met in Napa, and my wife Kelly always wanted a chalet in the mountains no less, and since she loved to cook… well, you can see what happened. I bought the land here and Jake helped me build this place." Jake opened the wine, tasted it, then poured Carrie a glass.

"This wine came from Fred's very own vineyard. It's down in the valley not far from my place." Jake said.

Carrie was taking all this in. "This is a wonderful place; I'm very pleased that Jake brought me here." She smiled at Jake.

The four of them sat visiting most of the afternoon. Kelly served her special dish, and Blackie came in out of the cold and lay in front of the fire. Jake told his friends how he had met Carrie, the silo ordeal and all. And then after many laughs and a few tears, it was time to head back to Oak Valley. Jake still had one more surprise up his sleeve.

Jake and Carrie left Kelly's and went down towards the valley. Carrie had had a glorious time. "Jake, I have never laughed so hard. That Fred is so funny; they truly are neat people."

"Yes, they're my best friends. Anyway, how about you driving by my place and looking it over. We can stop and pick up your truck on the way back."

"Sounds good to me," Carrie said, taking his hand.

They drove into the village and Jake stopped his truck by Carrie's. He got out and helped her to the door of her truck, reached down, and gave her a kiss. "Jake, do you want the whole town to see us?" As she said that, Mrs. Alden walked by.

"Hello, Mrs. Alden, how are you today?" asked Jake. The woman hurried on by, pretending she didn't see them.

Carrie and Jake both started to laugh. "You follow me, okay?" Jake said as he turned to go to his truck.

Ida stood at the café window watching Jake and Carrie. She couldn't believe her eyes. *I might have known Carrie Roundtree hasn't changed one bit since high school.* Just about anyone could have read her thoughts.

Jake drove down a long dirt road with grape vines on both sides. Carrie felt like she was in another world. Or maybe it was the wine. She didn't know. She kept following Jake till he stopped. Carrie kept looking for the house and then she saw it: this large house looking like a frame only made out of logs, four steps leading to a deck that went the full length of the house, tall windows on each side of the front door. Jake came to her door and opened it. "Well, this is it. What do you think?"

"Jake, I don't know what to say. It reminds of a Hansel and Gretel hide-away right out of a story book. I'm speech-less. Can we go inside?"

"Sure, but first..." He picked Carrie up in his arms.

"Jake, what are you doing?"

"Wait. You'll see, little lady." He moved to the front door, opened it, and moved inside, still holding her in his arms. "You are the first person to see my home and I want to do this right." Then he kissed her. *Jo, where are you now when I need you? I think I love this man.* He held her as she slid down the front of his body; she could feel his warmth. Reaching the floor she looked into his eyes. "Jake, I don't know what's happening here."

"I know, little lady. The first time I saw you at the service for Hank I knew I was drawn to you. I think we are an item. I mean I have all these feelings and I can't handle them. I just want to be with you, Carrie. I think I am falling in love with you. I have never felt like this before."

"I know. I have these feeling too. But, Jake, we mustn't let this go on. I live on the East Coast."

He took his fingers and held them up to her mouth, "Shush now, little lady. If it is meant to be, you and me, it will happen. Let's give it time, a few days anyway." He stopped and laughed.

"A few days. That's all we have, Jake," Carrie said turning away.

"Okay, then you know how you feel and I know how I feel. Let's just let it happen," Jake said pulling her to him, covering his mouth over hers.

"Oh, Jake, let's stop this before…"

"Yes, I know. So, do you want to go on a tour of my home?"

Jake took Carrie by the hand and led her through the house. She loved the stone fireplace and the wonderful kitchen. There was a huge table made out of logs that Jake had made; he had cut them in half. There must have been a hundred coats of varnish on the top. And the benches—he could seat ten people or more. They walked into the bedroom where the headboard had *Thompson* on it. He had even made that, hand carving the letters. There was a quilt on the bed. He told her his mother had made it. A bathroom separated the two bedrooms; the second bedroom was for his pop. It had a built-in desk and bookcases. A loft extended out over part of the living room; there were two twin beds up there. Large braided rugs lay on the living room floor, and the head of an elk was over the fireplace. A wine closet sat at one end of the kitchen. There were a wood-burning kitchen stove and an electric one.

"Why two stoves?"

"I like to cook, and I like to do my baking in the wood stove. Yes, I am telling you my secret. One of my hobbies is cooking and baking, and good wine."

"Jake, we have so much to learn about each other." Carrie walked to the door and stood there, wringing her hands together. "This is such a wonderful home, Jake. I love the log effect and to think you did all this."

"Carrie, you could have all this if you wanted to. Stay here, love, with me and Pop. We can build a great future with your farm and mine, and it could be one of the most outstanding vineyards around with Pop."

"Jake! Stop. Please. We really need to think this all out," Carrie said.

"I know, hon." Carrie heard him; the first time he had called her hon. She had to get home, remembering what Jo had said to her.

"I think I best go home now, Jake. I will see you tomorrow. I have some papers to look over. I promise I will think a lot on all of this. This is a feeling I have never had either and I like it." Carrie reached up and kissed him. Jake pulled her close to him; she ran her hands over his back. She didn't want to leave.

"Can I call you later?" he asked.

"If you wish." Carrie looked up at him. Jake gazed deep into her eyes. Carrie moved and opened the truck door and quickly got in.

As Carrie drove down the lane towards the farm house, tears were running down her face. She didn't know why she seemed to be sad, leaving Jake like that. She really wanted to stay with him. He was the man she needed in her life, but how confusing could it get for them? She parked the truck in the garage and Blackie jumped out of the back. She picked up the file she had gotten from the bank and walked to the front door.

Chapter Six

Carrie had been nervous about leaving the village and a little embarrassed, wondering how many people had seen her and Jake. She was unsure if Ida knew about them by now. Hopefully, Jake would take care of that matter.

She opened the door and stepped into the house still thinking about her feelings. Was she really falling in love with this wonderful man whom she had just met less than forty eight hours ago? Could this be true or was it just that she had been through so many things this past week?

She heard a noise and Blackie was barking. She turned and pulled the blind back and noticed a car leaving. What is going on, she said out loud.

Carrie opened the door and found a long white box with a pink ribbon on it. She picked it up and carried the box into the house, closing the door behind her. She sat it on the dining room table and took off the ribbon, opening the box slowly, pushing the tissue paper back. She found a dozen pink roses with a small card.

It read: *Thank you for a delightful day little lady.*

Love, Jake

Carrie picked up a rose and smelled it. *Bepo and Jake did talk about me. How else would he have known that pink was my favorite color and roses my flower.*

Carrie got out one of her grandmother's vases, filled it with water, and then arranged the roses carefully. She sat them in the center of the dining room table. They were so beautiful; the rose scent filled the room.

The phone rang, and Carrie answered it. Jake was calling to see if she had received her flowers. He hadn't been sure if he could count on Jimmy to deliver them, so he wanted to make sure.

"You know I want to see you, Carrie. Does that dinner promise still hold?"

"Sure, Jake. How about tomorrow night?"

"Okay, only if I can bring the steaks."

"Jake, what happened today…was it just something, you know, two people having a good time?"

"Carrie, it was more than that. I told you how I felt and I can say it again if you want."

"No, I understand your feelings. I have them too. I…only this has never happened to me. I have never had this feeling before and I barely know you."

Jake took a deep breath. "Well, I think we should spend as much time as we can together before you leave and see how it goes. Does that sound tolerable to you?"

"Oh, yes, I do want that, Jake. So, till tomorrow night. I'll be waiting. And Jake, I love the flowers. Thank you so much for them and today."

"You're welcome, little lady. Till tomorrow. Take care and good night." Jake hung up the phone.

Carrie was very excited; just hearing Jake's voice made her heart pound. Blackie was at the door whining, so Carrie let him in and then she looked at her watch. It was six. My, how the day had gone by. She sat down in Bepo's chair and thought about the day. It was so perfect. She couldn't remember when she had been happier. She felt so at ease with Jake, and his friends were like family. She couldn't wait till the next day.

Carrie got up early and went for a walk with Blackie. This time she stayed out of the barn. They walked to the pond and back and, as she came into the yard by the farm house, she observed the big oak by the garage. She looked up and saw the old bell; it was still there. When she was a child, she used to pull the bell at lunchtime so Bepo would come in from the barn. She remembered the bell rope pulling her off the ground, and then she would pull on it as hard as she could and up she would go again. She just stood there, looking the yard over.

She opened the gate and there was the old garden bed where she had planted corn with her grandmother. She walked around the rose garden; most of the roses were still there but needed to be pruned. That was her grandmother's favorite place. In her spare time, she was always working among her flowers.

Carrie was busy all morning. She cleaned up the kitchen, made the bed, and carried in more wood for the fireplace. She went through the wine cabinet to make sure she would have a good wine for the steaks. She had made herself a sandwich when she heard Blackie carrying on in the front yard. Carrie hurried to the door and opened it to find a strange man. Blackie wasn't going to let him come to the house.

"It's okay, Blackie," Carrie called to the dog. The man was carrying a briefcase and tipped his hat to Carrie.

"Hello, are you Miss Roundtree?"

"Yes, and who…"

"I'm Mr. Carter from the Wine Growers Association. May I have a word with you?"

"Would you like to come in?"

"Please." The man followed Carrie into the house with Blackie on his heels. He sat of the sofa and Carrie sat in Bepo's chair. "I have come out here, Miss Roundtree, to ask you some questions and to find out what your plans might be in regards to this farm."

"You see, Mr. Carter, I don't believe that it is any business of yours."

"Well, I know this sounds strange, but I was told you were leaving right away to go back to the East Coast." He removed his hat. "I am here to inform you that if you want to sell your land, part of it or the whole farm, there are people who would be very interested in it and would give you a good price." Mr. Carter cleared his throat.

Carrie stood up and paced the floor for a moment and then asked, "I know that my land is worth a lot; I have been told that investors would like it to develop vineyards and perhaps a winery."

"That's true, young lady. Besides it would be best to do so. After all, what would a city girl like you do with this old place," Mr. Carter said, looking around the room.

"Mr. Carter, I think you should leave. I haven't decided what to do with the farm as yet. And besides, it's my home, thank you," she said firmly and motioned him to the front door. Mr. Carter took out a paper.

"If you should change your mind, maybe these numbers on this paper will help you make up your mind." He handed her the paper and walked out the door.

Carrie called Blackie and shut the door. "Boy, they sure didn't waste any time, did they?" she said to the dog. Carrie opened the paper, took a deep breath, and then sat down on the sofa. One thousand dollars per acre. That was two hundred thousand dollars. She felt faint and had had no idea that the farm was worth so much money. Now what would she do? "Well, Blackie, we really have to think this one out. If this farm is worth that much, maybe its worth a lot more to us."

Carrie knew she had to forget about Mr. Carter's visit for now. She would have to talk to Jake and Jo and perhaps Mr. Temple. She just didn't know what to do. But today was a day she wanted to go well; Jake was coming for dinner and she had to plan for her guest. She set the dining room table, arranging the flowers at one end. She put two potatoes in the oven and made a salad. The wine was open so it could breathe, the rolls finished. Now all she wanted to do was take a shower and get dressed.

All Jake could think about was how he felt. He was useless all day; he couldn't get Carrie out of his head. He knew he was acting like a school boy.

He even drove into the city to the market place so he could get special steaks. He picked up a box of candy. He hand picked the wine; one of Fred's would do fine. *I hope I'm not overdoing it.*

Jake could think about nothing but holding Carrie in his arms. Somehow he had to keep her here. Anyway, she needed to keep the farm. He definitely wanted her to be in his life. Jake put on a new sweater in royal blue and a new pair of slacks, but he had to wear his boots. He grabbed his leather coat and out the door he went to the farm.

Chapter Seven

Carrie reached for the phone and dialed Jo's number. She knew she had better talk to Jo and tell her how she felt and about Mr. Carter's visit.

"Hello, Carrie, how are you, girlfriend?"

"Oh, Jo, I have so much to tell you."

"Really? Well, you better start at the beginning. Okay?"

Carrie took a deep breath and then filled Jo in on her day and the visit with Mr. Carter. "What in the world do I do now, Jo? The farm is worth so much more than I ever dreamed of." She sat waiting to hear Jo's response.

"Wow, I had no idea land was worth that much way out in the country," Jo said.

"I guess it's because of the soil. You can't just grow grapes anywhere," Carrie remarked.

"I think you best have a talk with your new boyfriend and find out some things, but I wouldn't tell him what Mr. Carter told you the farm is worth, not now anyway. You know what I mean."

"I guess so, but I really do trust Jake and, well, if I just didn't feel the way I do about him, you know? Jo?"

"Do you think you really are in love with him?"

"I think so; I know I just want to be with him, Jo," Carrie said softly.

"You haven't…"

"No, but that doesn't mean I haven't wanted to. Oh, Jo, what should I do?"

"Well, play it cool, honey. He sounds like a special guy, you know; and if he has fallen for you like you have him…well, I don't think there is a chance of stopping this romance."

"Jo, I better go. I think Jake just pulled up. Blackie is barking."

"Remember, take it slow, girl, and ask some questions, okay?"

Carrie knew what she meant. "Talk to you later." Carrie hung up the phone and opened the door.

Jake gathered up the steaks and wine and put the box of candy under his arm and walked to the door where Carrie was waiting for him, Blackie running along side of Jake. "Hi," Jake said.

As he pushed the door open, Carrie reached up and kissed him lightly on the lips. "What do you have here?" She reached for the package.

"Our dinner." He moved inside and closed the door behind him and followed Carrie to the kitchen. "Come here, little lady. Do you expect me to settle for that peck?"

"Hmmm, I guess not." Jake took Carrie in his arms and kissed her long and sweet. Carrie felt her heart race. *If this is what love is all about, I'm in a wonderful place and I feel so comfortable with this man. Yes, I love this man.*

Jake stepped back and told Carrie how beautiful she was and that he had wanted the time to fly so he could be with her. It had been one of the longest days in his life.

"I brought you this box also, and I'll put Fred's wine on the table," he said handing her the candy.

"Oh, Jake, I love these chocolates. Thank you so much." She set the box on the table next to the flowers.

"My dear, you will have the best. Carrie, I think we better get this dinner started before…"

"Yes, I think so." She started to blush. Carrie got out a large black iron skillet and gave it to Jake. She put an apron around him and they both giggled; she told him it was her grandmother's. Jake made himself at home and enjoyed fixing the dinner. They ate and sat at the table for a long while, sipping the wine. Carrie remembered what Jo had said and started to ask Jake some questions about the farm and the vineyards. She then told him about Mr. Carter.

Jake was happy that Mr. Carter had come to the farm. Now maybe Carrie would realize what the farm was worth and perhaps it would mean more to her now and she wouldn't second guess her decision.

"When are you heading back to the East? I know you said next week, but what day?"

"Perhaps in seven days, I guess. I have so much to think about—you!" She smiled. "And then the farm. If I keep the farm and move here to Oregon permanently," Carrie stated pushing her hair back, "do you think I could bring the farm back to life?"

"The farm is worth a lot, and you will have no trouble selling, but how can you, Carrie? Hank was so adamant about you keeping it, and you know how I feel, little lady. I want you to stay here and I will do everything I can to help you."

"Yes, I know, and I want to, but I just have to make the right move."

"You need some more time, Carrie?" Jake reached out for her hand.

They both got up and made their way to the living room. Jake had picked up the wine and the glasses. He pulled her down in front of the fire; they sat watching the dancing flames, not saying a word.

"This is so pleasant, coming back here to the valley and meeting you, spending time here in this old house with its memories. Your friends, Jake, are so great, and Blackie—what a friend he has become to me. I have to say this sounds like a wonderful life."

"It will be. The country does great things to a person," Jake said, pulling Carrie into his arms, holding her. Carrie felt the warmth of his body and she could feel his heart beat; she pulled away and he found her mouth and kissed her with love. Jake took Carrie's face in his hand and looked into her eyes. "You are the most beautiful person I have ever met and I know that I love you with my whole heart. I do believe that Hank had something up his sleeve. He talked about you to me every time I saw him; it was always Carrie this and Carrie that, and I feel he wanted us to be together."

Carrie felt the tears come into her eyes, and Jake took her into his arms and held her close as she sobbed. He knew she had to let go and this was the time to do it. Jake comforted Carrie, rocking her in his arms, knowing that she had to grieve for her grandfather. Then they sat in front of the fire, wrapped up in each other, talking about the past, where he came from, what they wanted out of life.

They sat for hours talking about likes and dislikes, inno-
cent things that brought them close like music and books
and, of course, food. The way the air smelled after a walk in
a warm rain. Sitting on the sand watching a sunset on the
beach.

Carrie told Jake about her parents, that she was a lot
closer to her mother than her father, and how hard it was to
lose her best friend. She told him about the accident and
how a part of her had died along with her mother and the
awful phone call to Boston.

Then Jo came into the conversation and how she was the
sister that she had never had, that they shared a flat and
worked together, and that she was from Canada and her
family lived in Vancouver.

Jake talked about his boyhood and how close he was to
his pop and that he wanted him in his life and to be with
him. He knew Carrie would fall for him; he was a wonderful person, full of love and big bear hugs. Jake mentioned
his mother and how close he had been to her and that she
had passed away with an illness just a few years back.

Jake got up and added more logs on the fire then sat
down next to Carrie. He looked at his watch and noticed it
was getting late. He pulled Carrie into his body, his hands
feeling her shoulders and her back. She felt warm and so
soft. Moving his face to hers, he kissed her cheeks and her
forehead and moved to her mouth, never wanting to pull
away. He sat back to look at her.

"Little lady, I don't want to rush you or want you to do anything you might regret. Lord knows that this has all happened so fast, but I need you and want you so very much. I need your body next to mine; I want us to be one." Jake kissed Carrie.

"I want that too, Jake. I'm staying. I can do this; I can run the farm with your help."

Jake stood up, picked Carrie up, and whirled her around the room. Carrie felt this warm feeling moving over her. Blackie started to bark with excitement. They stopped; Carrie slid her body down the front of Jake. She could tell he was a little excited himself.

"We can build a good life here together, hon, and Pop will be here too. We will be a family. I love you so much, Carrie."

She stood there listening to Jake, her world all coming together. And to think the silo incident had brought them together and Blackie would be with her. "I know that Bepo wanted it to be this way. Do you think he wanted us to be together?"

"I'm sure of it, little lady. That must be why he talked to me about you so very much, your life and all."

"Really? Just how much did he talk to you about me?" Carrie said smiling.

"Well, he told me about your wild teenage years. Boy-friends and how they wouldn't leave you alone." Carrie pushed at him in a joking manner.

"Oh, you! You are teasing me."

"Okay, Carrie, but I am sure of this…" He reached out and pulled her to him and kissed her firmly. "I love you, Carrie Roundtree, and I want you in my life as long as I live; it just feels so right."

Carrie touched his face with her finger. "Jake, I feel the same way. I'm in love with you and I want us to be to-gether." Carrie pulled Jake away from the fireplace to lead him towards the bedroom, but Jake stopped.

"No way, hon. Not this way. Let's wait. I want this to be a very wonderful moment." Jake looked at his watch, "You know I have to go to work in four hours and I really must be going. I would not be surprised if Mrs. Jenkins has the state police looking for me," Jake said, walking towards the door.

"Jake…" Carrie said. As Jake opened the door, she tried to convince him to stay, but she could see that he had his mind made up. Jake pulled Carrie to him and looked at her.

"My darling girl, I will see you very soon. I never say goodbye just that I will see you soon, and I promise the time will be right when we make love." Jake turned and walked to his truck.

"Hurry back and take care," Carrie waved. And to herself she added, I love you, Jake Thompson.

Carrie watched Jake drive out to the main road, thinking how lucky she was to have met him. Carrie had such passion for this man; she smiled to herself as she walked towards the bedroom, with Blackie on her heels.

As Jake drove down the lane, he kept thinking how insane he was. No man in his right mind would leave a beautiful woman like Carrie alone. And damn, she was so ready! But it had to be right and this was too soon. *Gee, man, I've only known her for seventy-two hours.* He knew they both loved each other; it had to be fate. This had all happened so fast, but it felt so right. He was ready for bed and a few hours of sleep, and then he would see her again and hold her in his arms.

Carrie lay in bed half awake. Blackie nudged at the blankets, his front paws pulling at the sheet. He finally succeeded and pulled the blankets off the bed then stood there barking at Carrie. "Hey, what are you doing? Blackie, stop it." He just stood there, wagging his tail and barking at her.

"Okay, I get it. You want out. What time is it, anyway?" She looked at her watch. "Good heavens, it's past noon!" Carrie got up, reached for her robe, and made her way to the door to let the dog out. She stepped out on the porch and took a deep breath of fresh air, reaching for the sky.

"Oh, what a wonderful day! Hello, world!" Carrie made her way to the kitchen slowly and put on the coffee.

Mrs. Jenkins watched Jake as he walked down the stairs into the parlor. "My, my, Jake you came in rather late, didn't you?" The firm smirk on her face changed into a friendly smile.

"I was with Carrie. We had an awesome day. I took her up the mountain and then up to Kelly's. We had a great visit and Kelly had lunch made, so we ate and then we left. I told her about my house, so we stopped there. She went on home and then I took steaks out to her farm."

"Really, Jake, you don't have to go into this with me."

"No, it's fine. I want to. We have really hit it off. She is so wonderful."

"Jake, are you telling me the love bug has taken a bite out of you?"

"Well, you know, Mrs. J, I wouldn't do anything to jeopardize this relationship," Jake said enthusiastically.

"I see," said Mrs. J.

"No, ma'am. I'm in love for the very first time in my life. And you will never guess. Carrie is staying in Oregon; she is keeping the farm and plans to run it. How about that for news?" Jake and Mrs. J sat for a while, Mrs. J asking Jake about Ida.

"Ida and I are just friends; we would have never had feelings like this."

"Really, you silly boy. Oh, my."

"Carrie Roundtree is the loveliest person I have ever known. Smart too. Hank told me all these things about her, her favorites things you know, or maybe he had her all picked out for me and knew that fate would step in and bring us together."

"Really, Jake, maybe he did." Mrs. J sat there thinking how it all fit. Maybe Jake was right after all. Hank was a good man and he had such warm feelings for his grand-daughter.

"I'm going over to see Ida and tell her about Carrie and me, and then don't expect me home tonight," Jake said winking at Mrs. J.

Jake left the boarding house and drove directly to the café. Several heads turned as he walked in. He knew Ida probably had seen Carrie and him in the truck. It was Saturday; the whole town was out and about and the café was rather busy. All the farmers knew Jake very well. He made his way to the counter, waiting for Ida to finish what she was doing.

"Ida, I would like to talk to you. Do you have a few minutes?"

"Why, Jake, can't you talk to me here in front of my customers?"

"Well, I would rather talk to you in private." He leaned over the counter.

"Really. Is this about the miss you were seen with in front of Doc's? You know the whole village knows about you and Carrie. You were acting rather...you know...in front of the whole world." Ida grabbed a coffee pot and took off across the café.

Jake stood waiting, with all eyes on him. Ida returned and looked at Jake. "You know, Jake, Miss Roundtree can have you. I really don't care if you want that pretty little thing. Go for it."

Jake could see a few tears filling Ida's eyes as she wiped her face. "Ida, I don't want to hurt you, but we were going no place. I know you can understand."

"Oh, great. Miss Farm Girl from the big city comes along and sweeps you off your feet. Really, Jake, are you that naive."

"Ida, you don't have to talk that way. I just wanted to explain. I thought you would understand. I thought we were friends."

"Not anymore, Jake Thompson. You can't play me the fool. I'm dumping you."

Jake was embarrassed, but he thought he'd better try to talk to Ida. The café was not the place. What was done was over. Jake turned to leave and several men stood up and clapped and waved their hats at him. Jake turned to everyone.

"Carrie and I are an item and she is keeping Hank's farm. I hope you all have a good day."

As Jake left, he tipped his hat then saw Ida leave the room with her head down. He didn't want to hurt her; he just had no feelings for her, not like the ones he had for Carrie. There must have been more to Ida's feelings than he thought, but now he had to concentrate on Carrie, Pop, the farms and the future. He was a happy man and could hardly wait to get back to Carrie's farm.

Carrie sat down at the desk to look over some papers. She opened the envelope that Mr. Temple had given her. She came across the bank book and opened it. She was shocked to find that it had over seventy five thousand dollars in it. All she could do was sit there and stare at it. *Why? Why didn't Bepo use some of this money to bring the farm back to life? It just doesn't make sense. I guess he lost interest, being so sick.* Carrie fingered the papers: bonds and stocks. She had no idea that her grandfather had stocks and bonds; some of these stocks were older than she was. Carrie had not an inkling what they might be worth. All of a sudden, she became frightened. Could she handle this? She had so much to talk about with Mr. Temple.

With these funds, she could do whatever she wanted to with the farm. *Bepo, I can do this. I wish you could be here to watch over me with Jake's help! And you, old lovely man, you did have a plan. You knew when I saw these papers I would move forward and keep the farm. After all, I am your grandchild.*

Carrie sat in her grandfather's chair, looking around the room. It needed paint and new carpet, and the lumpy sofa had to go. She could even have the piano tuned. All the repairs could be done, and even the outbuildings could be fixed and painted. *Wow! A lot of work and a challenge!* Who knows what I could do, even a new home maybe, she said out loud.

Carrie's parents had left her an estate, which gave her a comfortable income, plus her work; she could just about do anything she wished. *I best keep this information to myself for now. Jo was right. I guess I'm worth more that I thought. I can tell Jake in the future. I best go one day at a time. I love Jake, but it has only been a few days. I will know more before I leave to go east*

The dog began to bark, so Carrie pulled the drape back and saw Jake's truck pull up. A warm feeling came over her at the sight of this new man in her life. Carrie opened the door to meet him. He opened his arms, picked her up, and brought her to him, kissing her like he had been gone for weeks.

"I've been waiting for this, just to hold you." Carrie's feet came to rest on the ground.

"And I have been waiting for you too, Mr. Thompson." They walked into the house arm in arm. Blackie followed them with his tail wagging. Jake bent down and ruffled the dog's hair.

"Hey, he looks pretty good. How you doing, boy?" Blackie was pleased with the attention.

"The wind is coming up again. Maybe the storm didn't go through after all," he said.

"I filled the wood box, so we can have a nice fire."

"Did you have a good rest today?"

"I got up late and then I sat here and daydreamed about the farm and looked at this house. It sure needs work on it, Jake."

"I know, but that can come in time. We just need to get you back East and then home here where you belong."

"Will you take care of Blackie while I'm gone?"

"Did you need to ask?"

Carrie walked into the kitchen. "Are you hungry, Jake? I found some soup in the freezer. Mary must have brought it over. Anyway, it tastes pretty good."

"Hey, that's great." Jake sat the table and Carrie made a salad. *He sets a pretty good table and is helpful in the kitchen, a woman's dream come true.*

Jake found another bottle of wine and opened it then turned to Carrie and put his arms around her and pulled her to him. "I went to the café today and talked to Ida. I wanted to tell her in a nice way about us and how this just happened between us and guess what? The whole village knows about us and I think they like it."

"And what happened?" Carrie moved away from Jake.

"Well, she will come around and I think we will still be friends. She is a little hot right now, but don't worry. Okay?"

"Maybe she loved you, Jake? And she may be hurting."

"We never talked about love. We were just friends; you know, someone to play pool with or take to a dance."

"I see," Carrie said.

"Hey, you're not jealous, are you? Come here, hon. I love you, and this is a new beginning for us. Our future lies ahead of us and I want to marry you." He took her hands in his.

"Jake, it's a little fast, don't you think?"

"Is it, Carrie? I know we need to talk a lot, yet I know I want to be with you, no one else. I want a family and a special woman like you. I've waited, Carrie, for this person to come along and it's you, my dear."

Carrie could feel her face getting hot and flushed. She knew she wanted this man, this stranger that she had just met a few days ago, the man who saved her life, now the man she had fallen in love with. She could not bear to not have him in her life.

The two ate in quiet and sipped the wine. Carrie took Jake by the hand and asked him to sit by the fire, their special place. Their eyes met, both thinking the same thoughts, holding each other and wanting each other — to hold, feel, and explore each other's bodies.

They heard the shutters bang against the house; it had started to rain and the wind was blowing hard. The tree branches were creaking; a few had even dropped to the ground. Suddenly, the power went out and the firelight filled the room.

"I wanted this to be special, Carrie, our first time together," Jake said, leaning into Carrie.

"This is special, our little piece of heaven here in front of the fire. We have told each other our deepest thoughts about ourselves and our feelings right here. This feels right. Jake, make love to me now."

Jake fumbled with the buttons on Carrie's blouse and began kissing her neck; he removed her blouse and then her bra, looking at her well formed breasts. "I have never seen such beauty, my love. I hope you will not be disappointed."

"Jake, you are amazing. You are more man than I have ever dreamed about," she replied as she reached for his belt. None of his past experience with women had prepared him for what he felt at this moment. He kissed her bare shoulders as they moved out of their clothes. They both stood, looking at each other's bodies. The beauty they saw in each other was overwhelming.

Jake picked Carrie up in his arms and carried her to the bedroom and laid her gently on the bed. Then he lay next to her, holding her and making love to her. Their love was real and cherished. They became one in each other's arms, both content and feeling blessed to have found each other. They lay in each other's arms, falling asleep.

The storm woke them with the noise of the shutters slamming against the house. They could hear the storm outside and drifted into making love again.

Daylight came and Jake got up. He stood watching Carrie sleep; she was so beautiful. He was so full of happiness and love for this woman. He slipped into his pants, grabbed his shirt, and made his way to the kitchen.

Carrie woke to the smell of brewing coffee. She stretched her arms up over her head then felt beside her.

Jake was gone. She sat up frightened and then heard singing coming for the kitchen. "O, what a beautiful morning...," Jake sang at the top of his lungs. Carrie put her hand over her mouth and laughed to herself. *Wow, I know one thing; he sure can't carry a tune.* Looking at Blackie who was on the floor wagging his tail, Carrie reached for her robe and slipped it on. She made her way to the kitchen. The table was set with a rose in the middle. Jake was standing in front of the stove putting griddle cakes on the grill.

"Well, Mr. T, you really can cook! This is nice; I rather like this." Carrie moved close to Jake.

"My dear, didn't I tell you I love to cook? It's kind of a hobby of mine."

"You can do your hobby anytime." Carrie reached for a hug.

"Little lady, did I wake you?"

"No, the coffee did."

"That was a great night, don't you think?"

"Oh, yes!" Carrie looked up and smiled at Jake then kissed him. "Good morning, Jake. Pinch me. I think I am dreaming."

"Sweetheart, this is true and it is happening to us. When you get back from the East, we will have to have a wedding."

"Jake, is that a proposal?" Carrie said smiling. Jake quickly got down on one knee and asked Carrie to marry him. "Yes, Jake." He stood up and took her in his arms. "This is a dream. I know I will wake up soon."

"No, little lady, it is not a dream. You just told me you would be my wife." He kissed her gently. Carrie walked around the kitchen, her hand on her forehead.

"Jake, we have so much to do here at the farm: the shutters and the garage door."

"I think we need to fix the silo door first." He made a face at her. "I know a man who works around the farms and his wife helps out some. I hired him to help during planting. I bet I could get the both of them pretty cheap. What do you think?" Jake sat at the table while Carrie poured his coffee.

"Really, that would be good. She could help me clean up this farmhouse—new paint, drapes, and all."

"Good, I will get hold of him and see if I can hire them both. We may have to put in a trailer site as that's what they live in."

"No problem."

Blackie started to bark and Jake made his way to the front of the house. Mary was making her way to the porch. "Mary's here," Jake called out.

Carrie joined Jake and looked surprised, "What will she think, Jake?"

"Don't worry. I will take care of everything," he said as he opened the door.

"Hello, Mary. What brings you out this time of morning?"

"Well, I just might ask you, Jake Thompson, what are you doing here?"

"Come on in, Mary. The coffee is hot; you can join us," Jake said as he held the door open.

Carrie gave Mary a little hug. Then Mary followed her. The three of them sat at the table and Jake gave Mary her coffee. She knew that Carrie was in her robe, so her mind drew its own conclusions about what had occurred between the two of them.

"Well, Mary, we have good news. Carrie is keeping the farm and will make this her home as soon as she comes back from the East." Mary's eyes lit up; she got up and hugged Carrie.

"Your grandfather Hank is smiling down upon us today, child." Mary said.

"I just have to be here. I love the farm and this dog," Carrie petted Blackie.

"I can see that you two…well, I think maybe something is going on here, am I right?

"Yes, Mary, you are. Carrie and I have become an item. I love this girl and we plan to share our lives." Jake took Carrie's hand from across the table.

"That's good coffee, Jake. You be good to this lady here. After all, she is part of Hank." Mary got up and walked to the front door. "I will be keeping an eye on you, Jake Thompson," she said.

"Hey, that's okay. Mary, thank you for stopping by." Mary left in her usual way.

"Jake, why did she come over?" They both started to laugh.

"I told you I would take care of everything, remember?"

"She is something, isn't she? Comes and goes as she wants," Carrie remarked. "But she is a great person and helps everyone. And I'm sure Hank talked to her too." They finished their breakfast and Carrie got dressed.

The storm was over. Some dark clouds remained in the sky, but at least the wind had stopped. Jake asked Carrie if she would like to go for a walk, so they both put on their boots and heavy coats and left for the sheep barn, with Blackie on their heels. As they walked the farm road, they could see the ducks on the pond. Blackie barked and the ducks took off in flight. "Jake, look." Carrie pointed towards the sky. The ducks flew right over them.

"It won't be long now and they will be making a nest." Jake bent down by the side of the pond. "Look here, Carrie; see the prints? A coon was here, perhaps after the storm; these are fresh prints." Jake stood up and told Carrie that the coon would be back to break up the duck nest. They walked in the rutted, muddy road towards the sheep barn.

"What feeds the pond?" Carrie asked.

"Probably an underground spring," he said. They walked hand in hand.

"My grandfather used to have about two hundred sheep up here. I loved to come here and feed the lambs." They entered the barn. Carrie pointed out all the pens; some were broken down and the gates were hanging on their hinges. Just then, a loud clap of thunder sounded close by and hail beat down on the tin roof of the barn. Carrie held her hands over her ears. Then, just as it had started, the hail stopped.

Blackie came running inside the barn, barking and turning away from Jake and running. "Look, Jake, he wants us to follow him." Carrie ran after the dog. Jake reached a fence row where the barbed wire was strung out and loose. Blackie ran to a ditch. Jake made his way with the dog to find a deer trapped in the wire.

"Carrie, call Blackie back and I will try to let this poor critter loose." Carrie held the dog and they waited for Jake to help the deer. Then suddenly the deer made a dash and away she went, off into the woods.

"That poor thing, she was frightened to death," Carrie said.

"Well, Blackie, you did it again," Jake said reaching for the dog. "I guess we had better get back before we get caught in another shower." Jake put his arm around Carrie. As they walked towards the pond, Carrie pointed at a rainbow. Jake looked over at the fence rows, all overgrown with brush and broken posts lying on the ground. "One thing is for sure; we can keep busy in the off season cleaning up this part of the farm. It really needs new fences," Jake told Carrie.

They walked by the pond again and stopped to look around. The storm had caused some branches to fall into the water. "Here we have a mess to clean up. Jake, when I was a girl, this was a neat place to come to on a hot day," Carrie said bending down at the water's edge.

"Yes, I can see that this could be a fine place for us to come and relax in the summer. We will have to work on this spot, that's for sure." Smiling down at Carrie and pulling her to him, "I can see you in one of those little swim suits or maybe…"

"Jake Thompson, are you thinking about…"

"Now, now, little lady, don't put those thoughts in my head. I have a hard time as it is," Jake said as he kissed her softly.

They entered the barn where Carrie had been locked in the silo. She hesitated to look in this time, but she knew Jake was with her. They wandered around the barn.

"Did you ever have any horses here, Carrie?"

"Yes, we had Old Spot, but there is room for two. These old stalls look pretty good, don't you think?"

"Yeah, they would do. Just need a little cleaning up," Jake said.

"Jake, it would be so nice to bring some animals back to the farm. Do you think we could?"

"No reason why not. Do you like to ride?"

"I love to ride. Old Spot and I would go for hours at a time. Jake, there are two hundred acres here, and this big barn, room for a lot of hay. And then the milk house. We could use this in a few years for a wine shop and…"

"Wait a minute! Let's not get ahead of ourselves, hon. We have a lot of work to do."

"Oh, I know, but a girl has to dream a little and we can do this, Jake, together; I'm sure of it."

"Little lady, whatever makes you happy, we can work on it." They walked back to the house, with Blackie on their heels. It felt good to get out and look over the farm.

All of a sudden, Jake swept Carrie up in his arms and entered the house. "Jake, what are you up to now?"

"Little lady, I can't get enough of you and you're leaving soon." Jake sat Carrie down on a kitchen chair and reached for her boots, pulling them off. He took her coat off and threw it on the floor, took his own boots off, and then he led her to the fireplace. Carrie sat in front of the smoldering fire while Jake added more wood. They sat for a while, talking about the farm.

"Carrie, do you like kids?"

"Sure, I've always wanted children. I knew Bepo would love them. Farm life is great for kids."

"How many do you want?" Jake asked.

"Oh, about a dozen," Carrie laughed.

"Well, we better get working or thinking about that." Jake pushed his hair out of eyes. "Come here, woman," Jake whispered. They made love in the warmth of the fire and then lay in each other's arms.

The next few days, Jake and Carrie spent every minute together, moving him into his new home and making plans for the farm. With Mannie and Rosa working at Carrie's farm, Jake would have the farmhouse all painted and cleaned up before Carrie came back. Pop would be here and he would be surprised at all the news Jake had for him.

Carrie knew that she had to go back East and she dreaded the flight; it was so long. Then she had to talk to Alex; he was not going to be happy.

Carrie and Jake stood among the people at the airport waiting for Carrie's flight number to be called. They both were hurting, thinking about how awful it would be to be apart.

"I wish I was on my way back, Jake, instead of this." Carrie held onto Jake's hand and didn't want to let go. Suddenly, her flight number came up. Carrie felt sick to her stomach and tears started to fill her eyes.

"Look, little lady, I want to tell you something. I love you so damn much and I am going to miss you every minute you are gone so get everything settled and get back here.

Okay?" Jake wrapped his arms around her and kissed her twice.

"Jake, I will call as soon as I get to Jo's and every day we will talk, okay? I love you, Jake Thompson," she called out as she moved with the passengers boarding the plane.

Jake waved as he watched her board the plane. He moved to a window and waited till the plane took off and then watched as it disappeared into the clouds.

He walked slowly to the parking garage; he missed her already. He knew he loved her and wanted her back. Then he told himself to get with it. Pop would be in tomorrow and he had things to do. He knew the days would go by fast and he would wait for her phone call.

Chapter Eight

Carrie took her seat by the window, buckled her seat belt, and waited for the plane to take off. As the plane started to move, her eyes locked onto the ground rushing under the plane. She could hear the roar of the jet engines. When the aircraft lifted off, she felt the pressure in her back as the plane reached altitude and leveled off. She looked around and noticed the plane was at full capacity. The seven hour flight seemed to go on forever.

Carrie sat for a long time looking out as far as she could see, glancing below from time to time. Over the wing, she could see below through the fluffy clouds small cities and highways, lakes and rivers. Everything looked so clean and peaceful from so far above. She wondered as she looked up and saw such beauty: Would heaven be like this? And if so, she could feel close to her Bepo.

She reached in her handbag for the brochure that Jake had given her. A large log home was featured on the front cover. Fingering through the pages, she saw house plans in all sizes and stopped to stare at a four bedroom with three of those rooms in the loft. Liking the plan, she studied it: a large fireplace off the kitchen, a nice family area, and an office off the back of the house—just perfect for Jake.

Carrie closed her eyes. She pictured several children running about. Then she saw herself with Jake, sitting in a swing on the front deck on a hot summer night, looking over the newly planted vineyard; they were a very happy couple with their family. Carrie drifted off in a restless sleep.

Her dream changed. Now she saw a tall man standing by the entrance of the church. He turned and stared into her eyes. Who was this stranger at her Bepo's service? What did he want? Did he know her grandfather? She started to move towards him as he walked away. *Wait? Wait? Who are you?* Carrie ran to catch up with him, but he kept walking away into a deepening fog.

"Miss," the attendant whispered. Carrie opened her eyes.

"I'm so sorry. I guess I drifted off. Are we about to land?" asked Carrie.

"Yes, miss, in about ten minutes," the attendant stated.

Carrie sat up in her seat and fussed with her hair. She hated landings and hoped this one would be better than the last. Why on earth had this stranger come to her in a dream? She shook her head to clear it. She thought about how grateful she was for the past two weeks and how one's life could change. She thought about Jake and wished she were home on the farm. She smiled; nothing could get in the way of her happiness.

Carrie reached for her purse and placed it on her lap. The light came on overhead, signaling passengers to fasten their seatbelts and wait for the plane to land.

The plane sat down easily and taxied to the terminal. Carrie stayed in her seat, waiting for the other passengers to get up and leave. Soon it was her turn. She made her way forward, moving along with the other passengers, and stepped into the terminal. She watched people as they moved about. It was early into the evening rush hour and everyone was in such a hurry.

Carrie moved slowly with her bags, then she spotted Alex hurrying towards her. He reached for her one of her bags. Carrie was surprised to see him,

"How did you know Alex the time and all"

"I heard at the office I just thought it would be nice to pick you up."

"Yes it is I guess." Carrie forcing a smile.

Then he reached out to Carrie for a hug, but she pulled away. They moved to the parking garage and towards the van.

"Come on Alex: help me. Let's get these bags in the van and get out of here," Carrie said.

"Well, is that any way to greet me?" Alex gave Carrie an astonished look. He moved towards her slowly, picked up one bag, and put it in his van. Then he reached out to Carrie for a hug, but she pulled away again.

"Alex, fine; it's nice to see you. Okay? But I've had a very long day. Again Alex moved towards her for a hug. "Alex! People are everywhere. Will you stop this? Here, take this bag. Let's go."

He took the last bag and put it in the van. He walked around to his side, got in, and waited for Carrie to close her door.

"You're sure in a bad mood, Carrie." Alex looked at her.

"I know; I'm sorry. It's just, well, at least I'm here," she said.

"Was your flight that bad?"

"Yeah! Not too good." *A small white lie*, she thought.

They didn't say much as he drove the few blocks to Carrie and Jo's apartment. He parked in the underground parking lot and got out of the van. He lifted the bags out. Carrie picked up her shoulder bag and started walking. Alex picked up the other two bags, moving slowly as he lugged them towards the elevator door.

"What do you have in these things?" he complained. They rode up to the third floor, not speaking to each other. The elevator door opened and Alex carried the two bags to the door of the apartment. Carrie unlocked it. She hoped Jo would be home because she didn't want to get in to it with Alex. Not tonight anyway.

Carrie called out. "Jo, I'm back."

"Looks like were alone," Alex said as he set the bags down. "Now, why don't you say hello the proper way," he teased, taking Carrie in his arms.

Carrie felt the wet kiss on her lips. She put her hands on his shoulders and pulled away.

"Come on, Carrie. I've waited weeks for this moment. I've missed you, honey. Come on; let's make up for some lost time." Alex pulled her towards the bedroom.

"Alex! Please! I'm tired! You know I have had along day. Is that all you think about?" She raised her voice.

"Well, what can I say? I really missed you, and it's so nice to have you home. Come on, babe," he pleaded.

"Alex, things have changed, okay?" Carrie moved a few steps away from him.

Just then the door flew open. Jo walked in, her arms full of shopping bags.

"Hello, you two. I was trying to get home before you got in, but the store was packed with people."

"I'm so glad you're home," Carrie said, helping her carry the bags into the kitchen

"How was your flight, girlfriend?" She gave Carrie a big hug.

"It was great. Am I ever glad you're here. You came just in time. We have to get rid of Alex; I just can't talk to him tonight. Now I know it was a mistake to let him bring me home." Carrie said.

They both turned around to see Alex in the kitchen doorway, listening to the conversation.

"So, you want to get rid of me tonight, huh? You don't want to talk to me? And what did Jo save you from, Carrie," he said.

"Alex, I'm sorry. I didn't mean it like that. I really do need to talk to you. Like I said, things have changed since I've been away. Please try not to be so upset," she said.

"Now, you two, let's just sit down and visit a little. We should let Carrie tell us about her trip." Jo began to lead them over to the living room sofa, but neither of them paid much attention to her.

"No way, Jo. To hell with you, Carrie Roundtree! I can tell when I'm not wanted." He turned away with his hands on his hips.

Just then the phone rang. Jo picked it up.

"Hello. Yes, she's here. It's for you, Carrie."

"Hello? Oh, hi. I'm finally here; it was a long flight. And you know where I'd rather be."

"Can't talk, huh? Is he there with you now?" Jake asked.

"Yes, that's for sure," Carrie answered and then turned away from Alex,

"I'll call back about nine, okay? I love you, little lady."

"That will be just fine. Goodbye." She put the phone back on the receiver.

Alex paced around the room.

"Come on, Alex. Sit down. Let's try to talk about this without getting mad at each other," Carrie asked gently.

"So what has happened, Carrie? You want to tell me?" Alex stopped in front of Carrie.

"Jo and Alex—I have something to tell you both. I have decided to keep the farm and move out west. I've come here to give my notice to Mr. G."

"You're going to become a farmer? Give me a break," Alex said laughing.

"Alex, I know you're upset and all, but the farm has been in my family for so long…I just can't let someone else live on it."

"Carrie, you haven't a clue about farming," Alex said.

"Do you think you can do this?" Jo asked Carrie.

"Yes, but there's more. I have a neighbor who my grandfather wanted me to meet. He's going to help me with the farm. His name is Jake Thompson," Carrie said, looking at Jo.

"So Carrie, you're going to leave a career here in the city for a piece of dirt out west," Alex said bluntly. "And by the way, I know all about the money—the two hundred thousand—you turned down. I can't believe this is happening to us. Do you know what we could do with that kind of money? We could have a real life." He wiped his hair out of his eyes.

"Carrie, I didn't tell him," Jo said.

"No, she didn't. I overheard you two on the phone and put it all together," Alex said.

"I see," Carrie said firmly.

"Well, what about us? I thought we were going to have a life together."

"That's just it, Alex; you thought. We've been good friends and have spent some special times together, but we've never made any plans for the future. I'm glad we've been able to work together and still be good friends."

"Yeah, two years of my life down the tube helping you with your job. So, how old is this farmer guy?"

"If you really want to know, Alex, Jake is more than just a neighbor to me. We are committed to each other."

"What! You mean to tell me that you and this farmer— this has to be a joke! I thought you were smarter than that, and you fell in love with him in a week and a half?" Alex shook his head and looked away.

"Alex, Carrie is only trying to tell you how she feels," Jo said.

"Carrie, have you been touched in the head?" He pointed to his own. "Jo, can you talk some sense into her?"

"Hey, I'm staying out of this. But, Alex, sometimes people just have to move on," Jo said.

Alex threw up his arms is disgust, yelling at Carrie, "Why? Why? What do I do now? And how much do you know about this guy?"

"Alex, we were going nowhere. We work together and have some fun times; I just don't have any real feelings for you. We don't have a future," Carrie said, walking toward him. "I do hope we still can be friends."

"No way, Carrie! You're making a big mistake. You don't know anything about running a farm, taking care of animals, and all that stuff. I won't give you up. Carrie, you know how I feel," he said reaching for her. Carrie moved away from him and looked at Jo.

"Alex, I just don't love you and I never will. I don't want to hurt you. I do appreciate all your help at work but try to understand."

Alex moved to the door and opened it. "Carrie, I think you're mad. This isn't over yet," he yelled and slammed the door as he left.

Carrie turned to Jo, "I knew this was going to happen. I really messed up, didn't I?"

"What can I say, girlfriend? You know how I feel about Alex. I thank God you have come to your senses. I just hope he won't carry this any further," Jo said.

"He can't do anything. I just told him how I feel. He has to understand that."

"So, it's nice to have you back, even for just a little while. Now tell me all about the past two weeks and about this new, wonderful farmer in your life," Jo said with a little giggle.

"I do have a lot to tell you, Jo." Carrie's voice was filled with excitement. "I love him so much. I know it's hard to believe this—it has happened so fast—but if you met Jake and talked to him and saw what a wonderful person he is and he is so sincere, I just know you would grow to think of him as a brother. I know, who would have ever thought this would happen to me? I mean, the farm and Jake."

"Honey, I'm happy for you and I can hardly wait to meet this man of yours. So tell me everything and don't leave anything out." Jo sat back and got comfortable. The two of them sat for a long time, Carrie telling Jo all about the farm, Blackie, and Grandfather's service. She told her about Jake, his friends, and the house he was building. Then she mentioned the strange man at the café and at the service.

"Who do you think this man is?"

"I have no idea. He must have just been a friend of Bepo's. He never came up to me or anyone else there. He left as soon as the service was over. He was tall and very distinguished looking. Oh, well, who knows? Maybe some-day we will run into each other again. It is strange. I get the funny feeling I should know him." Carrie flashed back to him sitting in the café and then she told Jo about the dream.

"So, girlfriend, when do you really have to be back in Oregon?"

"I hope Mr. G will let me leave in two weeks. What do you think?"

"He's a neat old man and a good boss. I bet he'll understand," Jo said.

"I hope so, Jo," she said but her eyes betrayed the sadness she felt at leaving her best friend.

"I will miss you, Carrie. Maybe I should transfer out west, my parents being in Canada," Jo laughed.

"Jo, that would be wonderful. Will you really think about it?"

"I just might, Carrie; we have always been pretty close. I hate to see you go so far away. I might need to keep tabs on you," she winked.

The phone rang.

"Hello?"

"Jo, I need to talk to Carrie. Put her on please."

Jo handed the phone to Carrie. "Guess who?"

Carrie took the phone reluctantly.

"Ah, I really feel bad for the way I acted. Carrie, you were right. I want us to be friends after all, you know?"

"Good, I would like that, Alex." Carrie nodded her head at Jo.

"So, how about you meeting me at the pub tomorrow night for a drink and we can talk," Alex asked.

Carrie covered the phone with her hand and whispered to Jo. "He wants me to meet him tomorrow night."

Jo stood up and shook her head no.

"Alex, I really don't think it would be a good idea."

"Come on, Carrie, for friendship. I promise I won't talk about you and your new found love."

"Well, okay. How about right after work, say six?"

Jo shook her head at Carrie in disapproval.

"Hey, that's just great. See you at work."

Carrie put the phone down gently and then looked at Jo.

"Carrie, I hope you know what you're doing," Jo said. The phone rang again.

"Hello?"

"Hi, little lady," his voice sounded strong on the other end of the line. "Oh, Jake, it is so good to hear your voice. Thank you for calling back. I've been waiting."

"It's great to hear your voice, too, hon. I've missed you all day and so has Blackie. How was your flight?"

"It was fine and the landing was good too."

"I bet you two ladies have really been talking it up."

"I had to tell Jo all about us, the farm, and some of our plans. Oh, Jake, I can't wait. These two weeks will take forever."

"Now, hon. I'm sure it will go by fast enough. You have a lot to do, packing and all."

"I know. When will you call again?"

"How about Sunday? Pop will be coming in sometime in the afternoon and then you can talk to him, too."

"That sounds nice," Carrie said.

"I guess I'd better go, huh," Jake said.

"I know. I love you, dear man."

"And I love you, little lady. Till Sunday."

Chapter Nine

Alex sat thinking about Carrie. He kept going over the past several years with her in his head. He had become Carrie's friend and had helped her with some of her work at the paper. They often worked on articles together. The two of them had been getting involved. He thought that going to the movies, taking in a dinner now and then, and sometimes going to the theater was being involved. He knew Jo didn't care much for him and he felt the same about her, but he knew he had loved Carrie for a long time. Their sex was good, when it happened. Carrie always had a way of putting him off or had some excuse. She was right; he never had talked about the future. He had taken her for granted. He had really thought she knew how much he loved her.

Alex got up and poured himself another drink. "Damn you, Carrie Roundtree. You'll pay for this. This won't happen to me again. Once is enough." He thought about the ex-girlfriend who had put him through the same thing when he lived in Idaho. Then he thought about the money. *All that money and I can't touch it. All down the tube.* He threw his drink against the wall, the glass shattering and the amber liquid splashing all over.

A farmer! She must be crazy. What does he have over me? Some dirt to plant grapes in? Shit.

He went to bed, trying to get some sleep. *No woman is going to dump me,* he kept saying over and over in his mind.

The night seemed to drag on and on; no matter how hard he tried, he could not sleep. Finally, the alarm clock went off at six thirty. Alex showered and dressed to leave for the paper.

That day he was the first one in Mr. G's office. Alex straightened his tie and tucked in his shirt as he stepped into Mr. G's office.

"Good morning, Alex." Mr. G said, sitting behind his desk.

"Good morning, sir."

"So, did you want to see me, Alex?"

"Ah, yes. I thought you might like to know about Carrie."

"My Lord, she's not hurt or something, is she?" Mr. G said.

"No, sir, she's just fine. But I was hoping you might talk to her. She wants to leave the paper."

"Oh, really? Alex, she hasn't been in yet, so I haven't talked to her." Mr. G looked puzzled.

"I hate to see her leave, Mr. G. Will you talk to her?"

"Alex, I'm sure Carrie can explain things to me. Let's give her a chance. Now I think you'd better get to work," Mr. G said firmly.

Alex left Mr. G's office. *That sure didn't do any good. Damn the old man.* Alex sat at his desk with Carrie on his mind. What could he do to get her to stay? If she didn't, she sure would be sorry. He would give her one more chance. Tonight he would ask her to stay and give up this farmer. If not, well, he would think up something. He would have to convince her to sell the farm and come back to Boston; he just knew they could have a good life.

Jo and Carrie were laughing as they walked into the office. Carrie didn't even say hello to Alex. She went right to Mr. G's office and knocked on the door.

"Hello, Carrie, welcome back! We missed you," he said.

"Yes, I missed the paper and you too." Carrie smiled as she looked around the office. She sat down in front of Mr. G, placing her folded hands firmly in her lap to hide her nervousness; her palms were already sweating.

"Carrie, what is it?"

"Well, sir, I want to give my notice. You know my grandfather passed away, and he left me a farm in Oregon. It has been in the family for many years. I have decided that I want to go back to live there." She looked right at Mr. G.

"I see," Mr. G said. "Go on."

"I have a neighbor who has offered to help me out there. I do appreciate my job, but I feel that I need to go back to Oregon."

"You know, Carrie, the cat has already been let out of the bag. Alex came in and asked to me to try and stop you."

"Mr. G, I am sorry. I wanted to tell you myself. I don't know why he did that."

"Well, he does have a little crush on you," he said, raising his eyebrows.

"I know. However, I've told him how I feel. There is someone else in my life now." Carrie smiled.

"You know, Carrie, I think you are a very brave young woman and I admire you for wanting to run that farm. When do you want to leave?"

"In two weeks, if possible."

"I think we can arrange that. I will just have to give Alex more work," Mr. G. laughed. "But you will keep in touch, won't you?"

"Yes, I will. Thank you, sir." Carrie got up and shook Mr. G's hand, then turned, and left his office. She walked right by Alex and went to her desk, giving Jo a thumbs-up as she started to catch up on her paper work.

Alex left the office early, about four. On his way out, he stopped by Carrie's desk and reminded her about their date.

Carrie looked at her watch around five thirty. "Jo, I'm leaving now. I'll be home no later than seven thirty. I hope to make this as short as possible," Carrie told her.

"Carrie, are you sure you want to do this? Maybe I should come with you." Jo looked worried.

"Heavens no! He wants to be friends and that's all I want. Anyway, see you soon, girlfriend." Carrie waved as she left.

Carrie took a cab to the pub and arrived at about ten to six. She walked into the dark, smoked-filled room looking for Alex. She saw him, standing up and motioning her to a table in the back.

"Here I am. Come sit down right here, Carrie. I'll go get you a glass of wine."

Carrie noticed he was staggering as he left to go to the bar. He had been drinking straight shots; several empty glasses were sitting on the table. She wished she had gone home; meeting Alex was a mistake.

"There you go, Carrie." He placed a wine glass in front of her and sat down. "Now, Carrie, let's have a little talk," he said.

"What do you want to talk about, Alex? My job and how you told Mr. G I was leaving?" Carrie could feel her face get hot with anger.

"Now don't get upset, Carrie. I just thought he might ask you to stay. Maybe he would give you a raise or something. You know that I want you to stay, honey."

"Alex, I told you I was leaving."

"I know, but I do want to be a friend even if you don't love me. Carrie, I do love you and I need you. We can go right now to my place and talk all about it. I know we can make this work."

"Alex, I'd better go. This conversation is going nowhere."

"So you're telling me that you and that farmer guy are serious?" Alex took another shot with a look of disgust and amusement on his face.

"Yes, we are Alex. Please understand. You said you would!" Carrie started to get up to leave.

"I know what I said, but can't a guy try?"

"Alex, I'm flattered that you say you love me. But it just won't work. Now let's not fight about it, okay?"

Alex looked at Carrie. He thought he hated her.

"Alex, let's go now. You've had too much to drink."

"Okay, you're right. Maybe I should walk it off. Let's walk you home and then I can catch a cab."

Carrie watched him set some money on the table. He took her arm and led her through the crowd of people. The pub was very busy, the people loud and pushy. They made their way to the door. As they stepped outside, Carrie took a deep breath and hoped the fresh air would help Alex clear his head. Then he would let go of her arm. But he continued to pull her along with him.

Carrie felt his hand firmly around her arm, holding her so tightly it hurt. They walked down the street. She moved gently and tried to pull away, but he just held on with more force.

"You know, Carrie, I don't want it this way. What can I do to change your mind?"

"Nothing, Alex; it just won't happen between us. I am sorry. But we can be friends. We still have to work together for a couple of weeks; then I will be gone and you can forget me," she said again while trying to pull her arm free.

They continued down the dark street to the corner, waited for the cars to pass, then crossed. Alex led her about half a block then quickly pulled her into a side alley where darkness surrounded her.

"Alex! What are you doing? Stop this right now! Let me go! You're drunk!"

"Oh, you think I am, huh? Well, let me tell you something," he said as he pushed her hard up against the brick wall.

Carrie felt her head hit the brick, making her dizzy. He pinned his body up against her, taking her arms and putting them over her head. Forcing her mouth open, he kissed her hard and long. She struggled beneath him, but he just kept pressing his body against her harder. She kept fighting to get away, not knowing where his strength was coming from. She could feel his manhood hard against her. Fear ran through her body and she knew she had to get away from him. She strained to look past him for help, but there was no one in sight.

Suddenly he pushed her to the pavement, his body on top of hers. He pressed his mouth against hers again, his hand reaching for one of her breasts. Carrie couldn't stand the smell of the alcohol on his breath; she felt sick. All of a sudden, he let her go and stood up.

She brushed her hair out of her face, took a deep breath, and started to get up. But he leaned down and grabbed her hair, pulling her head up to face him. Then he hit her in the face with his fist. The searing pain stunned her and for a moment she was unaware of where she was.

"No woman is going to dump me, Carrie Roundtree. You had this coming to you. You're a tease and you led me on." He touched his face gingerly and looked down at his fingers to see blood. "You bitch! You scratched me," he hissed.

Carrie could barely hear his words; pain racked her face and body. "Please, Alex," she cried, "don't hit me anymore! Let me go, please. Okay? We can talk this over; I won't go back to Oregon. Please! Just don't hit me again," she pleaded.

"You're not worth it, bitch!"

Carrie just lay there waiting for him to leave.

Alex moved away from Carrie, then stumbling, he turned and came at her again. He kicked her in the side several times, each blow harder than the last, sending waves of pain crashing through her body. Then he turned and left. She could hear him laughing, staggering off into the darkness.

Carrie pulled herself up the wall, her fingers clawing each brick to help her stand. Blood ran down her cheek. Pain jolted her body with each breath. She felt her way along the wall till she could see the street lights then stumbled and fell in the street. Carrie heard a horn honking loudly and the sound of brakes screeching. She tried to get up but collapsed back to the pavement just as the car came to a halt in front of her. A man got out and ran over to her.

"Miss! Miss!" That was the last thing she heard.

The stranger stood by Carrie's limp body, yelling for an ambulance.

Carrie woke up staring into two bright lights overhead. She was in an unfamiliar, scary place.

"Jake, Jake..."

"Hold still, please. We need to help you," the doctor said.

"Where am I?"

"You're in the emergency room, miss."

A police officer stepped into the room. "How long will it be until I can ask Miss Roundtree some questions?"

"Just about finished here," the doctor stated.

Carrie could feel something on her face, a bandage she assumed. She took a deep breath and yelled in pain. "My side? What happened to me?"

"You don't remember, miss?" the officer asked.

"No...wait...yes, I do. Alex, he..."

"Carrie, I'm Dr. Brookmire. I would like to keep you over night for observation. You have two broken ribs and a possible concussion. I am also concerned about your left eye. That's why there is a bandage over it. I want to get a better look at it in the morning. You were hit pretty hard. I'm moving you to a room upstairs," the doctor said.

"Will you call my friend? Her name is Jo Hamilton; her name and number are in my purse." The doctor nodded. "Thank you."

"Officer, don't stay too long. Miss Roundtree needs to rest." Then Dr. Brookmire left the room.

The police officer asked Carrie all kinds of questions. Who was Alex? How long had she known him? Had he ever hit her before? Where did he live? Carrie gave him all the information she could and then was asked to sign a complaint against him. She didn't hesitate. The officer left but told her he might need more information.

A nurse came in and helped Carrie into a wheel chair then wheeled her upstairs to another room. Carrie lay in her bed on her right side, talking to the nurse.

"I just don't understand why he did this to me." Taking her hand and wiping her tear-stained face. The nurse comforted Carrie while she rested.

Jo was eating a sandwich and catching up on some reading when the phone rang.

"Hello?"

"Is this Jo Hamilton?"

"Yes."

"This is University Hospital. You have a friend here, Miss Roundtree; she is asking for you."

"What happened? Is she okay?" Jo sat down in fear of what the woman on the other line might say.

"Yes, she'll be fine. But she will need to stay overnight. It would be good if you could come down."

"I will. I'll be right there."

When Jo walked into Carrie's room an hour later, Carrie was sound asleep. Jo pulled up a chair next to the bed and sat down. Carefully she took Carrie's hand in hers. The nurse came back into the room.

"What happened?" Jo asked.

"Your friend here was beaten pretty badly by her boyfriend, I take it. I do believe the officer will be back," she said.

"Oh, my God. Alex did this? How could he?"

"Jo, is that you?" Carrie slowly opened her eye and looked up at Jo.

"Yes, honey. I'm here, Carrie. I won't leave, sweetie. What happened?"

"Alex, he…he…drug me into an alley and…" Carrie started to cry.

"Oh, Carrie, I wish you would have listened to me. Or I should have gone with you."

"I know. Oh, I hurt so bad; he kicked me. The doctor said I have two broken ribs and my eye…Jo, he hit me so hard and he was so drunk. I don't know where all his strength came from.

"Hush, honey, you need your rest," Jo told her.

"I will, but first will you call Jake?"

"Sure. You want me to right now?"

"Please. Jo, why did Alex do this to me?"

"I don't know, honey. He's just all mixed up, I guess," Jo said.

"He had a lot to drink; he was a mad man."

"Carrie, did he..."

"No, thank goodness. He just wanted to hurt me because I love Jake and I'm leaving him. Jo, I didn't know he loved me. He never said so. I even told him I would stay if he would just quit beating me. I didn't know what to do, Jo."

"Carrie, I want you to rest. I'm going now to use the phone, but I will be back. I'm staying with you, okay?"

"Okay. Hurry, Jo." With that, she closed her eye and drifted off into sleep. Jo looked at the nurse.

"The doctor gave her a sedative," the nurse told her. "She should sleep for a while."

Jo nodded and left the room, making her way to the nearest phone booth.

Alex heard the knock on the door. It woke him. He pulled himself out of the chair where he had fallen asleep and stumbled over to the door. When he opened it, he saw two policemen standing there.

"Yes, what do you want?" Alex rubbed his eyes and yawned a little.

"Mr. Alex Blane?"

"Yes, what is it?"

"May we come in?"

Alex stood back and opened the door to motion the officers into his apartment.

"We need to ask you some questions?"

"Yeah? What for?"

"Do you know a Miss Carrie Roundtree?"

"Sure, I work with her. Why?"

"Where were you about two hours ago, around seven?"

"Ah, I guess I was leaving the pub," Alex stated.

"Were you and Miss Roundtree together?"

"Yeah, we had a drink and then I left and came home. She was still there, I guess, talking to some people she knew."

"Can you tell me how that stain got on your shirt and that scratch on the side of your face?

"Oh, that. Gee, I really don't know. I must have bumped into something," he said quietly.

"Mr. Blane. I think you better come with us down to the station. We need to ask you some more questions," the officer said.

"Sure thing. Let me get my coat." The officer escorted him to his bedroom and, when Alex started to change his shirt, retrieved the bloodied garment and took it with him to the station.

The officer met Jo outside Carrie's room. "We just picked up Alex Blane. I thought you'd want to know," he said.

"Thank goodness! He shouldn't get away with this." Then she continued down the hall to call Jake.

As the doctor left Carrie's room, he asked the police officer to follow him a few feet from the room door. "I think this young woman was attacked by a man called Alex. No rape but one hell of a beating," the doctor said.

Chapter Ten

Jake heard the phone ring, waking him from his slumber. He reached for the lamp and wiped his forehead and eyes before picking up the phone.

"Hello. Carrie, is that you?"

"No, Jake, it's Jo, Carrie's friend."

"Is something wrong?"

"Yes, I'm afraid there is, Jake. Carrie's in the hospital. She's okay, a little shook up, and has a few cuts here and there."

"My God! What happened to her? Was there an accident?"

"Well, sort of," Jo said softly.

"Please tell me what happened."

"I don't know how to tell you except to just spill it out. Alex attacked her and left her in an alley. She walked in front of a car, but the driver was able to avoid her just in time. She keeps asking for you, Jake."

"Oh my, why would he want to hurt her? My poor Carrie…"

"Carrie was just trying to tell him about you and how she loved you and wanted to move to the farm."

"Has anyone turned him into the police?"

"Yes. Carrie signed a complaint. I hope to talk to an officer soon. They have him in custody already," she said.

"Thank God. How did this happen?" Jake's voice resonated with concern.

"I guess Alex was just mad and went crazy thinking Carrie was leaving. She agreed to meet him at the pub down the street. He led her to believe that he wanted to be friends and that they could talk it all over. He said he wanted to be happy for her. Carrie had no reason to think differently." Jo was shaking and felt sick to her stomach. Talking about what had happened to her best friend upset her again.

"You tell Carrie I'm catching the next plane east. Tell her I love her and I'm on my way." The line went dead.

Jo hung up the phone, thinking how fortunate Carrie was to have a man like Jake. He truly was the man she had been told about.

She stood for a moment, trying to compose herself. She was having a hard time taking all this in—her best friend and a co worker who she would have never guessed would do such an unforgivable thing.

Jo walked slowly back to Carrie's room. As she opened the door, she could see the doctor leaning over Carrie's bed, talking to her, trying to tell Carrie she was in the hospital and she would have to stay at least the night. Carrie just wanted to go home.

Jo moved towards the bed and, trying to calm Carrie down, agreed with the doctor. The doctor then ordered the nurse to give her another sedative to help her sleep. Jo pulled up the chair and sat down. The doctor told her that Carrie would be just fine but she needed her rest.

Jo sat for along time holding onto Carrie's hand. She was so mad at Alex. How could he do this to her best friend? She sat watching Carrie, her face all swollen and her eye bandaged, curled up in a fetal position. Jo then curled up in the chair to spend the night with the sister she had never had and her best friend.

As morning dawned, Jo got up and stiffly moved to the window. As she watched the sun coming up over the city, she turned to hear Carrie call out.

"No! No!" Carrie thrashed about on the pillow.

"It's okay, Carrie honey. You're in your room here in the hospital, remember?" Jo said reaching for her hand.

"Jo, what time is it?"

"It's about seven, hon."

"Do you know what time Jake will get here?"

"No, honey, I don't. But he will be here soon. You really should rest," Jo said as she fluffed up her pillow.

"I'm so sore all over and my ribs hurt."

"I'm sure you hurt all over with him kicking you like that."

The police sergeant came into Carrie's room about nine o'clock.

"Hello, Miss Roundtree. I'm Sergeant Wilson."

"Hello. Are there more questions?"

"No, ma'am. We just wanted to let you know that Mr. Blane is now in jail and he will be there till his arraignment which may take a few days.

"So now what will happen to him?" Carrie asked.

"Depends on the judge," he said.

"They won't turn him loose, will they?" Jo said looking right at the officer.

"I doubt it, ma'am. This Mr. Blane is in a lot of trouble. I think he'll be sentenced to the state prison for this," the Sergeant said.

Jake packed a small bag and left a letter for Pop, who would arrive sometime during the day driving his old truck and pulling a trailer behind it. Jake talked to Mannie and told him to be at the house about noon to wait for Pop. By 3:00 a.m., he was on his way to the Portland airport.

He got his boarding pass and looked at his watch; it was five in the morning. He would soon be on his way to Carrie. He thought about how much this woman had been through and now this. He would bring her back home as soon as he could. *If only I would have gone east with her, this would not have happened. My poor Carrie! God, please let her be okay.*

Alex sat in his jail cell. He was due in court so an attorney could be appointed for him. He would meet with him and talk about the incident and how it all got out of control with his drinking and his anger. Alex could tell his attorney how he felt about Carrie and how sorry he was that he had beaten her so badly. He just didn't know what had gotten into him; he was so mad and hurt.

The iron cell door slammed open. Alex stood waiting.

"Come on, Blane," the jailer said. "It's time for you to go before the judge."

He made Alex bend down and put the shackles on his feet and then cuffed his hands in front of him. Alex walked in front of the jailer, shuffling his feet along. A man opened the door to the court room.

As they entered the bailiff called the court to order and then the judge introduced himself. "I am Judge Anderson. Mr. Blane do you have an Attorney.

"No Sir, I do not,"

"Okay then, the court will appoint you one. You may meet with him and return to your cell."

Carrie awoke looking at Jo, who was asleep in the chair. The nurse came in to take Carrie's blood pressure and Jo stirred.

"Hi, girlfriend. How are you feeling?"

"I don't feel so good. My side and there's this bandage over my eye. Why is it there, Jo?"

"Well, honey, Alex hit you in the face. Your lip is split and the doctor wants you to see a specialist about your eye. He has some concerns."

"What kind of concerns?"

"He just wants to make sure your eye is okay, honey. He can't tell too much now because of the swelling, but in a few days it will look just fine."

"I think I understand," Carrie said, feeling her face. "Jo, do I look awful?"

"Honey, like a truck ran over you," Jo tried to laugh.

"Is there a mirror in here someplace? I want to see my face."

"Oh, Carrie, why not wait a day or two," Jo said.

"No! Jake is coming and I have to see how I look."

Jo took the mirror out of the drawer and handed it to Carrie.

"Jo, I look awful! I can't let Jake see me like this. You have to keep him away," Carrie cried.

"Carrie, the man loves you. He has come a long way to be with you. You have to be strong."

"He won't want me now after all this mess. Damn Alex! Why did he do this? I trusted him." Carrie put her hand on her face.

"Carrie, listen to me. In a few days you will look just fine. You have to give it some time, honey. Now Jake will be here soon."

"What time is it?" Carrie asked.

"It's about one in the afternoon."

Jo continued to sit with Carrie, talking about the life ahead of her and their hopes that Alex would be put away forever. They speculated about how soon Carrie could leave to go back to Oregon. Jo brushed Carrie's hair and put a little makeup on her face.

Then the doctor entered Carrie's room and looked at her chart. "Well, Miss Roundtree, I see you're awake now. How are you feeling?" The doctor reached for her hand to take her pulse.

"I'm very sore. My side hurts pretty badly," Carrie said.

"You know, that is one break that really takes nothing but time to heal. I want to keep you another night just to be on the safe side, I am still a little concerned about your eye.

"How soon can I travel?"

"How far?" the doctor said.

"I live in Oregon and I would like to go home," Carrie replied.

"In a few days and if you take it very easy and get a lot of rest. Then I want you to see a doctor in Oregon in two weeks."

"Very well," Carrie said.

"Okay, I'll be back in the morning; we will take the bandage off your eye then and take a good look at it. You get some rest and not too much company."

"Thank you, doctor," Jo said. "I will make sure she gets a lot of rest."

The doctor smiled at Carrie and left the room.

"There, that wasn't that bad," Jo said.

Carrie pulled the sheet up around her neck.

The door swung open and there stood Jake. He went right up to the bed.

"Carrie, honey, I'm so sorry. I came as fast as I could," Jake reached carefully for Carrie.

"Oh, Jake, I don't want you to see me like this."

Jake held on to Carrie, kissing her forehead and her hands, looking at her. "I love you, Carrie. You're still the prettiest woman in this town, as far as I'm concerned."

"Jake, this is Jo, my friend. She called you."

"Hello, Jo. Thank you so very much for letting me know about all this. "Carrie, how are you honey?"

"I'm okay, I guess. The doctor says I can go home to-morrow and then we can go back to Oregon in a few days," she said, holding on to Jake's hand.

"She has to see a doctor in Oregon in two weeks, but the ER doctor will see her in the morning," Jo said.

Jake sat on the edge of Carrie's bed, listening to her as she told him how the incident with Alex happened. Just as she was getting to the alley part, a man entered the room from the prosecuting attorneys office. Jake stood up and introduced himself and then stepped aside to listen to him.

"Hello, Miss Roundtree. I hope you're feeling better." I am Carl Hudson from the D.A's office.

Carrie smiled as best she could at the man.

"Miss Roundtree, I wanted to stop by and let you know about Mr. Blane."

"Yes, what about him," Carrie asked.

"Well, he went to court today and the judge appointed him an attorney. It will be awhile before he comes in front of the judge to hear his case. So we just wait."

Carrie's whole body trembled thinking about Alex she just wanted it all over with.

"Now, honey, you can't let this bother you. We'll be out on the west coast. He's not going to come out there," Jake said.

Jake paced around the room and turned to the officer. "This could take some time. Will you keep in touch with me sir? Handing him his card.

"Sure will," he said looking at Jakes card.

"This is just hard to take in," Jake said.

"Sir, this wasn't his first time in trouble or the first attack."

"What first attack?" Carrie asked.

"You see, he had a problem in Idaho, but the woman would not press charges against him, so the judge couldn't use that against him. I am truly sorry, Miss Roundtree.

Carrie just sat there in shock. Jake held her hand. Jo walked out of the room with Mr. Hudson.

"Carrie, I want you to listen to me," Jake said. "I will never let anything happen to you, honey. I will always be here for you. You can count on that. Okay? I don't want you to worry." He kissed her on the cheek and held her gently.

"I love you so much, Jake." Carrie said, her eyes filling with tears.

"I know and I love you, little lady. It's going to be all right. We'll be home in a few days. We have a wonderful life ahead of us," Jake said.

Jo entered the room again and sat down in the chair. "Well, Alex is at least put away for now, girlfriend."

"I just never dreamed he could do a thing like this. Jake, we worked together for two years," Carrie told him

"Yeah, but Carrie, there was always something funny about him. You see, Jake, our girl here has a heart of gold and believes that all people are kind," Jo said.

"Yes, I know," Jake said.

Jake and Jo stayed with Carrie until she fell asleep. Then Jo excused herself and told Jake she would wait for him in the lobby. Jake stayed for a while longer looking at her, hurting inside because of her pain. He wished he were lying in that bed.

Jake stayed until Carrie woke and then he talked to her about the farm, and about his house. A nurse came in and told him that Carrie needed her rest and that he should leave. Jake kissed Carrie softly and then joined Jo in the lobby.

Carrie woke up as the nurse came into the room, the doctor right behind her.

"Good morning, Miss Roundtree. How are you feeling this morning?" he asked.

"Better. I think my head doesn't hurt as much and I slept pretty good. Can I go home now?"

"Well, let's take a look at that eye," the doctor said. He took off the bandage carefully and cleaned around the eye. "Well, now, that doesn't look as bad as I thought. A good night's rest really helped. Your eye is a little swollen and a little black and blue, but there is no sign of blood in the eye. And how are the ribs?"

"Sore, but only when I move," she answered the doctor.

"You will hurt for sometime. The ribs heal slowly. It just takes time. Now, when you get home, I want you to rest and no lifting or bending. I still want you to see a doctor in two weeks. If you have any problems, you have your friend take you to a hospital, understand?"

"Yes. Can I go home now?"

"I'll sign the papers. I think you should stay here in the city the rest of the week before making the trip to the west coast," the doctor stated.

"That should be no problem, doctor," Carrie said.

As Jo and Jake walked in the room, Jo was surprised to see such a change in Carrie.

"My, my! Look at you, girl! No patch on that eye and sitting up in the chair! I bet you're ready to leave this place," Jo said.

Jake walked over and kissed Carrie. "Good morning, honey. You look so much better and you still are so beautiful," Jake said.

"I can go home now. The doctor is signing me out of here; he just told me to take it a little easy."

"Yeah, we talked to him. We know how easy," Jo and Jake looked at each other and smiled.

"We plan on spoiling you, kiddo." Jo smiled at her friend.

The next few days Carrie rested in the apartment. Jake sat with Carrie for hours. They talked about Alex, the attack, her leaving the paper, and her work. Carrie knew this had been a hardship on Jake because he should have been working in his vineyard and getting ready for Pop.

Jo and Jake did a lot of packing preparing for the move west. Carrie and Jake took several long walks and stopped in at the sidewalk cafés. Jake and Jo made special dinners for Carrie and bought flowers and brightened up the apartment. On Monday, Jake took Carrie back to see the doctor. He said she could travel and that he was really surprised at how well she was healing. Jake made their reservations for Portland.

It was March 1st. The week had sped by and Carrie and Jake were packed and at the airport.

"Jo, I'm going to miss you so much," Carrie said.

"I know; me too. You just get better. I just may be out west sooner than you think. I love you, girlfriend. You take care," Jo said

"Don't worry, Jo. She's in good hands. We'll give you a call when we get to the farm. I have Mary coming to stay for a few days, and I know she will really make her rest," Jake said, winking at Jo.

"They're calling our flight, Jake. We'd better go," Carrie said.

As Jake and Carrie started to board the plane, Carrie looked back at Jo, waving at her and blowing her a kiss.

Carrie took the window seat and leaned against Jake as they waited for the plane to take off.

"Jake, somehow I will make this all up to you, coming here for me like this," she remarked.

"My dear little lady, I wouldn't be here if I didn't care so much for you. You are my life now, Carrie. I love you. Have I told you how much?"

"Yes, you have, at least twenty times today and I love it." She held his hand tightly in hers.

The plane started to taxi. Soon they were airborne and on their way to Portland. Carrie fell asleep with her head resting on Jake's shoulder. While the trip seemed long for the both of them, they knew a new life was about to start for them. They were leaving Alex and Boston behind them.

The day finally came for Alex his day in court. He had met with his attorney several times and had admitted that he was wrong. The jailer came for Alex and again he was cuffed and put in shackles.

His Attorney was waiting for him and motioned for him to sit down by him.

The court was called to order by the bailiff. Alex was asked to stand and give his Plea.

"Guilty sir," he said.

The judge looked over some papers; then he lifted his head and looked at Alex.

"Mr. Blane, did you hit Miss Roundtree and beat her like this?" The judge looked at the photos in front of him.

"I believe you should see these? Bailiff, show these to Mr. Blane." The bailiff took the photos and handed them to Alex. He looked them over then hung his head.

"Now answer me did you do this to Miss Roundtree?"

"Yes Sir I did." And I am sorry, but."

"I don't like what I see here Mr. Blane I see you have a problem from the past seems something like this happened in Idaho, also you have an anger and alcohol problem."

"Yes Sir."

You will be sentenced on the 10th of next month, please check the calendar Bailiff. He picked up his gavel and hit it on his desk and said "Dismissed."

Alex was removed from the court and was taken back to his cell.

Chapter Eleven

Carrie sat close to Jake, her head on his shoulder, as they drove towards the village. Darkness was starting to settle in and lights were a welcoming sight. Jake turned down Roundtree Lane. He passed Carrie's farm, then Mary's, and then turned onto the lane that led to his house. He parked his truck in front.

"Carrie, honey, wake up," he said, kissing her on her forehead.

"Oh, I must have drifted off. Are we here already?"

"Yes, little lady, we are home. Look, there's my pop. He saw us drive up. He looks great, doesn't he?"

"He sure does, and he seems excited to see you." Carrie moved over to her side of the front seat as Jake got out, came around, opened her door, and helped her out.

Pop walked down the steps of the house and came towards Jake, his arms open. "My son, I have waited so long. It is so good to see you," he said as he reached for Jake and gave him a big bear hug. Then he turned to Carrie. "This is the little woman you told me so much about. I can see why you've taken to her; she is a beauty. I'm Pop," he said, reaching for her. Carrie started to hold out her hand to shake his, but he drew her into a huge hug.

"Easy does it Pop." Jake said.

"Well, Pop, it's nice to meet you and so good to be home again. I'm so sorry Jake wasn't here to meet you, you know, the day you arrived. I guess all my troubles…"

"Now we're not going to worry about that now. We're all here home safe and sound. You know, I just don't like my family way up there," he pointed towards the sky.

The three of them entered the house. All of a sudden, Carrie heard Blackie barking as he ran up the steps of the house and jumped up at her. Jake scolded him, but Carrie bent down and hugged him anyway, stifling the moan that barely escaped her lips as she bent down.

"Now, Carrie, you sit here on the sofa," Pop said as he fluffed up a pillow and handed it to Jake.

"Pop, I'll be taking Carrie home to her farm in a few minutes, but I wanted to see you, old man."

"Hey, none of that old man stuff."

"So tell me Pop, how do you like the house?" Jake asked, as he pulled up a chair close to Carrie

"It's really a lot more than I expected. These log homes, well, you know…," Pop said, looking around the room.

"So how about the farm and the vineyard?" Jake got up and walked over to the kitchen. He poured Carrie a glass of water, then walked over to her, and handed it to her.

"Thank you, Jake, I've been waiting to have a good glass of cold well water." Carrie reached for Jake's hand and smiled up at him. "Have you met Mary, Pop?" Carrie asked.

"Oh, yes, that woman has just about drove me batty. You know, she thinks you should eat soup every day at noon. I bet I've had a dozen different kinds," Pop said.

Jake laughed. "He hates soup!" And they all laughed, Carrie grasping her side. Blackie came over and put his nose on the edge of the sofa, nudging Carrie to be petted.

"Blackie boy, I missed you too. Have you been a good dog for Pop here?" She messed up the hair on his head.

"Now that is a special animal," Pop said.

"Yes, we sure know that. We'll tell you about how smart he is but another day. I really should get this little lady home. I know she's pretty tired. It's been a long day for both of us," Jake said as he helped Carrie up off the sofa and they walked to the door. "Pop, I think I'll stay at Carrie's tonight and make sure she gets some rest. I know that Mannie and Rosa are at the farmhouse, but Carrie hasn't met them yet," Jake said.

"That's fine. We have all day tomorrow to catch up on everything. Besides, I know you're just down the road. Now you two run along and, Carrie, I do hope you feel better real soon. I'm sure that woman will be here very early with some buns or something. I think she likes my coffee," he said, half clearing his throat as he glanced away from the couple. Jake and Carrie looked at each other and smiled.

"So I'll see you about eight then, Pop. Sure nice to be home. Keep the coffee hot," Jake called out as he opened Carrie's door and helped her into the truck.

When Jake and Carrie arrived at the farmhouse, Mannie and Rosa were standing there waiting for them, both very nervous about meeting Carrie. Jake had left Rosa a note, asking her to make sure the house was in order.

"Rosa and Mannie, this is Miss Carrie Roundtree and, believe me, we are truly glad to be back," Jake said.

"I'm so happy to meet you both and glad you're staying here at the farm," Carrie said, as she moved to Bepo's chair and sat down, Blackie right on her heels.

"Miss Carrie, can I get you something?" Rosa asked.

"No, thank you. I'd just like to visit for a while; then I think I better lay down. I am rather tired."

Jake and Mannie stood by the fireplace, talking farm business while Rosa visited with Carrie, thanking Carrie for letting them stay upstairs in the farmhouse.

"What would you like for breakfast, Miss Carrie?"

"Rosa, let's just skip breakfast in the morning. I will probably sleep in, so you and Mannie go ahead. We can talk about our house plans tomorrow. I think I better go rest now. It's been really nice to meet you. I'm so sorry I didn't get to meet you before my trip."

Carrie got up and said goodnight. Jake stayed a few minutes talking to Mannie.

Carrie stepped into her bathroom to wash up a bit before going to bed. Standing in front of the mirror, she removed the dark glasses she'd been wearing and stared at her face. Her eye was now yellow and blue and, while it still looked awful, was somewhat better than before. *Damn Alex Blane. I hate him for doing this to me, so why does he still haunt me?*

She returned to the bed, slipping out of her clothes and into a silk nightgown, and pulled back the blankets. She was climbing into the bed when Jake entered the room.

"Here, hon. Let me help you," he said, reaching for the blankets, pulling them up around her. Then he sat on the bed. "We're home, little lady. I love you so very much. It feels so good to be here with you at the farm. Now we can think about getting you well. I want you to rest up tomorrow. I'll be going to my place and spending the day with Pop, you know, going over the farm and all. Rosa will be right here close by. All you have to do is call out to her." Jake kissed her.

"Oh, Jake, you are so silly. I'm just fine. Really. It's just these darn ribs; they hurt when I move around. Now why don't you get undressed and come to bed with me. I want you beside me," Carrie said.

"I'll be right back; I'm going to let Blackie out for a short run and then lock up."

Carrie's dark hair lay around her on her pillow. She pulled the blankets up around her and snuggled down in the bed. Then she closed her eyes.

Jake closed the front door quietly. He and Blackie walked slowly to the bedroom turning off the lights as they moved along. Jake entered the room and just stood still, watching Carrie. She was sound asleep and so very beautiful. She looked like a small child under the blankets. He was such a lucky man to have found this wonderful person who would soon be his wife.

About midnight, Jake roused from a very sound sleep when he heard Carrie tossing in the bed and moaning. Then she cried out, "No! No, Alex! Stop this! Why do you want to hurt me?"

"Carrie, honey, wake up. You're having a bad dream, sweetheart. It's okay. I'm right here, hon." Jake took Carrie in his arms to comfort her; she was shaking. She looked up at Jake and then started to cry.

"Why, oh why, is he haunting me? Jake"

"It's going to get better; I promise, love. You've been through quite an ordeal. I tell you what; let me hum you a song. You lay here in my arms and try to go back to sleep." Carrie closed her eyes, listening to Jake hum a sweet song, but she didn't know the name. Soon she was sound asleep.

The 10th of March came rather quickly for Alex and he would soon know what his fate would be. He appeared in front of the judge.

Mr. Blane I have reviewed your case and I find that you will spend two years in the state prison with a chance of parole in one year. You will take classes in anger management as well as alcohol treatment. I do not want to see you back in my court again. Case dismissed. Alex was lead away.

Jack received the phone call from Mr. Hudson. He waited till dinner was over and Pop and Mary arrived then they sat around the table.

"I have something to tell you all."

"Is everything okay," Pop asked.

"I received a phone call from Mr. Hudson today- Jake reaches for Carrie's hand and I have news about Alex."

"Oh Jake why didn't you tell me." Carrie said.

"Well I wanted to tell everyone, it seems Alex will be spending two years in the state prison."

"No, that is not enough Jake." Carrie got up and moved around the room.

"It's what the law set Carrie, there is not a thing we can do about this."

"It doesn't seem fair."

"He is put away now Carrie and he will have to stay out East, and when he gets out we can put the restraining order out on him. I believe we have nothing to worry about."

"Okay if you say so, "Carrie sat down at the table again.

"He sure should have received fifty years if I were that judge." Mary said. They all looked at Mary.

"Well you're not the Judge." Pop said.

The days seemed to fly by, but Jake knew he had to go to the city. He took Carrie into Portland to see an eye specialist. Thankfully, her eye had healed with no permanent damage.

Carrie was feeling more like herself now. Her ribs had healed and she was making all kinds of plans for the farmhouse and farm. She and Jake spent every spare moment together, but most evenings they had dinner with Pop. Often Mary would join them. Although Pop and Mary got along, Pop stayed his distance and hid if he saw her coming. Jake and Carrie joked about it.

As the days passed and the work in the vineyard was caught up, Jake started thinking about the future. He wanted Carrie to be his wife and wanted to be with her every night, just not now and then. He missed her slim body lying next to his. It was time to make some plans.

Chapter Twelve

Jake called Kelly and asked her to meet him in the village at the café. April had been a busy month. Now that Carrie was feeling herself again, he knew it was time for him to have an open house. He needed a woman's advice on how to arrange for the party. He had given a lot of thought to this special surprise.

They sat in a booth by the window. Ida was not around. "Kelly, I need your help. I want to give Carrie a ring, but I want it to be very extraordinary. Do you think a nice party and an open house would be right, you know, together?" Jake pushed his hair out of his face. "I can call Jo, her friend in Boston. They're like sisters. I thought you could invite whoever you think might like to come. I thought it would be a good way for people to meet Carrie and to see my new home," Jake said.

"Sure, I'd love to, Jake. Fred can help, too, with the food. We just need to set the date, so do it."

"How about May 1st, say four in the afternoon?" Jake said. Kelly smiled and nodded.

"Good. I'll get busy. How many people do you want? If we leave someone out, we'll hear about it. After all, the whole village has been wanting to see your log home," Kelly stated.

"Yes, you're right. I think I'll just leave that up to you,"

"Okay. I'll get the invitations out and will let them all know the open house party is a secret," Kelly said.

Jake drove back to the farm smiling; he felt real proud of himself. He knew he could pull this off with Kelly and Fred helping.

As soon as he got to his place, Jake called Jo. She was thrilled. She had a vacation coming up so she could take it then and would arrive on the last day of April. She would stay in the city till the party so she could really surprise Carrie, and she'd use the time to check out the Oregon papers and apply for work. She had already made up her mind to make the move to the west coast; she would be closer to her family and to Carrie. Besides, things had changed at the paper in Boston after the problem with Alex.

Jake then drove to Carrie's and parked by the rose garden. "Carrie, where are you?" He called out, remembering she was going to work outside.

"Jake, I'm out here in the garden," she called back.

Carrie was bent over, her knees in the dirt and her hands digging little holes so she could plant the seeds.

"There you are, my farm girl," he said.

Carrie stood up and Jake started to laugh.

"What's so funny, Mr. Thompson?"

"Well, you must have half the garden on your face," he said as he wiped the mud off her cheek, then pulled her to him, embracing her as their lips met.

"You are the most beautiful woman and I just love that farm girl look you have with you're red bandanna on and these big sloppy overalls."

"So tell me what you think of my garden?"

"Well, we may eat a lot of lettuce and beans," he said.

"Isn't it great, Jake? I've enjoyed this so much. My grandmother used this very same spot for her garden."

"You really have a green thumb. Hey, when are we going to be alone, I mean really alone! I need you, little lady."

"I know, Jake. How about a walk up to the sheep barn," Carrie said, pulling him towards the barn road.

They half walked half ran towards the barn, down past the pond and up the dirt road. Mannie was at Jake's place and Rosa was working in the house. They could be alone at last.

They entered the barn and made their way to the back to a dark hay-filled corner. Jake helped Carrie undress; then he lay beside her. He knew all the special places that pleased her, his hands moving over her body. It felt good to be together as one, the love they shared, lying in each other arms, just holding onto each other, not wanting the moment to come to an end.

"That was the greatest, coming here to the barn. It's kind of naughty, don't you think? And exciting," Jake whispered.

"Well, you might call it out of wedlock," she said.

"Not for long, little lady. We have to think about that date. Before the harvest, in June maybe." he said.

"Really, Jake, that's not far away." They dressed and then walked hand in hand back towards the house.

They found themselves standing by the pond.

"A gazebo would fit perfectly here," Jake mentioned. "On hot summer nights, we could come and sit by the pond. Mannie and I could build one."

"Oh, Jake, it's a grand idea. When can you start?"

"Soon, hon, real soon," pulling her close to him.

Meanwhile, the days seemed long and filled with activity at the farm. Mannie fixed fences and had orders from Carrie to get more of the garden plowed. Mannie loved to plant things so he took care of the rose garden and set out bedding plants. Carrie often stood and watched him; he was very good at his work.

Rosa and Carrie talked about Mexico and Rosa's family and how she met Mannie; they had both come to Oregon to work in the fields, Rosa with her parents. She met Mannie at a church picnic in Woodburn. They were married three years ago and bought their trailer so they could go from job to job. Being on the farm seemed like home to them.

The house was coming together. Mannie had moved the old treadle sewing machine from the second floor to the dining room for Rosa to use in making draperies. The carpet people were coming, and the new appliances were being delivered. The old farm house was looking pretty good. It was more like a home to Carrie now.

Mannie and Rosa moved back to their trailer. It was parked up by the barn, so now Carrie had her house to herself and she and Jake could spend more private time together.

At least twice a week, she had Rosa fix a good dinner and invited Jake and Pop and sometimes Mary. She so wanted them to be friends; however, Mary seemed to want it more than Pop. Still, Carrie had no idea of all that was going on around her in secret.

Jo arrived in Portland on time and checked into a hotel. She still had time to apply at the largest newspaper in the city. She changed quickly, putting on a dignified linen suit, and made her way downtown.

She sat waiting eagerly in the outer office. When her name was called, she followed the receptionist into the head editor's office.

"So tell me, Miss Gordon, why do you want to work here in Portland?"

"Mr. Blackley, I have family close by in Vancouver, British Columbia." He sat behind his desk, looking over the folder Jo had handed him.

"I see your résumé is very good…I do have an editor leaving. He is retiring. Can I reach you at this number?"

"No, not for at least a week. I'll be staying with my friend for the next week. You can reach me at this number," she said, handing him her card with her phone number written on the back. "I will be going back to Boston then. You can, however, get in touch with Mr. G. before then. He knows I want to make a change."

"Very well, until you hear from me," he said, shaking her hand.

Jo left the paper and went back to her hotel. She called Jake, but he wasn't home so she left word with Pop. Jo was so excited to see Carrie and the farm; it would be a long wait until four tomorrow afternoon.

The preparations for the open house and Carrie's surprise were all ready. Kelly and Fred were to arrive at Jake's about two in the afternoon with the food. Kelly had made her famous Italian cheese pie and had had a nice cake made in the city. Fred had brought some of his number one prize wines that he had made.

Jake was nervous, trying to think of a way to keep Carrie away from his house. They were sitting at Carrie's kitchen table finishing a sandwich when Jake said, "Hey, let's go mushroom hunting this afternoon. It's such a nice day out. We might even find some wild flowers."

"Jake, if I didn't know it already, I would think you were a romantic,"

"Well, I have a free afternoon and you better take advantage of it," he said.

Jake and Carrie ran through the weeds and tall grass in the back timber. Carrie fell down on the grass and Jake rolled beside her, pulling her close.

"I have a mind to make love to you right now," he said as he kissed her.

"Well!"

"Oh, you're a bad girl, Carrie Roundtree. You know I want to." Jake kissed her hard on the mouth. "I can't get enough of you, my love."

"Oh, Jake, I love you so much."

Afterwards they lay watching white fluffy clouds moving across the deep blue sky.

"This is a little bit of heaven, don't you think, little lady?"

"Where are all these mushrooms?"

"Come. I'm not sure there are any, but look at the purple wild iris and the bachelor buttons." He   picked the flowers and handed them to Carrie. It was three thirty. *The guests would be arriving soon. I better get Carrie back to the house. But how?*

They walked rather slowly back towards her house, counting their blessings and thinking about Hank and Pop and how sad it was they hadn't met.

"Hon, let's take these flowers and show Pop," Jake said, as they walked into the back of the house. "I told him we might be over and he said he would make his famous chili for us. He wouldn't take no for an answer so I think he misses you coming over and all."

"Okay. Let me wash up." Carrie left Jake standing in the kitchen. He fidgeted, hoping not to give anything away. He looked at his watch again; it was four thirty. He knew it was time to leave for his house.

"Are you all right, Jake? You look funny. Was this afternoon too much for the old man?" Carrie tickled him and then laughed.

"No way, little lady, but you do bring the best out in me. You know that, don't you? We better leave or Pop will be coming after us."

The grapes were leafing out and the fields were green. But as they drove up the lane, Carrie saw that things didn't look right.

"Jake! Look at all the cars! What do you suppose is going on? I hope it's not Pop," she said.

Jake parked the truck, got out, walked around, and opened Carrie's door. When they reached the top of the steps, the door flew open and Jake picked Carrie up in his arms, carrying her across the threshold.

"Surprise!" yelled people from all around the room.

"For you, little lady. Welcome home to Oak Valley," Jake said. Then he kissed her and set her down gently on her feet.

Carrie didn't know what to say. She looked around the room. There were Mr. and Mrs. Temple, Mrs. Foster, Doc, Gene, Fred and Kelly, Mary, Mrs. J., and people she did not know. "Did you know about all this?" Carrie looked up at Jake. "Wow, Jake you really pulled this one off and picking wildflowers! You…you…," Carrie reached for him.

"I couldn't have pulled it off without Kelly and Fred. They did a lot of the work. Well, everyone, take a good tour of the house and then we will drink to our future," Jake said and watched his friends move about the house.

A bit later Jake gathered all their friends around. He and Fred poured the champagne. He handed Carrie her glass and made the toast. As Carrie tipped her glass to sip her champagne, she stopped.

"There's something in my glass." Carrie looked puzzled.

Everyone became very still; Jo slipped out of the hall-way and came up behind Carrie and just stood quietly.

Jake got down on one knee. As Carrie took the ring out of her glass, she handed it to him.

"Little lady, will you do me the honor of being my wife?

"Yes, I will Jake Thompson," she said, tears running down her face.

"What's wrong, hon? Jake asked.

"Oh, this is so silly. I wish Jo were here," she said.

"I am!" Jo shouted behind her.

"Jo! Oh, I'm so happy you're here! Oh, Jake, you are something, and I love you!" Carrie hugged him; then she turned and hugged Jo, each laughing and crying at the same time.

As Carrie showed off her new engagement ring, she saw Ida coming through the door. Ida walked right up to her.

"I'm really very happy for the both of you. You got a good man there," Ida said as she stretched her hand out to shake Carrie's.

"We're happy you're here, Ida," Jake said as he walked up. "Here, let me get you a drink."

Jo came over to Carrie. "Well, girlfriend, I have never seen you glow like this. He is a handsome man. Does he have a brother?"

"No, not that I know of. Have you met everyone?"

Carrie went around the room introducing Jo and even met several people she hadn't known before.

"Carrie girl," Pop said.

"Yes."

"I am so very happy for you and my son. You are the daughter I never had," he said.

"Thank you, Pop. I love you like my own father, and I will always be here for you," and she hugged him.

It was going on ten when most of their friends started to leave; Fred and Kelly cleaned up. Pop had already said goodnight and gone to bed. Then the five if them sat around the fire, talking about the grape crops and a new winery.

Jo sat amazed, listening to all this farm talk and watching her friend, seeing how happy she was. "So, have you two thought about a date?" Jo asked.

Jake looked at Carrie. "Soon," he said, holding her hand.

"We have to wait till Jo moves; you will be my maid of honor, won't you?"

"You need to ask?" Jo chided.

"Kelly, will you be one of my bride's maids, too?" Carrie asked.

"I would be honored."

"Well, Fred, that leaves us. Fred, you will be my best man, and I can ask Gene to stand up with us," Jake said.

"Hey, that's a good wedding party. Now how about the date?" Fred said.

"Well, hon, it's all up to you," Jake looked at Carrie.

"Oh, gee, I don't know. Maybe a month or two? Do you think we can have everything ready by then?"

"Just so it's by harvest time," he said.

"My lucky number is seventeen," Carrie said.

"So that's it, June 17th," Jake smiled.

"This has been some day. All our friends and even some new ones and Jo being here. I couldn't be happier!" Carrie said.

Chapter Thirteen

At the end of the week, Jo had definitely decided to make the move west. She was going to go back to Boston, pack her things, and return in two weeks. That way she could help with the wedding plans. When Jo returned, they would go to the city shopping for dresses.

Jo was busy packing for her move to the West, and she was happy the day finally had arrived. She was excited about the move and would be close to her family in Canada. She had arrived at the airport a little early and decided to sit and wait and do some reading. She found a seat near a window sat down and dug in her shoulder bag for her book and started to read.

A tall well built man took the seat next to her Jo couldn't help but notice how good looking he was just then she dropped her book. The man bent down and picked it up.

"I do believe this is yours" he said.

"Oh, thank you" Jo said. The man asked Jo.

"Are you going to Portland also Miss?"

"Yes I am."

"The city of roses is a very lovely place to visit this time of year.

"Yes I know I am moving to Portland to be near friends and family." She stated.

"Have you lived in Portland a long time?" Jo asked.

"For awhile I have a law office on the West side."

Just then Jo's flight number was called.

"Here is my card if you ever need a lawyer in the city." He got up rather quickly and moved ahead of Jo.

"Thank you," Jo took the card and dropped it into her bag, then got up and followed the man towards the gate, he was to board first as he was flying in first class. Jo was happy to be seated and now it wouldn't be long and she would be at the farm.

Carrie and Jake had decided to have the wedding ceremony held at their special place by the pond, so Mannie started building the gazebo. Mary asked to do the wedding cake and the reception, which would be held at the old farmhouse. Carrie asked Pop to give her away.

The old farmhouse was looking pretty nice: new carpet, new kitchen floor, new appliances—Carrie and Rosa were still trying to figure out the new range; this was a real challenge for both of them—new paint and drapes. Carrie was pleased and relieved she'd finished it all before Jo's return. Now she had to work on the second floor. She wanted to get the front bedroom ready for Jo as she was going to stay at the farm till she had a job and a place in the city.

As rushed as these two weeks were, Jake stayed at the farmhouse sometimes. The couple sat by the fire on chilly nights, dreaming about the future, talking about the party and how special it had been, and speculating about Mary and Pop, who were now talking to each other. It seemed Pop was more open to Mary since the party. Now he could see how much she cared about his family.

Carrie climbed the steep stairs, hoping to clean out the front bedroom closet.

She pulled several old boxes out to the middle of the room and had just started digging through them when she heard Jo. "I'm up here, Jo. Come on up," she called.

"What in the world are you doing up here?"

"Hello to you too, girlfriend."

"I guess you're stuck with me now," Jo said.

Carrie got up and gave her friend a hug. "Bepo had all these things packed up. I'm not sure what is up here, but I wanted to make some room for you so…"

Carrie sat down on the floor opening the first box. Jo joined her; they sorted clothes and looked at old pictures: pictures of Carrie when she was a small child, of her and her

Bepo, of old Puddles her pet dog, and of her on her first bike that Grandma and Bepo had hid in the milk house. Then Carrie pulled out a family Bible; she opened it, reading her mother's name on the inside.

"Oh, Jo. Look,"

Jo took the Bible. When she did, an envelope fell out. Jo gave it to Carrie, who carefully fingered through the envelope, noticing that it held several old letters.

"What do you think, Jo?"

"I don't know. Should we read them? Maybe they're love letters that your dad wrote years ago," Jo said.

"This is so strange. Do you think we should, you know, being both my parents are gone?" Carrie was trembling.

"It may be nice to see what he wrote to your mom," Jo replied.

"Well, here goes." Carrie took one letter. Jo watched as she opened it. Carrie read it to herself and stopped. "I don't understand."

"What do you mean?"

"Here. You read it."

My Dear Carol,
I'm so sorry I had to leave you last night. I really do want you
in my life and, under the circumstances; I'm not sure how long
we will be able to see each other. I know it's very hard on you,
my darling. I just can't live without you. We have to do some-
thing. Please tell Andrew about us. Think about this, my
dearest. I will take you away from here and we can start a new
life.
Your loving Paul.

Carrie sat there, not saying anything.

What did it mean? Another man? Who was Paul?

"Carrie, are you all right?"

"I guess so, Jo. Does this mean what I think it does? My
mother was having an affair with a man named Paul? Look.
It's dated three years before I was born. Oh, my God, Jo!
What do we do?"

"Well, maybe the next letter will tell us more. You don't
want to stop now, do you?" Jo asked.

"I guess not. Maybe this is a mistake." She opened the
next letter and handed it to Jo. "Here you read it, please."

My Dearest Carol,
I miss you so very much. I want to see you. Can we meet at the
usual place this Saturday afternoon? I need to see you. We need
to talk.

> *Love,*
> *Paul*

"Well, that didn't tell us much." Carrie opened the next letter.

Dear Carol,
I'm so happy we had the chance to get away from town. I will
never forget our wonderful day, holding you in my arms and
loving you. We have to tell Andrew. People only find this kind
of love once in a lifetime. Please tell me we will spend the rest of
our lives together. Till we meet again, my love, on Sunday.

> *Lovingly yours,*
> *Paul*

Carrie sat holding the letters. She was shaking and felt herself breaking into a cold sweat. Jo took Carrie's hand in hers.

"Carrie, it's okay. This is in the past, honey. You're mom must have left these letters here for a reason. I think we should read on," Jo said.

"Jo, how could my mother do this to my dad? I just don't understand. I'm so confused," Carrie said as she handed Jo the next letter.

"So, do you want to read on?

"Yes.

Dear Carol,
I am shocked. Why is Andrew doing this to us? Church or no church, this is wrong. Why won't he let you go? I am happy that you told him everything. I know how hard this must be on you, my love. This hurts me so very much. I wanted you in my life ; however, if I can't have you, I will take my baby. At least I will have a part of you. My parents will pick up the baby at the hospital; they will have papers for you to sign. If you change your mind, you can write to me. I am shipping out for awhile. Carol, you will be the only woman in my life. I will always love you. If I don't hear from you, I will know that you don't want me. I will never see you again and you will never see your baby again. At least our baby will have one parent who loves him. I hope you can live with yourself and find some happiness.

Paul

Carrie sat still, tears running down her cheeks. Jo handed her the letter, noticing the return address was 2310 Market Street, Salem, Oregon.

"Carrie do you know what this means?" Jo asked.

"No, I just can't think right now. How could my mother do this...Oh, my God in heaven! She gave her baby away!" Carrie said, reaching for Jo and embracing her.

"Carrie, I think the reason the letters were kept maybe was so you might find them someday or she was going to tell you or something," Jo said.

"Jo, do you know what this means? I may have an older brother or sister somewhere."

The excitement pounded in her chest. "Wouldn't that be something? We have to find this person somehow. That poor man. He sounded like he really loved my mother. This is such a shock. Do you suppose no one knew of this, not even my grandparents?" Carrie said. "My grandfather, being from the old country and being a Roundtree, knew. I just know it."

"There is only one way to find out if this is all true. We have to find this Paul," Jo told Carrie.

"But how, Jo? All we have is an address to go on and that was over thirty years ago."

"We can go to Salem, look up the address, ask questions. Carrie, we have to find out who this man is and where he is today?"

Just then Blackie barked.

"That must be Jake. I have to tell him."

"Here we are," both Carrie and Jo called from the stairway and headed towards the kitchen. "Jake, come sit in the kitchen. I have something to tell you."

Jake removed his hat, ran his hand through his hair, and moved towards the table.

"You're not going to believe this," she said as she and Jo sat down. "Jo and I found these letters upstairs when I was cleaning out the closet." Carrie put the letters on the table in front of Jake.

Jake listened to Carrie and Jo, amazed at what they had found. He agreed that if Carrie had a sibling, they had to go to whatever means necessary to find this person. Salem was a good start.

"So now you two ladies can be detectives," Jake said with a flat laugh. "I'm sorry I just had to be a little funny here," reaching for Carrie's hand and smiling.

"This is serious," Carrie smiled back.

The next morning, Carrie and Jo left for Salem, which was about fifty miles from Oak Valley. They stopped at a market, picked up a city map, and proceeded to find the house on Market Street.

"Jo, what if the house is gone? It's been so long. We'd come to a dead end."

"Watch for the numbers. There is 2308; we're getting close. It sure looks like an old neighborhood and run down. There, there. Stop."

"Jo, the house is empty and the windows are boarded up." Carrie's heart sank and she felt sick. "What do we do now?

"Well," Jo said. Carrie parked the car as they looked around. "See that old man working in his flower bed? Maybe he might know something."

They got out of the car and walked up to the man.

"Sir? Sir?" Carrie said. The old man kept working. "Sir, can you hear me?"

"Sure, why are you shouting?"

"I have a question and hope you may help me."

The old man got up and looked at Carrie.

"Have you lived here along time?" Jo asked.

"Most of my life." The old man looked at them over his glasses.

"Sir, did you know the people who lived in that house? Number 2310?" Carrie looked at him hopefully.

"Of course, I did. They moved. Why you want to know?"

"Well," Carrie said, "they could very well be lost family."

"Mr. and Mrs. Higgins lived there. Nice folk, they were."

"Did they have any children?" Jo asked.

"Yes, they did. They moved to be near their son, I believe somewhere," the old man removed his hat, "somewhere in Colorado. I used to get a Christmas card from them, but that stopped around five years ago. I'm not much on writing. Always left that up to my wife. She's not here anymore. She's gone."

"Do you remember what town in Colorado?" Jo asked.

"Well, it was a big one, you know, the mile high one."

"Denver," Jo and Carrie said at the same time.

"Thank you, sir. You may have helped me find some of my family." Carrie reached out and gave the old man a hug.

As the two women jogged back to the car, the old man put his hat back on and smiled to himself; then he started working again in his flowers.

As Carrie and Jo headed back to Oak Valley, Carrie exclaimed, "Jo, we did it! Now I think we can find this Paul Higgins. Let's just pray that he still lives in Denver. Jake will know what to do. I can't wait to get home."

Jake was pacing the floor, waiting for Jo and Carrie to return, wondering what they would find, if anything. He heard the car drive up and met them at the front door.

Carrie hugged Jake. "We may have found something," she said as the three walked to the kitchen.

Jake got out cups and poured coffee for all of them. Then he sat down at the table with them as Carrie told him her news.

"So what do we do next, Jake?" Jo said.

"Just think, I may have a sister or brother out there," Carrie said.

"Yes, you may, so let's get working on this. Now, little lady, let me take over. I will find someone to find this

Higgins, and then we will know and go from there. It may take some time, so you need to be patient."

"Okay, but this will be difficult."

"Well, we have a lot to do with the wedding and all," Jo stated. "We have a trip to Portland to buy dresses, Carrie, and I am sure we can find a lot to do. I have to find an apartment, you know.

"I know and we can start in the morning."

Jake and Carrie sat in the lawn swing in the yard under the old oaks; it was a lovely Sunday spring day. When the letters came up in the conversation, Carrie had a hard time not thinking about them. Her mother must have been a very unhappy woman.

"Jake, now that I think about it, my mother was always very close to me. In fact, we were like sisters sometimes," Carrie said.

"Were you close to your dad?"

"Not really. I always felt closer to Bepo. It sure would have been good if I could have read the letters my mother wrote to Paul. Everything is so one sided." She snuggled close to Jake as a light wind came up.

"We'll find this man, little lady," Jake said, holding her face in his hands.

As the days rushed by, Carrie and Jo made their trip to the city. Carrie found her wedding dress, a lovely white satin full ankle-length dress, off the shoulder, with little seed pearls around the neckline. Jo picked out a light pink taffeta dress for her and Kelly.

The vineyard was in full dark green foliage with the grapes beginning to set on. Pop continued to visit with Mary, giving him well-deserved rest from all that he did around the vineyard and farm. He always found something to keep him busy with both farms.

Carrie had Pop over for coffee and hot buns and learned about Jake's childhood and his mother.

Many evenings Jake and Carrie packed up supper and went to the newly finished gazebo. Carrie had had Pop and Mannie plant Oregon grape and large ferns around the steps. Pop had added some sweet William and lily of the valley. If all went well, they would be blooming in a few weeks.

Bricks bright red in color were laid around the front of the steps; it was a truly wonderful setting for a wedding. The large oaks in the background gave lots of shade. The sun sparkled off the pond, Carrie and Jake's favorite place for many refreshing dips after long days in the vineyard.

Jo found a small apartment near the downtown area and took the job at the *Oregonian* newspaper.

Jake and Carrie were sitting at the kitchen table going over some business papers and Jake thought he better tell Carrie."

"I want to tell you something Carrie,"

"What is it Jake."

"Well with the farm's and all, I decided to take a leave from the office."

"Gee, I am surprised you haven't before now, you put in so many extra hours I really don't know where you find the time."

"Then you feel okay about it?"

"Jake, of course. Do what ever you want." Carrie reached and squeezed his hand.

When the phone rang. Carrie rushed into the dining room to answer as she did every time it rang, hoping for news of her sibling.

"Hello," and then she listened intently to what the voice on the other end of the line had to say.

She walked slowly back to the kitchen, excited yet apprehensive at what she had just learned.

"Jake, they found Paul Higgins in Denver. Temple wants to see us as soon as we can get to town. The investigator is there now."

"Well, there's nothing stopping us. Let's go." Jake picked Carrie up and twirled her around the room. "See, I told you, little lady, we would find him."

Jake and Carrie arrived at Mr. Temple's office where the investigator they had hired sat waiting.

"We found your Mr. Higgins in Denver. He has been there for twenty-two years. He owns a hardware store, has no children living at home or in the area, and he is married," the investigator said.

"No children," said Carrie sadly.

"Well, he didn't talk much until I mentioned Carol Roundtree's name."

"What did he say?" asked Jake.

"I had a good feeling when I told him that Carrie had some letters that a Paul Higgins had written. He said he would meet with you, but only with Carrie, at the Denver airport. All I need to do is set up a time."

Chapter Fourteen

Paul walked slowly to his car. He felt rather ill. His life was sure to change now. Why? Why had Carol kept those damn letters? Why had he even kept his? He thought the past would never come out. He had forgotten about Carol. No, he was kidding himself; every time he looked at Brad he could see Carol's dark eyes. He hadn't told Brad because he had made that promise to her. Now he could lose his only son. *How can I tell Brad that his mother gave him away?*

As soon as he arrived home, Paul made arrangements to fly out to Portland at the end of the week. He would see Brad on Friday and stay the weekend.

Brad Higgins sat at his desk. He had opened his own law office several years ago. He had always thought Portland was a great city; he liked the music, the art, and the great Columbia River. The City of Roses was truly a beautiful place to live. He was preparing a case and was due in court the first of the week and had a meeting with a partner in twenty minutes. His secretary buzzed him.

"Mr. Higgins, your father is here to see you."

"Really? Please send him in," he said.

Paul opened the door and walked into the comfortable but distinguished office. Brad met him and shook his hand.

"Dad, what's wrong?"

"Now does something have to be wrong for me to come to see you?"

"Well, no, but you normally call first," Brad said.

"I know but something has come up. I need to talk to you and spend some time with you." He sounded rather nervous.

"What is it, Dad?"

"Well, I think we should talk tonight after you get off work."

"Okay, you know where the key is. Go on out to the house and I'll be there about six. I have a short meeting first and then I'll be home," Brad said.

The intercom buzzed. "Mr. Higgins, your party is waiting in the conference room."

"Thank you, Sara. I'll be right in," Brad said. "Dad, I'll see you about six." He patted his dad on the shoulder and walked him to the door.

Paul reached for the key and unlocked the door. His son's home was very nice, three bedrooms with a daylight basement in Candle Hills. Brad's law practice had done very well. He was very proud of his son. It took long, hard work to get where he was today.

Paul made himself a scotch and sat down in the easy chair. He took a drink, set his glass down, and closed his eyes. He could see that unhappy young girl with her big dark eyes and her wet hair dripping with rain. He hadn't been able to keep his eyes off her. Paul remembered her offering to share a booth in the crowded bus depot diner. The image disappeared when he heard the front door open. Brad was home.

"I'm here," Brad called.

"I'm in the living room," Paul replied.

Brad hung up his coat and set his brief case in his study. He made himself a drink and joined his dad.

"Sounds like you've been very busy, son," Paul said.

"Yes, I've had some good cases that have lingered on. I hope to have a break soon. I was hoping to get over to see you and mom. By the way, how is she?"

"She's fine, busy with the store. You know how hard she works," Paul remarked.

"Yes, I do. I wish you could get her to slow down," Brad said

"Well, you know your mother."

"So, what is it that brings you to Portland?"

"Well, something happened a long time ago. I need to talk to you about it." Paul got up and started to pace.

"Dad, I can see you're really upset about something. Now sit down and let's talk about it," Brad said.

"When I was in the army, I would take the bus on weekends from Fort Lewis down to Salem to my parents'. One rainy day I stopped in at the bus depot diner. It was full of people, and I kind of ran into this beautiful girl who offered me a seat at her booth. We sat and waited out the rain till my bus arrived. The following weekend, she was there again. We sat together and visited. She was very unhappy and seemed to be lonely. This went on for a while and we became friends. Well, really more than that."

"I see," Brad said.

"Well, I found out she was married." Paul got up and paced the floor again.

"Dad…"

"No, I have to tell you, Brad. Please listen."

"But Dad..." Brad said.

"I have to say this, Brad. I just hope you'll understand. You see, I made a promise and I had to keep it. I told you a lie when you were a little boy. Brad, your mother didn't die when you were born. God, I hope you don't hate me."

"Dad, I would never hate you," Brad said.

"Your mother died five years ago in an auto accident. I just found out about it from a lady named Carrie Roundtree. She lives in Oak Valley."

"Yes, Dad I know."

"You...know?" Paul's voice rose sharply. "But how?"

"I read in the newspaper about a Hank Roundtree. He passed away, and he had a granddaughter named Carrie Roundtree. I went to Oak Valley. I even saw her several times. I just couldn't bring myself to talk to her. You see, Dad, I found the letters that Carol wrote you. I knew she was my mother."

"Oh, son, I'm so sorry. I should have told you so long ago," Paul said.

"What. That my mother didn't want me? What kind of nut was this Andrew? Ever since I found out, Dad, I've just felt so blessed. I thought about you being so young and in the army and taking on a baby. You raised me alone till I was five. Then you married Mom," Brad said.

"Brad, you've got it wrong. Carol wanted you, but her husband had a wicked hold on her. She was forced to let me take you, and I promised not to tell you. Miss Roundtree feels her mother left the letters in her Bible so she would find them."

"Is that why you kept yours?"

"I'm not sure why I saved them. I just forgot about them, I guess. I can tell you one thing; you were made out of a special love. Carol was the soul mate I needed in my life. It took me a long time to heal. She was a kind and sweet girl, just very unhappy. I made her happy for a while. Your grandma and grandpa really helped me a lot."

"So, what does this Roundtree woman want?"

"Well, she has no family, and she hopes you will contact her. You are her brother," Paul said.

"Yes, I know. I saw the family plot. That's when it hit me that my real mother was dead. Carrie Roundtree...she was alone at the cemetery."

"She's getting married soon to a farmer. I believe he owns a vineyard," Paul stated.

"The only thing I really missed was not having a grand-father. I wonder if he knew about me," Brad asked.

"No, they sent Carol away till you were born. I believe everyone was told she was away taking care of an Aunt. I was told I would not find her in Oregon. My parents picked you up at a meeting place. I was back east at the time, finishing up my army tour," Paul said.

"You know, Dad, that Hank Roundtree was very well liked. In the café in Oak Valley where I ate, that's all you heard about the man, about how great he was. It's amazing how much a person can learn when you just sit on the sidelines," Brad told his Dad.

"I really feel bad about this, but I guess you knew. Why didn't you come to me?" Paul asked.

"I don't know. I was afraid to hurt Mom. I figured you must have had a pretty good reason not to tell me. I just had to put it together. I thought Carrie must not have known this about her mother. She didn't need to be told and hurt, so I was going to leave it until I saw her in Oak Valley. Believe me, I think in due time, I would have asked you about the letters," Brad said.

"So, what now Brad?"

"Well, I have this case going. I really can't think of much else. But I will get in touch with her sometime in the future. Did you like her, Dad?"

"Yes, she seems to be a very caring person. She looks a lot like her mother. She had real feelings towards me. She was rather worried about me. You know, she traced us from the old address in Salem. Some neighbor told them that we moved to Denver."

"Yeah, well, I guess she really wants to meet me," Brad said.

Chapter Fifteen

Carrie sat in the lawn swing thinking. *I wonder when Brad will call. Maybe he doesn't even want to meet me. I have so many things I want to talk to him about. I think Paul Higgins is a wonderful man. I will never forget the sadness in his eyes. I'm still having a hard time thinking my father sent that baby boy away. My mother had to be so very unhappy when she met Paul and very vulnerable. Poor Paul, he must have loved her so much. Raising a child alone was a real challenge. I wonder what it was that made my parents drift away from each other. I'll never know. If Bepo had known, I'm sure he would have told me I had a brother.*

Carrie was startled from her reverie by the phone. She rose from the lawn swing and ran into the house.

"Miss Carrie, its Miss Jo."

"Yes, I'm coming," she said taking the phone from Rosa. "Jo, I've been waiting for your call."

"So how are things going out at the farm?" Jo asked.

"Oh, I think good. We have just about everything finished, just the flowers and last minute things need to be done."

"Have you heard anything from Brad?"

"Every time I hear the phone ring I think maybe it's him. Jo, maybe he doesn't want to see me," Carrie said softly.

"Now, girlfriend, he probably has to get used to the idea. And you really don't know when Paul told him. You have to be patient," Jo said.

"Yeah, I guess you're right."

"Well, I'd better go now. I still have some unpacking to do," Jo said.

"Okay, you take care. I'll see you soon, girlfriend. Tell that good-looking man of yours I said hi."

Carrie sat back in the chair. *Two weeks! Just fourteen days and then I will be Mrs. Jake Thompson.*

Mary and Carrie went over the cake decorations: a two layer white cake with custard filling and white icing. Fresh pink roses from her grandmother's garden would adorn the top.

Carrie and Rosa walked through the house checking everything once more. The drapes were hung and Carrie had bought a new sofa. She had Rosa put fresh flowers on the dining room table every day. Mannie had planted little flowers all around the front of the house. He had even painted the old milk house. And the gazebo by the pond was just outstanding.

Carrie looked out the window and saw Pop go driving by in his truck, honking his horn. Jake was behind him but stopped at the end of the driveway and called for Carrie.

"Hey, what's up?"

"Come with me, honey. Pop has something for you," Jake said.

Carrie got into the truck and rode with Jake past the barn. She could see Pop backing up his truck towards the pond. Jake got out and ran over to help him lift a large box out of the back of Pop's truck while. Blackie barked and carried on the whole time.

"Pop! What have you got in there?" Carrie asked.

"Girl, this is something I really gave a lot of thought to. I always have just loved these birds." As he opened the box, two large white swans came out slowly and walked right to the water. They glided across the pond as if they belonged there.

"For you, daughter. Do you like them?" Pop asked.

Carrie stood there with her hands over her mouth. "Oh, Pop, they're wonderful. What can I say? I love them. Will they come to me?"

"I'm not sure. It will take a few days. They have their wings clipped, and I'll have Mannie build a shelter for them. We don't want something wild to get them. I'm sure we will need to keep an eye on them. Now the pond has its very own family of birds, with the other ducks and all," Pop said.

"Pop, I love you. Thank you so much. You did this for the wedding, didn't you?"

"Well, kinda, but I thought the pond needed something else. The next thing I want to do is get some fish," Pop said.

"Oh, Pop, you are something," Carrie said, hugging him tightly.

That evening Carrie and Jake walked down to the pond to see the swans. As they arrived, the birds swam to the far end of the shoreline. Jake and Carrie stood with their arms wrapped around each other, watching the two swans.

"This is perfect for the wedding, isn't it, Jake?"

"Yes, little lady. The gazebo and the flowers and ferns are just perfect. Just a few days to go, my sweet."

The days seemed to fly by. Jake had made plans for a get away to Mount Hood for a short honeymoon. Jo had arrived back on time and helped Carrie finish all the little last minute details.

Carrie had finally had time to show Jo the farm. They had taken an afternoon and walked to the barn where she had shown Jo the silo; the door had been repaired and bolted so no one could go in.

Jo loved to sit and read by the pond; it was a haven. She had nearly another two months before she actually started her job at the *Oregonian* and loved being on the farm. It was so relaxing compared to almost any other kind of vacation she could have taken. And she had time to spend with her best friend to boot. Then, too, the time between the wedding and her official first day of work gave her time to get her own apartment in the city ready.

Jake decided to stay at his house the week of the wedding. He really just wanted to stay out of the women's way. When Mary was there, four was too many. Jake and Pop worked around the farm. Plus they had to go into the city to pick up their tuxedos. Jake still had to deliver his wedding present; he had bought Carrie two white horses. She would have another dream fulfilled.

Carrie woke up to the chirping of birds outside her window. The sweet scent of roses from the garden filled the morning air. The sun gleamed on everything. It was a lovely day for a wedding.

She could smell coffee coming from the kitchen and had just started to get out of bed when Rosa came in.

"Oh, no. You don't get up, Miss Carrie," Rosa said, setting a tray in front of her.

"What's this, Rosa?"

"This is what Mr. Jake wants," Rosa said. Carrie took the tray and saw the card on the plate. She opened it and it read:

My wife to be, this is our day. I love you with all my heart. I have missed you so very much this past week. We will be together now forever. See you at the gazebo.

Love J.

Carrie folded up the card and put it on her side table; she took the rose and drew in its wonderful scent. "Yes, this is our day, my love," she said out loud and smiled.

As Carrie was eating, there was a knock at the door.

"Come in," Carrie said with her mouth full.

"Well, how is our bride feeling this morning? You look very happy, girlfriend," Jo said as she bent down and kissed Carrie on her forehead.

"Look what Jake had Rosa do; I'm having breakfast in bed." Carrie laughed.

"What a man! I hope I can be so lucky, girlfriend." Jo pulled up a chair.

"You will. I will just have to start looking around for you."

"Oh, no, you don't, girlfriend!" Carrie winked at Jo. "Carrie, this is the day. It's finally arrived."

"And look at the weather! It couldn't be more perfect. Everything is ready, girlfriend, it really is happening. Jo, I'm so grateful and I feel so privileged to have you here with me."

"Girlfriend, I'm here to help you today. I am at your call," Jo said.

Carrie and Jo laid out the dresses. Carrie took her mother's pearls out of a small box and put on a ring of her grandmother's. "Something old, Jo; this was my grandmother's ring." She put it on her right hand.

"Jake, I can't find my socks," Pop called.

"Pop, I put them in your shoes. Here, let me help you with your tie," Jake said.

"Well, I have to get going; I need to get the buggy. I hope Mannie has the horses all hitched up. You're sure those horses will do what I want them to do?"

"Pop, everything is going to be just fine. You would think you're the groom here," Jake said.

"Well, it's not every day my son gets married. There, do I look alright?"

"You look great, Pop, and that tux really will make the ladies take notice."

"I'm afraid it's a little late for that, my boy," Pop said.

"Well, let's get going. I guess we are as ready as we can be."

They drove to Carrie's farm and parked at the barn. People were starting to arrive and were enjoying the wedding setting of the pond. Mannie had the buggy all hitched up; Mary had made flower wreaths and had had Mannie put one on each horse. She even had one for Blackie.

Carrie stood in her dress in front of the mirror while Jo adjusted her veil. She put the necklace around her neck and stood back.

"Oh my, Carrie, you look so wonderful," Jo said.

Kelly entered the room. "Wow, Carrie, you look like one of those brides on the front of *Bride Magazine*," giving her a little hug.

The three girls started towards the living room with Rosa and Mary helping Carrie with her dress.

"Rosa, is everything under control? Mary, are you sure about all the chairs and the food?"

"Now, Carrie girl, don't worry so much. This wedding is going to go like clockwork. The yard is so nice; Mannie has worked so hard. And this girl here, Rosa, has been working since dawn. It all has come together. Now you just stand here. Your ride will be here any minute. Here is your bouquet."

Pop got in the buggy. Mannie had it turned so all Pop had to do was drive the buggy to the house, around the rose garden, then stop in front of the house. Mannie climbed up and sat with Pop and they were on their way.

Jake and Fred were at the pond. People were still arriving and parking out in the barn lot. The gazebo was decorated with white satin bows and flowers. The swans were curious and swam close to the edge of the pond.

The guests were seated and the candles were lit. The minister was waiting on the steps in front of the gazebo.

Pop stopped the buggy in front of the house. Mary opened the front door. "Oh, my God in heaven! What is this?" she tried to look surprised.

Carrie walked towards the door and looked out. She put her hands over her mouth, trying to hold back the tears at the sight of the two white horses and Pop driving this buggy. "I can't believe this! Jo, Kelly, look!" she pointed at the buggy.

Pop got down while Mannie held the horses. He then walked toward Carrie, his arms opening to meet her with a hug and a kiss. "Daughter, your buggy awaits you," he said smiling at her.

"Pop, the horses? Are they ours?"

"I believe they are yours, my dear, from Jake. They're pretty nice, don't you think?" he said.

"Oh, that son of yours! He is so amazing! Now do you know how to drive this thing?"

"Don't worry. Mannie will be leading them," Pop said.

The three ladies got into the buggy, Blackie running ahead. They moved slowly enough for Mary and Rosa to follow behind. Pop sat on the seat proudly, as if he were really in control of the two white horses.

They reached the pond area and stopped the buggy. Pop helped the women down and they took their places. First Blackie walked down to the pond as Jake called him, then Kelly in her light pink taffeta dress and summer straw hat. Jo, with a darker pink dress, walked slowly behind her towards the gazebo where Jake, his groomsmen, and the minister stood. Guitar music, played by a friend of Jake's, filled the air. Everyone stood as Carrie stepped out on Pop's arm. A light buzz of oohs and ahhs filled the air. The guitarist began the "Bridal March."

Carrie walked toward Jake, her eyes never leaving his face. She reached the steps of the gazebo and handed her bouquet to Jo. Pop took her hand and gave it to Jake, who stared nearly dumbfounded at his beautiful bride. She was so gorgeous. He couldn't believe this was happening! The most precious gift he would ever receive was being handed to him.

Brad waited till all the guests were seated and the wedding party had reached the gazebo before parking his BMW and walking down to the pond. He sat on the last row. *Well, sister, I guess this is your special day. You have a new husband and a new member to your family. I've waited so long to meet you. I promise you will never be alone again. I wish you many blessings.*

"Jake William Thompson, do you take this woman to be your lawful wedded wife, to have and to hold, till death do you part?" the minister asked

"I do," Jake said, looking at Carrie.

"Carrie Ellen Roundtree, do you take this man to be your lawful wedded husband, to have and to hold, till death do you part?"

"I do," Carrie said.

"Let us pray."

After the vows were said, Jake took Carrie in his arms and kissed her. Blackie let out a howl, causing all the guests to laugh.

"Ladies and gentlemen may I present for the first time Mr. and Mrs. Jake Thompson," the minister announced. And as the audience applauded, Carrie threw her flowers. Jo caught the bouquet.

Jake took Carrie's arm and led her back down the aisle to the buggy, nodding and smiling to their guests along the way. Brad slipped back among the other guests so Carrie wouldn't notice him. He wanted the time to be just right.

When they reached the buggy, Pop was waiting in the driver's seat. Jake picked Carrie up in his arms and lifted her inside.

"Jake, the horses…"

"Later, my love," and he kissed her as the buggy pulled away and headed back to the house.

Jake helped Carrie get down and followed Mary's instructions about where to stand for the receiving line. Rosa was busy setting food out, and Mannie was tying up the horses. A couple of minutes later, the guests started arriving from the pond.

Brad stood in back of the line. When it was his turn to greet the bride and groom, he walked up and took Carrie's hand. She looked at him strangely. "You...I know you," she said.

"Really?" Brad said.

Carrie reached for Jake's arm. "Jake, this is the man I saw in the café and at Bepo's service."

"Yes, I was there," Brad said.

"Oh, my...you're Brad Higgins, aren't you?"

"Yes, I am Carrie," he said.

"Jake, this is my brother," Carrie said. Tears streamed down her face.

Brad held out his arms to Carrie. They embraced and held each other while Jake and Jo looked on.

"And, you're that guy I met at the airport, oh my goodness if I only would have looked at your card." Jo said, with a blank look on her face.

"Yes that would have been something, I sure didn't know you were family," Brad said. Brad smiled at Jo; he had a hard time not thinking more about her, but at this moment he was concentrating on Carrie. "I hope I didn't do something wrong," he looked at Carrie. "I just thought it might be nice to meet you on your wedding day," Brad said.

"This is so wonderful, Brad. I have waited for weeks to hear from you. How is Paul?"

"Dad? He's doing just fine. I think he is relieved somewhat. We'll talk about that later. This is your day, Carrie," Brad said.

"Everyone, may I have your attention?" Jake asked. The guests gathered around. "This is a very special day, our wedding day," he stated to the crowd, smiling at Carrie with love in his eyes. "And to make it even more special, Carrie and I have just met someone for the first time. This is Brad Higgins, Carrie's brother, a new member of our family," Jake said, reaching for Brad's hand.

All of the guests clapped and cheered as Carrie and Brad hugged each other. Then Pop began tapping a spoon on his glass, knowing that Fred and Rosa had just finished passing around glasses of the prize wine he had contributed to the reception.

"To my son, Jake, and my new daughter. My son, your mother would be very pleased with your choice of a bride.

May you two have many happy years and give me several grandchildren. Soon," Pop said.

Then Fred raised his glass. "To my best friend and the reason Kelly and I came to Oregon. Our very best to you both. We love you," Fred said.

Carrie and Jakes Friends and neighbors finished their wine and moved on through the receiving line, congratulating the newly married couple, ready to savor the wonderful foods on the buffet: smoked ham, fresh baked bread, and several salads. Then there was the wedding cake.

The afternoon sped by. Carrie and Jake visited with all their Oak Valley neighbors. Carrie wanted very much to talk with Brad, but she noticed he and Jo were sitting at a table alone, laughing and having a good time. She smiled to herself. *Wouldn't that be something?*

Finally, as guests started to leave, Jake and Carrie wandered over to Jo and Brad. "Now, Jo, you told me about a man at the airport. Don't tell me this is the man?" Carrie said.

"Yes, in the flesh. If I had remembered to look at that card he gave me, we would have put this all together," Jo said.

"Yes, you silly girl," Carrie laughed.

"Brad, I hope we can get away soon, just the two of us, and have a good talk. I have pictures to show you, and I want to tell you about your grandfather," Carrie said.

"I would like that very much. You really know how to have a celebration. Someone went to a lot of work," Brad said.

"Well, there was Mary, who is a neighbor and a dear friend. Then Rosa and Mannie who work for us between Jake's farm and mine."

"So tell me, where is your farm, Jake?" Brad asked.

"Just down the road a piece, on the other side of Mary's. I have a vineyard. Your sister here wants to put one in along with her grain fields. You need to come out and visit us and we can show you both farms," Jake said.

"Are you two taking a honeymoon break?" Brad asked.

"You see, I have a little surprise for my bride. As soon as she changes, we can get on our way," he replied, kissing Carrie softly.

"Jake, where are we going?"

"Now, no silly questions," Jake said.

"Brad, did you see the white horses? Jake gave them to me. I have to go see them, please, as soon as I change," Carrie said.

Mannie had taken the horses to the barn and put the buggy away. Rosa had cleaned off the tables with Mary's help. All of the guests had left all except Fred and Kelly, Jo and Brad. As soon as Jake and Carrie had changed, they all walked up to the barn to see the two white horses.

"Jake, they are so attractive. Look how they have made themselves at home," Carrie said.

Jake opened the stall and took Carrie inside. She rubbed the neck of the gelding. "I just love them. Thank you so much, Jake. Now our farms have some animals." Carrie walked out of the stall.

"Do you ride, Brad," Jo asked.

"I did when I was younger. Something tells me I might just have to spend some time here at the farm," Brad said.

"Brad, you missed so much here on the farm. I grew up here, well most of the time, all vacations and the summers," Carrie remarked.

"When you get home from your trip, give me a call. We can meet and talk. I really should get back to the city; I have meetings in the morning. It's been a great day, Carrie. I wish you the very best, and I'm looking forward to spending some time with you. Thank you, Jake. I hope to see the both of you soon," Brad said as he walked towards the house.

Carrie walked with him, holding his hand.

"Thank you, Brad, for making my wedding day complete. This has been one of the happiest days of my life."

"My pleasure, sis," he said smiling.

Carrie's mouth opened slightly and her eyes widened. Then she smiled. She felt so relaxed with this man.

Jake joined Carrie as Brad got into his car and stood with their arms wrapped around each other as he drove down Roundtree Lane.

"Sweetheart, this has no doubt been the most spectacular day in our lives. Now it's time to leave, little lady."

The limo that had arrived just moments before sat waiting for the two of them. After they climbed in, the driver headed towards the city.

"Jake, don't you think a limo is a little much," Carrie said.

"Nope, not for my wife. Besides, as you know, we haven't a car yet. Now wouldn't it look funny for me to take my new bride off on her honeymoon in a truck?" he asked, pulling her towards him.

"Jake, I'm so happy. This has been the grandest day! And what about that Brad? Isn't he nice and so handsome? I knew something was special about him, even back at the café months ago."

"Come here, Mrs. Thompson." He took Carrie in his arms, pressing her body against his, kissing her and then holding her.

"Now will you tell me where we are going?" Carrie asked.

"I thought you might like the mountains. It will be dark when we get to the lodge."

"Lodge? Really? Oh, I never thought you would do this, Jake. I have always wanted to see the mountains. This is fantastic."

The two of them sat close to each other enjoying the night lights of the city in the distance; the moonlit sky was brilliant. As they drove around the mountain curves, every so often they caught glimpses of the snow-capped mountain.

The limo pulled up in front on Timberline Lodge, and the driver opened the door for the newly weds. Carrie and Jake walked slowly into the lodge.

"Jake, it's just as I thought. So rustic. Look at this fireplace. And the view even at night. This is so wonderful," Carrie said.

"Slow down, little lady, we have four days to enjoy it all," Jake said.

Jake took the key and made arrangements for the driver to come back in four days. Then he picked Carrie up in his arms and walked up to the second floor to the bridal suite. He opened the door. As he set her down, Carrie's body slid down Jake's. She could feel the hardness of his manhood. He kissed her on her neck, then softly on her mouth.

"See what you do to me, little lady. I love you so much."

Carrie took Jake's hand and led him to the window. The snow-capped mountain gleamed in the moonlight, the snow glistening like precious gems.

"Oh, Jake, this is so romantic. I love you, my darling, so very much."

As they kissed, Jake began to undress her. First, he unzipped her dress and slowly drew it off her shoulders to slip silently to the floor. She drew her arms tighter around his neck as he unhooked her bra. She stepped back barely an inch and let the lacy confection drop, and then pressed her breasts against Jake's chest. His fingers found the band of her lacy panties and slowly drew them down over her firm buttocks. He trailed kisses over her breasts, down her belly to her womanhood, and across her thighs as he carefully removed the panties from around her ankles. As he stood back up, Carrie stepped back, letting him sear her body with the unbridled desire in his eyes as she stood naked in front of him.

"Such beauty, my love," he said as he picked her up in his arms and laid her on the bed. She lay and watched lovingly as he undressed hurriedly, her breath becoming shallower as she waited for him to relieve the aching deep within her that only he could fill. As he lay beside her, their bodies intertwined, making them one, each touching every special place to give pleasure to the other, each hungry to satisfy each other—a night they would never forget.

When they were exhausted, they held each other closely. Tired from the long bliss-filled day, they fell asleep cradled in each other's arms, dreaming of their future lives together.

Carrie slipped out of bed very quietly and made her way to the bathroom where a large tub awaited. She turned on the water, added some bath salts, slipped on her robe, and reached for the phone to order coffee and juice from room service. She was standing in front of the window looking at the spectacular view when she heard Jake.

"I want to remember this picture of my wife looking out that window with the mountain in the background. You are so lovely with your hair falling onto your shoulders. Come here, wife." He reached out for her.

"Honey, I have a hot bath running for us. They have a huge tub and it's full of scented bath salts waiting for us." Carrie tickled him.

A knock sounded at the door. Carrie opened it and took the tray. She was surprised to see a bottle of champagne.

"Jake, did you order this?"

"Nope, I think it comes with the suite." He got up and reached for his robe.

Carrie turned off the water in the tub, letting her robe fall. She pinned up her hair and stepped into the water.

Jake opened the champagne, poured a glass for him and Carrie, and took off his robe to join his wife.

"Now this is really something," he said, taking his toes and touching Carrie's.

They ate breakfast in the dining room before going for a walk. The weather was very cool with a hint of rain. The walking trail led them through tall fir trees. Green ferns and Oregon grape grew as ground cover. Squirrels ran in front of them and birds sang as if to welcome them into their kingdom.

Soon they stopped to admire the mountain and breathe in the smells of the trees and fresh mountain air.

"Jake, this mountain air is so refreshing. What an exceptional day. Look, the birds seem to follow us. Do you suppose they know we are in love?"

"Mother Nature is a wonderful thing. See the spring flowers are just now blooming; they're late up here on the mountain. I guess we'd better start back. We've come a good three miles," he said.

They walked hand in hand back to the lodge, warming themselves for a few minutes in front of the fireplace as soon they as walked in. Jake ordered a bottle of wine and a tray of cheese with bread and crackers. They sat for a long time by the fire, resting in each other's arms.

The days seemed to fly by, with daily walks, hours in front of the nice warm fire on the chilly summer nights, and meeting new people from the city. There was even a good card game of gin rummy. They made love and planned the new log house they would build. Jake told Carrie to pick out a house plan; then he and Pop would find time to lay out the plot for it. He hoped the knoll behind the barn in front of the pond would be satisfactory. They talked about the farms, deciding to let Rosa and Mannie live in the old farmhouse while Carrie and Jake lived with Pop during the construction of their new home.

Finally it was time to return to the valley. As they drove back, Carrie remarked, "If heaven is like the past four days, I will really work hard to get there."

"Let's not hurry, love. Maybe in a hundred years," Jake said as he kissed her.

Chapter Sixteen

Pop was waiting for Jake and Carrie when they returned. Rosa had moved all of Carrie's personal belongings to Jake's log home. Pop could hardly wait for his children to be with him. Rosa had fixed a large roast with all the trimmings, and Pop had set the table. It was a very nice home coming for the newly weds, but the fun was over and now the farm work had to start.

Blackie barked at the limo as it drove up in front of the log house. He ran around the big car like an excited pup. Carrie bent down and wrapped her arms around the dog.

"Blackie! We're home now boy, I missed you," Carrie beamed.

"Welcome home my children, come tell me all about your trip."

"It's nice to be home Pop, but we sure had a good time. It was very restful," Jake said winking at Pop.

With the wedding now behind them, Jake got up very early in the morning, sometimes before daybreak. He and Pop were busy walking over the slopes checking for drainage or working the grain fields and planting cover crops. The summer was at its hottest. August looked to be Oregon's driest month of the year, and the grapes were setting on.

The phone rang, Carrie answered.

"Hello, Carrie? It's Brad. How was your trip to Mt. Hood?"

"It was wonderful. It was so nice up in the mountains. How are you Brad?"

"I'm fine, I was wondering if we might get together. We can have that talk. I've caught up some on my cases, and have some free time now," Brad said.

"Brad, that sounds great. How about this weekend," Carrie asked.

"That's good. I can come out Saturday morning."

"Good, but plan on staying the night Brad, okay? I would like to show you the farm."

"See you then." Brad hung up.

Carrie sat with a smile on her face. It had been about a month since she had seen Brad. Now she would be able to have that special visit. She wanted to show him her family photo album and tell him about Bepo.

Since Jo found an apartment close to her new job. Carrie and Jake hadn't seen much of her, as she was very busy with her new job.

Carrie was up making the bed and being lazy. She didn't really feel too good, so she had slept in. Jake was worried about her. He had noticed she wasn't feeling well. She felt dizzy and her stomach was upset. She sat down on the side of the bed. The room went round and round but it passed and she finished making the bed. She thought and wondered if she might be pregnant.

That Sunday started out grey but the sun broke through and burnt off the clouds. Around mid-morning, Brad drove up to the log house. Carrie watched his car wind the circular driveway and then watched him slowly get out of the car and look around. Blackie ran out to meet him with excitement jumping all around him.

"Hello Boy." He reached down and fluffed Blackie's head. He liked the looks of the house. It had a nice open deck across the front and the vineyard was just marvelous. The grapes hung heavy and full on the vines. It was rather quite around the farm. Carrie heard Blackie and came to the door. Jake and Pop were over at the old barn tending to the horses.

"Brad, it's so good to see you," Carrie said reaching for his hand.

"It's good to see you," he said.

"I see you found us okay."

"Yes, it was a nice drive. This is a neat place. I've never seen a log home before." As he spoke he looked around, letting his eyes sweep around the whole lot, the house itself and then settle back on Carrie.

"Come on in Brad, I'd like to show you around," Carrie motioned to Brad.

Carrie took Brad through the house and the loft. She showed him the log home plans that she and Jake were going to build.

"I have my family album. I thought you might like to see some pictures." Carrie sat at the table, waiting for Brad to take a chair.

Carrie opened the picture album. On the first page was a wedding photo of her parents. Brad looked at it carefully.

"My, she was very pretty wasn't she?"

"Yes, she was."

"You know Carrie, you look a lot like our mother."

"Yes, Bepo always told me that." She smiled at the memory of him.

"Who is Bepo?"

"My grandfather, Hank Roundtree. It's a shame you didn't have the opportunity to have known him."

"When I was in the cafe, his name was spoken often. I can tell that he was well thought of," Brad said.

"You would have loved him, Brad. He was a kind person and very caring," Carrie said pointing to a picture of him.

"Brad was it hard to learn about me?"

"Well, Dad had it the hardest. He had to tell me. You see, I found the letters our mother had written him. I knew about her for a long time. Then I read about Hank Round-tree who had passed away. When I put it all together, I came to Oak Valley to his service. That's when I saw you at the grave sight. That really got to me."

"Why?"

"You were there all alone with no family around you. I didn't figure it out until you left and I walked up to the grave. Then I saw the head stones, the family plot, your parents, and the dates. I knew then that my mother was dead and it made me sick. I guess I always thought I would meet her someday. I just have a hard time trying to figure out why she gave me away. Don't take me wrong, I'm happy to have my dad, he's great." Brad nodded his head, seeming to reassure himself.

"Brad, why didn't you try to find me after the service," Carrie asked.

"Well, I knew I would have to tell my dad that I found the letters. I didn't want to hurt my adoptive mother; I love her very much. I knew you didn't know about me, and I felt you would just be hurt. So I decided to wait. Then that day came when my dad told me about your visit to Denver. My poor dad, he really had a hard time telling me, but it was also a relief. I guess he made our mother Carol a promise."

"Brad, my mother would not have given her baby away without being forced to. My father must have had some kind of hold on her. She was a loving person. She and I were very close, she was always more than my mother, and she was my best friend. I feel those letters were kept in her bible knowing that someday I would find them. Why did your dad keep his letters?"

"He said he put them away and forgot them, but I have a funny feeling he was wanting me to find them, too. He told me Carol was the love of his life and it took him several years to get over her."

"Brad did your dad tell you how our parents met." Carrie squinted her eyes at him.

"Yes, on a rainy day, sharing a booth in a diner at the bus depot. My, mother must have been very unhappy. I guess we will never know."

"No, I guess not."

"So, is this you on this big white horse?" He pointed to a photo in the album.

"Yes, that's spot. She always managed to dump me out in the pasture, and then she would run up to the barn and watch me walk. I hated that horse." Carrie laughed.

"This is Bepo and our grandmother. I always stayed here at the farm on vacations and holidays. My parents were both teachers and were always working. I loved the farm, you know, I just decided to keep it a few months back. I almost sold it," Carrie stated.

Carrie and Brad sat for several hours just talking about her farm life as a child. They looked at all the family pictures together. Brad told Carrie about his childhood and how he had worked his way through law school. He told her that he grew up in the hardware store helping his parents.

Carrie took Brad tour of the farm. They found Jake and Mannie at the sheep barn mending a gate. Brad heard all the farm stories. He couldn't believe at one time there were two hundred sheep on the farm. They walked by the pond and then to the horse barn.

Jake told Brad how he and Carrie met. He was amazed about all the things that had happened to Carrie, and how brave she was. They saddled up the horses and went riding.

Brad and Carrie would always bring the conversation back to their mother, and wondered how things could have been different. They rode over most of the farm and through the timber on the edge of the North Slope. Carrie told him about her dream of a vineyard and perhaps a winery.

"Well, Brad, how did you like the ride?"

"It was great, only I will never walk right again." He laughed.

The two of them brushed the horses down and put the riding gear away, then walked to the house. Carrie noticed a car in the circle drive. It was Jo's.

"Look who's here Brad, Jo must have gotten tired of the city."

Jo and Jake sat at the kitchen table. Jo wanted to come out to the country to get away from the hot summer day in the city. She knew she was always welcome and didn't need an invitation

Brad opened the door for Carrie and they entered the kitchen.

"So here you are. Did you have a good ride," Jake asked.

"Yes, it's been awhile but I really think I liked it. This country life could grow on me," Brad said.

"Hi Jo, glad you came out girlfriend. You remember Brad."

Jo looked at Brad and smiled as she saw him pulling up a chair for himself and Carrie.

"Yes, how are you Brad," Jo asked.

"Good," he smiled.

"Hey, why don't I fix some steaks? It's a great night for a BBQ," Jake said.

The two couples sat under the oaks and visited. Jo and Brad seemed to talk more than usual, like they were old friends. It was a nice summer evening and Carrie was thrilled to have Brad around. Their talks were something she had long been waiting for. Carrie showed Brad the upstairs bedroom, and Jo went back to Jake's.

The sun came up bright red over the vineyard. Jake sat reading the paper at the table enjoying his morning coffee. Jo sat on the front deck of the log home admiring the country life, thinking, *I guess we may have fooled Carrie and Jake. No one knows that we have been seeing each other. Brad, you are such a handsome man and I think I'm falling for you.*

Carrie walked out on the deck, yawning.

"I thought I heard you get up. Jo, I need to talk to you."

"Gee honey, you know I'm always here for you," Jo said.

"Isn't he wonderful," Carrie said, more to herself than to Jo.

"Who?"

"You know, Brad," Carrie replied.

"Yes he is girlfriend, did you two have a good talk?"

"Yes, I think so, but..."
"Is something wrong?"

"I feel kind of guilty. Bepo was his grandfather too, and he left me everything. You know what I mean?"

"Well, yes. But I don't think that means anything, you were here for your grandfather and he didn't even know about Brad. Plus, Brad has his family, too," Jo said.

"Well, maybe someday I can do something special for him," Carrie said.

"You shouldn't Carrie. You need to let your relationship grow. You know he's not hurting for money. He has a very good law practice."

"How do you know that?" Jo looked at Carrie and smiled.

"We sort of, you know."

"Jo Hamilton, have you been seeing my brother and not telling me about it? Shame on you," she scolded, hugging Jo.

The phone rang and Jake reached for it.

"Hello."

"Hi Jake, it's good old Fred. How are you two newly weds doing?"

"Hey, just great. Now that the harvest is in, I hope to spend more time with my bride. It was a long month," Jake said.

"Yeah, I know what you mean. Kelly and I saved a row of our finest to pick and harvest. We thought it might be fun to have a picking party and crush the fruit. And of course a lot of Kelly's fine cooking, how about it?"

"That sounds really wild Fred. So when is this party?"

"This weekend, October 1st," Fred answered.

"You can count on us Fred," Jake said.

"Oh, Kelly wanted Carrie to ask her brother and her friend Jo, and bring Pop, too. I want to pick his brain," Fred said.

"I'll tell her Fred. See you Saturday," Jake said.

"Jake, this is the time to tell Fred and Kelly about the baby. They've been trying for years to get pregnant and I think they kind of gave up hope. That's all she talks about, I wonder why they don't adopt," Carrie said.

Jake drove up the mountain pass as they talked.

"'I don't know. Fred doesn't say much about it. Maybe our baby will help things along for them."

"Well little lady, or mommy, our baby…. you make me so happy," Jake said, reaching for Carrie's hand.

"It will be wonderful our very own family little feet pattering around and daddy getting up in the night."

"Oh really" Jake said with a laugh.

"It will be nice to see Brad again. I feel close to him, even in just this short time," Carrie said.

As they pulled in front of the Chalet, they noticed that Brad's car was there along with several others. Pop had been rather quiet on the drive up.

"Pop, you didn't say much coming up the mountain," Jake said.

"Doing a lot of thinking. You know me, all that winter work in the vineyard ahead of us. We'll have to start soon you know."

"Now Pop, have a good time today and meet some new friends. Hey, is Mary coming up?" Jake said with a mischievous look in his eyes.

"How would I know? Haven't seen her for a while, I think she is out of sorts with me," Pop remarked.

"That's too bad. I wish you would make an effort to be nice to her for Carrie's sake," Jake said.

Fred met them at the door of the Chalet, handing out wineglasses. He told everyone to drink up and then they would go to the small vineyard in the back. He handed out baskets and gave everyone a knife. He showed them how to pick the grapes, and then they would empty them in a large barrel back of the Chalet.

"Now Fred, do you really think we will get in there in our bare feet and stomp these grapes," Jo asked laughing and pointing to the barrel.

"Here, have another glass of wine Jo, and then you will feel like it," Fred said handing her a glass.

They all washed up their feet and then took turns stomping the grapes. Fred told them all they would get some of the wine that they had stomped. They had fun laughing and doing a little dance while they stomped.

It seemed like hours before the grapes had been stomped to mush. Kelly had set out a feast for their guests. They all sat around eating Kelly's famous Italian cheese pie and home made pizza. Jake leaned over to Carrie.

"Now is the time. Do you want to tell or should I, mommy?"

"Go ahead daddy," Carrie said, reaching for his hand.

"Everyone, Carrie and I have something to tell you."

"Really," Jo said.

"Yes, Carrie is pregnant, due next March."

"Hip, hip, everyone drink up to Carrie and Jake," Fred said as he went around again and filled everyone's glass with his Pinot Noir. The guests gathered around them congratulating them on the new baby. Kelly seemed a little sad.

"I'm so happy for you Carrie, I only wish it would happen to me."

"Gee Kelly, it will hon, I'm sure of it. If not, why don't you adopt?"

"We're thinking about it. Fred thinks he's getting too old for a baby, so we might take an older child," Kelly said.

"I think that would be really special," Carrie said.

Pop was over in a corner talking to Fred about the wine he had made; he even gave Fred a few hints. He was hoping he and Jake could get a winery started down in the valley, perhaps out of the old barn.

Brad and Jo went for a walk and ended up in the tall firs, enjoying the summer coolness of the mountain.

"This is a great place to cool off on these hot days. What a great party." Brad paused and got a playful look in his eye." I wonder if my feet will stay purple?"

"Me too, Brad. You'll look funny going to work with purple feet," Jo said kidding him.

They stood for a moment looking at each other.

"Jo, you know, I think I'm falling in love with you."

"I know, me too."

He took Jo in his arms and kissed her sweetly. This feeling was special and he had never felt so at ease.

"Will you be my girl Jo?"

"I'd love to Brad."

"You know, when I met you in the airport I had a tug at my heart different than any other feeling. I had a lady friend for a long time, but this is something I have a hard time explaining. I want you in my life from now on Jo Hamilton."

"Wow! What can a girl say to that," she said reaching for him and giving him a hug that ended in a long kiss.

They walked back to the Chalet, hand in hand then arm in arm, giggling about little things.

Carrie noticed a change in Jo and Brad when she saw them walking back.

"Now you two! Do you want to tell me what seems to be going on here?"

"Well, my sister dear, since you're family and all and Jo is like a sister to you, we have just committed ourselves to one another," Brad said looking into Jo's eyes and smiling.

"You two make me so happy," Carrie said hugging them both.

"Brad, you must come out to the farm and see the plans for the new house, they're breaking ground next week. We hope to be in it by Christmas, and Jo we have to start planning the nursery."

"I know, maybe I can come out next weekend. How about you Brad?"

"I believe I can handle that," Brad said. Jake caught up to them.

"Well, little lady, you think we'd better get home? I think Pop is a little tired," Jake remarked.

They said their good-byes and thank you and got in the truck to go home.

The month of October was a busy one. A lot was going on at both farms. On the weekends Jake and Carrie would find themselves going for long horseback rides. The leaves were golden in color now and the cool fall air was refreshing. Brad and Jo spent a lot of time at the old farmhouse. They took over the upstairs, enjoyed long walks and quiet time in the gazebo. They enjoyed reading and watching the swans. Brad even brought some work from the office with him from time to time.

Jake and Carrie were busy going over a few changes in the log home, making sure things were being built right. Carrie was so excited as the house took shape. The master suite was her favorite room in the house, with its fireplace, his and her vanities and a small library. Jake's office was just off the kitchen. Her dream house was truly being built. By Thanksgiving Carrie seemed to really start to show. She had an appointment with Doctor Reese. She drove into the village to see him. She was feeling great, but a little too fat, she thought.

Carrie entered the doctor's clinic. She was called into the office. Dr. Reese listened to the baby's heartbeat with a puzzled look on his face.

"Well now, what do we have here," he said.

"Is something wrong Doctor," Carrie asked.

"No, but I do believe there may be two babies in there. I hear two beats."

"You're kidding aren't you," Carrie said.

"No, I want you to go to the city to a specialist and they can tell you more. I'm just an old country doctor."

"Well, if you think I should."

"I'll make the appointment."

Carrie drove home thinking, *two babies, how wonderful. I didn't know there were twins in the family, what a blessing. I can hardly wait to tell Jake and Pop.*

Jake took off his shoes and propped up his feet. It had been a long day and he was very tired. Soon he fell off in a rest full sleep. Pop was busy in the barn making a wood cradle for his first grandchild. He was a very happy man. He was counting the days until the birth.

Carrie drove up and parked. Blackie came running out to meet her. She opened the front door and saw Jake sleeping in his chair. *Poor darling, he is so tired. He looks so grand and I love him so. And now there will be four of us, I'm so happy and blessed.*

"I thought you drove up. How was the doctor's appointment?"

"Well daddy, are you ready for a heaven sent blessing?"

"What do you mean?"

"The doctor thinks we should go to the city to see a specialist. We might be having twins." Carrie grinned at Jake.

"What did you say?"

"You heard me, twins," Carrie said.

"Oh my gosh honey, are you all right," he asked, feeling her belly.

"I'm just fine, or we are. Isn't it wonderful Jake! Twins."

"Wow, wait till I tell Pop. Now he has to make two cradles," he said laughing. "Come here mommy."

Later that week their trip to the city specialist confirmed that Carrie was carrying twins. The doctor told Carrie to stay off her feet some and get a lot of rest, as twins can come early.

November came and so did the fall rains and wind. Pop and Jake, with Mannie at their side, worked in the vineyard long hours in mud to their ankles. They pruned most of the year's growth off the vines so they would be ready for the next season. Thanksgiving was a great holiday for the Thompson's. Mary, Rosa and Mannie had become like family. Jo would be joining them as well as Kelly and Fred. Jake went to the city and purchased a twenty-pound turkey. Rosa and Mary would do all the cooking and preparations.

Jake and Carrie walked through their new home, still not finished, but thinking that by Christmas they would be able to move in and have their first holiday. The house was large and cold. The rock fireplaces were being put in, and the windows were installed.

"My dear, your house is really taking shape."

"Oh yes Jake! It's going to be a great home for our children. Carrie and Jake moved to the front deck and leaned against the rail then Carrie took Jakes hand. I love it, it is splendid, don't you think?"

"Little lady whatever you want, this is your dream come true. And for giving me not one, but two babies! Carrie I love you so much."

Jake pulled her close to him and they both looked out over the vineyard.

Chapter Seventeen

Alex paced the cell floor, wringing his hands, thinking. *Just a few months to go and I will be up for parole. I've got to get out of here, this place is driving me crazy, and besides I shouldn't even be in here. Damn that Carrie Roundtree, I've got to get out and get even. I must think this through very carefully, maybe a few phone calls first. Why should she be so damn happy with her new farmer when I should be with her still working at the paper? If she would of just listened to me I know she would of loved me. I'm not that bad of a guy, a few bucks in the bank, and man all that money she came into too, that farm would of sold for a bundle! We would have had it pretty darn good.*

"Okay you flea bags, line up here when your doors come open. You get one phone call. No pushing and stay in line," the guard stated as they walked in formation to the phones in the day room.

Alex waited for what seemed like hours to take his turn. When he reached the phone he placed a call to information in Oak Valley Oregon, he wrote the phone number down. There was only one Roundtree listed—Hank. Alex dialed slowly.

"Hello?" Rosa said.

Alex said nothing. It wasn't Carrie on the phone.

"Miss Roundtree please," Alex asked in a polite voice.

"She no live here. She at new farm. Call Thompson farm," Rosa said, and hung up.

Alex immediately started to dial again.

"Hey! You can't do that. You already had your call." It was the prisoner behind Alex, yelling and pulling on him.

"Okay, okay," Alex said in a rough voice. So it would take some more time before he'd get to talk to Carrie. If that was the case, time was something Alex had plenty of.

Alex made his way to sit down in the day room. He didn't have any visitors. People mingled about with their loved ones. Once he thought that maybe Jo Hamilton would come see him, but no one visited Alex Blane.

Alex thought about how lonely he was but that was okay, he was used to it. He thought about his childhood all the times he had to stay alone at night while his mother was out going to the bars. He put his head down on the table. It was four p.m. when the guard had them line up to go back to their cells; he would try again for a phone call next time.

Alex sat in his cell writing on a piece of paper, over and over again the way a student might have to in class when the teacher catches them at something. Carrie Roundtree.

The next day he leaned up against the concrete wall in the exercise yard.

"Hi."

"Yeah. Who are you?"

"Bob Kindle," The tall man stated.

"Alex Blane." He shook the man's hand.

"Want a smoke?" he asked Alex.

"Sure," Alex said even though he didn't smoke. It was one of the many things Alex had picked up some coming inside the joint.

"What you in for?"

"A woman put me here," Alex answered.

"That's funny," Kindle roared with laughter. He slapped Alex hard on the shoulder. "Me too."

"Yeah, well I will get even somehow. No woman can get away with this. I come up for parole in a few months."

"My parole comes up next week, and then I'm heading home to the West."

"What part of the West?" Alex asked.

"Washington State," Kindle said wistfully while puffing on his cigarette.

They stood together a long time, talking about paroles and what might be ahead of them. Alex had an idea.

I wonder if it will work, he thought, staring into the gathering dusk with his hands on his hips.

Chapter Eighteen

Jake sat at the kitchen table with Pop, going over the daily chores. It almost sounded like he was checking them off as he said them on some mental list.

"Have you seen Mary?" Pop interrupted. His tone betrayed his interest.

"Uh, no," Jake said, coming out of it. "We haven't seen her in a few days."

"I think I'll stop in and see her on my way to the barn, when I let the horses out," Pop said.

"That's good, Pop. Make sure to tell her to stop over. I think Carrie misses her some, they are so close.

Pop loaded up some things to take to the barn. He wanted to get an early morning start on his chores, and then he would work on the second baby cradle. But first he would stop off at Mary's.

He drove up and parked and made his way to the back door. Mary always had a good cup of coffee on the stove. He was trying to make up to Mary. He knew how he had treated her badly and he felt bad. After all she was an old woman with a strong personality like his.

He knocked on the door but no one answered except the two dogs that ran to the door and barked. Pop opened the door and went in but stopped when he saw her spread out on the floor.

"Mary, can you hear me, it's Ed?" he said frantically, kneeling down next to her.

"Oh, what happened?" Mary was clearly dazed as she sat up and looked around. "I was trying to get that big bowl down out of the top cupboard I guess I fell off the stool."

"Looks like you may have passed out," Pop said, visibly relieved that she was okay. "I guess I came along at a good time," he said with a wink. "You lay still here," Pop told her.

"Don't you go telling me what to do, old man!" Mary said jokingly but with a look in her eyes that showed she meant it.

"You just stay put, you hear me!"

Pop dialed the familiar number and after a ring he heard Carrie's voice. "Hello?"

"Carrie, I'm here at Mary's. She took a fall off a stool. I think you and Jake better come down here and look her over. She wants to get up but I told her to stay put, don't know how long she'll mind me, you better hurry," Pop said.

"Okay, Pop you cover her up with a blanket, we will be right over." Carrie said, as she called out to Jake.

A few minutes later, Jake and Carrie hurried in the back door of Mary's house. Pop was sitting on the floor beside Mary and they were both laughing.

"Well, what do we have here Pop? Mary, how do you feel?" Jake asked.

"I think I'm just fine but this old man here won't let me get up."

"Okay let's try," Jake said.

"Oh, my foot hurts. I don't think I can stand on it." Mary said.

"I better call Doctor Reese," Carrie said.

Carrie and Jake sat with Mary waiting for the Doctor. When he arrived and examined her he could see that her ankle was sprained. Since she seemed fine otherwise, he told her to stay off her foot for several days and make an appointment in a week.

Jake and Carrie insisted that Mary come live at the farmhouse to let Rosa take care of her for a few days.

After they got Mary settled in at the farm, Jake took Carrie back home. They both laughed at how nice Pop was treating Mary.

"Did you see how the two of them were laughing when we walked into the kitchen?"

"Yes, I did. Maybe those two will finally become friends. You know my Pop. Strong headed like a mean bull!" Jake said. "Tell me, mommy. How do you feel this morning?"

"Jake I don't know how much bigger I can get. Sometimes these two babies feel like they are fighting in here." Carrie rubbed her belly. It was true. She had always been a slim woman and this extra weight was a strain on her.

Pop visited Mary every morning, had his coffee and did his chores at the barn, and then would stop by again in the afternoon. Sometimes he and Mary would play checkers. Carrie and Jake noticed how close they had become. Many nights he would stay for supper and Rosa always set an extra plate.

Everything else moved along at its own pace. The big house was about finished; Carrie and Jake took several trips to the city, picking out some furniture, like two cribs for the babies. Rosa and Carrie made dozens of diapers and little kimonos, and as soon as they could move they would work on the nursery.

Brad and Jo, with the help of their friends Kelly and Fred, came and helped Carrie and Jake move into the big house. It was a special day for Carrie. She made sure Jake brought his bed set that he had made. After the weekend, they were settled in.

Pop was already complaining about being alone but seemed to like the idea of having his own place, and Mary had promised to come and cook for him from time to time.

Jake and Carrie sat in front of the fireplace, looking about the room. Jake had put a lot of work into the fireplace mantel; he hand carved the design and then painted several coats of varnish. The family photo's in their oval frames sat on the mantel. A large red and blue braided rug lay in front of the fireplace

"Oh my gosh," Jake said.

"What?"

"My elk head has to go over the mantel. I forgot to move it."

"No, no Mr. Thompson! Not a stuffed head in our house," Carrie said in a kidding tone.

"Well if you insist. It does rather look good where it is," Jake said, apparently conceding. "Anyway, maybe Fred and I will have to go deer hunting," he said.

"Ouch!"

"What is it?" Jake asked, "Are you okay?"

"I think that one must be a boy. Here, feel."

"That's great! Hey, do you think they can hear us?"

"I don't know. Why don't we sing to them," Carrie said.

The two of them sat there singing a lullaby. Jake held Carrie close to him and they talked about Christmas and where they would put a tree. Then Jake got an idea.

The next morning Jake arrived at the barn early, he and Mannie hooked up the horses to the buggy. Then he pulled up to the front of the house. Carrie had put a coat on and waddled like a duck across the deck. Jake took her hand as she walked down the steps and helped her into the buggy, tucked a blanket around her then drove up to the sheep barn.

The cold December air felt crisp on their faces and the sky was dark like maybe snow would fall at any minute. Jake drove to the tall timber past the sheep barn and over a slope. He stopped, got out and helped Carrie down. Then they walked through the trees till they saw it.

"There, Jake. That one, it's perfect."

"Kinda big don't you think?"

"No, Hon it's perfect. It has to be spectacular for our first Christmas in our new home," Carrie said.

Jake took out a saw and Carrie watched him cut the tree down. He wrapped rope around the branches and tied the tree to the back of the buggy. Carrie sat in the buggy all bundled up and she could feel the snowflakes falling onto her face. Jake drove the buggy slowly, enjoying the ride. The two white horses pranced along as if they two were enjoying the outing. The next afternoon Pop and Jake made a stand for the tree and brought it into the house. It stood a good seven feet tall.

"Pop, Thank you for helping Jake, this is the perfect tree," Carrie said. She stood back admiring their accomplishments.

Jake took Carrie to the Doctor in the city for her seven month check-up. She was to come in every week from now on. The babies were growing just as expected and Carrie was getting bigger and bigger. She was to stay down as much as she could and take long naps.

Jake stopped long enough to get some tree decorations and when they arrived home Carrie was rather tired. Jake gave her orders to stay on the sofa.

"Honey, let's have Pop and Mary over to help decorate the tree. Maybe Brad and Jo would like to come too. I would love to have the both of them for the holidays," Carrie said.

"Yes, me too. And if you don't care, Fred and Kelly have always had Christmas with me."

"We'll have a great holiday with family and friends. And just maybe we'll have a white Christmas."

"Well, if you look outside I believe we're getting started on your order Mrs. Thompson." Jake helped Carrie to the window, putting his arms around her.

It seemed that Oregon was going to have another cold winter. Pop and Jake winterized the out buildings at all three farms. They filled the sheep barn with hay for the winter. Meantime Mary was up and around doing all kinds of baking. Hundreds of her special decorated Christmas cookies and her famous date bread and fruit cake filled the kitchen. Carrie felt too fat and was very uncomfortable, and really could care less about food. Jake waited on her, rubbed her feet in front of the fire and would sit with her for hours.

On Sunday night before Christmas, Pop and Mary, Jo and Brad, and Fred and Kelly all helped Jake and Carrie decorate the tree. The men put fir boughs on the deck rails, and hung up some outside lights. The log home was beautified with such colorful decorations.

The Christmas tree was decorated and was lovely; the scent of pine filled the house. Christmas Eve was here and Carrie had records laid out to put on the Victrola. It truly was a white Christmas. You could smell the homemade chili that Jake had been making all day.

Pop had arrived with Mary. Jo and Brad were sitting by the fire talking about how neat it was to see Pop and Mary friends at last. Jake was beginning to worry about Fred and Kelly even though Fred did call to say they might be a little late. The roads were snow covered; however, Fred knew how to handle a vehicle under these circumstances. They all sat waiting and visiting and being grateful to be together. Just then they heard a car.

"Here we are," Fred said as he opened the door.

"Where's your wife?" Carrie asked.

"Oh, she's coming. Now I want you all to sit down, we have a surprise in store for all of you."

"Sure thing Fred, what is it?"

"Okay, Kelly come on in," Fred said.

Kelly walked in slowly with a little boy standing beside her. He seemed afraid. But Kelly assured him he was among family.

"Everyone this is Benny our new son. He's just four years old. Benny this is Uncle Jake and Aunt Carrie," Kelly said.

Jake got up and bent down and reached for his little hand.

"Benny, this is a special moment for me. Welcome little fellow," he said, giving him a little hug.

Carrie had tears running down her face. She could see how proud Kelly and Fred were. She went to Kelly and embraced, her wishing her happiness.

"Benny, I'm Aunt Carrie and I've been waiting to meet you honey," she said, hugging him.

"We're so happy for you guy's. And I even think he looks like you two. What a Christmas gift," Jo said.

"We wanted to wait and bring Benny here tonight because we heard Santa was coming, right Jake?"

"That's right. We better put out some cookies and milk. What do you think Uncle Jake?" Carrie stated. Benny's eyes seemed to light up and he looked up at Kelly.

"Can we?" he said in a whisper.

"I bet Aunt Carrie has some cookies in the cookie jar," Jo said.

Mary made her way to the little boy and held out her hand.

"Benny, you can call me Nana. And if you will come with me, I bet we can find those cookies and we can set a place at the table for Santa." The little boy took Mary's hand reluctantly.

"Fred and Kelly. Wow we're so happy for you! Tell us how and when?" Jake asked.

They took off their coats and pulled up chairs around the fire.

"We got this call from our lawyer," he smiled at Brad and nodded his head.

"No way! And you didn't tell us Brad!" Carrie exclaimed, clearly not upset.

"Hey, I couldn't. This just all fell into place, and I couldn't enjoy my work more. This is one case I'm proud of," Brad said.

Before long, it was time to put Benny to bed; Kelly sat with him till he fell asleep. Then Jake and Carrie started to bring out some gifts and put them under the tree. Fred made several trips to his car as did Brad. The tree was overwhelmed with gifts. Every one retired except Jake and Carrie. They sat alone for a while admiring the tree. Jake looked at his watch and saw it was midnight.

"What a Christmas! Little Benny sure is a handsome boy."

"I'm so happy for Kelly," Carrie beamed. "She has wanted a baby for so long and to think my brother was able to help them. He really is a cutie! She did tell me at their party they might adopt. Oh Jake it is so wonderful."

"This has been an incredible year, just as if it were made just for us, my love. You have made me a very happy man. Nothing could spoil the love we have for each other," Jake said hugging her.

Just then the phone rang. Jake got up and answered it.

"Hello," Jake said. No one seemed to be on the line. "Hello?" he said again. Still no one was there. He held the phone in his hand. "Must have been a wrong number. Sort of late for a caller, don't you think?" he said looking at Carrie.

They both got up arm in arm moving towards the bedroom. Undressed, Carrie sat on the side of the bed waiting for the back rub that had been promised. Jake rubbed in the lotion.

"I must be the luckiest mother-to-be in the world. That feels like heaven hon, thank you so much," Carrie said reaching for him.

They held each other all night and woke to the smell of coffee. They both got up and slipped into robes and slippers and peeked around the corner. They watched little Benny as he walked down the stairs. He first went to the table. The milk was gone and only one cookie was left with a big bite taken out of it. He picked it up and held it up to Fred and Kelly.

"Look, he ate out of it and the milk is gone. He really did come," he said smiling at his new parents.

Jo and Brad came down the stairs joining in on the fun of opening gifts. Just then the front door opened.

"Hey, wait for us," Pop said as he and Mary came into the house.

It truly was a great morning watching the little boy with his gifts, and the love that was growing between him and his new parents and new family.

The holidays came and went, the winter weather hung around and the snow turned into rain. The days were long and dreary for Carrie. She felt miserable. Jake was never far from her side. The Doctor had decided to keep Carrie down. She had long naps, and Jake would read to her for hours about how to take care of twins. Jo and Kelly had painted little teddy bears on the nursery wall. Both cradles were in place, with piles of diapers folded and ready. Now it was just the waiting, and that was the hard part. Jo and Brad spent weekends at the farm helping out wherever they could so Jake could stay at the house and be with Carrie.

When the day arrived Carrie, was sitting up in bed.

"Jake! Jake!" Carrie yelled.

"I'm coming!"

"My water just broke!" Carrie said loudly.

"Okay," he said as he entered the bedroom. "Are you sure?"

"Well if I'm not, I must have really wet this bed" she said.

Jake went back into the kitchen and reached for the phone.

"Hi, Doc. It's time. Carrie's water just broke," he said in a shaky voice.

"I'm on my way, we may not have time to move her to the city so I'll bring a nurse with me and we should be there in twenty or thirty minutes. Keep her comfortable and stay with her." He said.

While Jake was by the phone, he called Pop.

"Now hon, the Doctor is on his way. He's bringing a nurse and he said just take it easy."

"Sure, daddy, I'm ready to get these babies out of here. Oh my back hurts Jake. Rub it okay?"

Carrie rolled over onto her side, Jake worked on her lower back, then the pain started, sharp unbearable pain. Carrie rolled over onto her back, grabbing the bed rail.

"Hang in their honey. The Doc said twenty minutes."

Just then Mary entered the room, with Pop on her heels.

"Well, so it's time Carrie girl. Old Mary is here honey so you hold onto my hand. I don't think you should push till the doctor gets here," Mary said lovingly.

Carrie yelled out a loud cry.

"Pop I think you better get Jake out of here. Bring the doctor in as soon as he gets here," Mary said.

Mary changed the linen, and put a wet cloth on Carrie's forehead, holding her hand and giving her encouragement to wait till help arrived.

"They better hurry Mary. I can't wait much longer. These babies want to meet their new family. Oh! My! Where are they? God please let this pain stop," she yelled.

The doctor and nurse entered the bedroom; the Doctor examined Carrie and determined she was about ready to give birth. Soon two new little babies would be coming into the world. The nurse was preparing Carrie, and the Doctor gave Carrie something for pain.

"Carrie, you are going to feel some very hard pains, but I don't want you to push till I tell you. Okay?"

"I just want them out of me. Please hurry, it hurts Doc. Oh Mary, why did I let Jake do this to me? Why oh why! Damn..." Carrie gripped Mary's hand.

"Nurse get ready, here we go. Okay Carrie, I want you to bare down, do you hear me, now. PUSH!"

Carrie strained as hard as she could. She took deep breaths and pushed as the Doctor told her to. The sweat beads on her head had made her hair wet, so Mary kept wiping her face and holding her hand.

Jake and Pop were pacing the floor. Jake shrugged as he heard Carrie scream. He felt her pain, covering his hands over his ears. Blackie would bark, wanting to go into the bedroom and finally Jake had to put him outside. Pop sat trying to give Jake some comforting words. It seemed like hours, he sat worried thinking *why hasn't that doctor let me know something?*

"Okay here comes the first one, push Carrie now."

The doctor reached for the baby, then handed her to the nurse. She was crying very loudly.

"We have baby a girl, Carrie, and she looks just fine. Now here we go again. Let's go for the other one, now push hard," the Doctor said.

Carrie worked very hard and did just as she was told. The baby was another girl. Carrie laid back spent from the hard work of delivery. The nurse cleaned both babies and handed them to Carrie, one under each arm. Then Mary went to get Jake and Pop.

Jake entered the room he couldn't believe his eyes. He knelt down by the bed and cried.

"Oh, Carrie you are so wonderful and these two baby daughters, they are so perfect. Are you doing okay?" he said kissing her.

The doctor told Jake the babies were in good health. One was five pounds and one five and a half.

"Mommy, look at our daughters! They are identical twins."

"Jake are you happy with two girls? I'm so sorry I didn't give you a boy."

"Hey, I am the happiest man in the world! Two girls! What a gift from God, Carrie. They are so beautiful my love," Jake said kissing both baby girls.

Pop just stood holding Mary's hand grinning from ear to ear. He was a very proud grandfather.

"Here Pop, do you want to hold your granddaughters?"

"Not yet. They're just too small. But I can look at um," he said smiling and thanking Carrie.

Chapter Nineteen

Spring was Carrie's favorite time of the year. There were thousands of colorful little flower buds everywhere and plants all around the farmhouse were about to bloom. Jake had bought twelve laying hens and Pop was busy building a chicken house.

Rosa and Mary were watching the twin girls as Carrie drove towards Oak Valley. The car she was driving wasn't new, but Jake did a good job of finding a good, late-model four door.

Jake had give Carrie a few errands to run and then she was going to the post office.

Carrie sat the package on the front seat, then she noticed there was no return address, and it was postmarked from Seattle. She wondered about it. She didn't know anyone from Seattle. It had her curiosity up. Oh, well, she thought, it'll wait until I get home.

She made her stop at the hardware store, picked up the items for Jake and then started back toward home. She had a good feeling being away from the farm. It had been awhile. The two babies kept her pretty busy, and the nursing didn't help. The girls were now eight weeks old and you could see how they had grown. Jake was as happy as a king seeing those first smiles. Real smiles and not gas, Carrie thought and giggled to herself. He was a perfect father.

Pop would come by in the evening just to rock Ellen. She loved to be cuddled. Carrie felt the bonding between Pop and the babies was well under way.

As Carrie drove towards the farm, the vineyards were turning green again and coming to life. She was content. This spring Jake was putting in the second vineyard; the new plants were arriving any day now.

She drove up, parked the car in front of the house, and gathered up the mail along with the package.

"I'm home. Where is everyone?" she called setting the package on the table then taking her coat off.

"We're in here," Mary called from the bedroom.

Mary sat rocking both girls under her arms. Rosa was folding diapers on the bed.

Carrie carefully took Carol and then Ellen and laid them in their cradles and then motioned Rosa and Mary to the kitchen.

"So, tell me how did it go?" Carrie asked.

"Just fine, a little fussy but not much," Mary told Carrie as she put on her jacket.

"Thank you so much. It was nice to get away by myself. Oh, and look! I even have a package." She picked it up and started to open it.

She unwrapped it carefully to save the hand - writing and postmark, so she could show Jake. Maybe he would recognize it and know who sent it.

She reached for the scissors to cut the tape away.

"That box sure has a bad smell to it Carrie. Maybe you better wait for Jake," Mary said just as Carrie opened the top of the box.

Carrie carefully pulled some paper back, then looked in the box. Instantly the color left her face and she sat down in the chair gasping for breath. Mary took the box.

"What in the devil is this? It's just a bad joke or something." Mary wrapped up the box and took it out side; she wanted Jake to see this.

"Miss Carrie are you fine?" Rosa asked.

"Mary? Who, who would do something like this to me, sending me a dead rat. It makes me sick." She got up and got a glass of water. "Maybe you better stay till Pop and Jake get back from their meeting. It should be any time," she said.

Mary made some tea and the three of them sat waiting. Carrie just sat thinking. I wonder if Alex had anything to do with this. He's my only enemy, but he's still in prison. Would he be that mean?

Before too long, Jake opened the front door of the house with Pop trailing right behind him.

"So, what are you ladies up to? Looks like you may have lost your best friend," Jake said bending to give Carrie a kiss.

"Jake, there's a box on the back porch. You better take a look," Mary said.

Jake and Pop went to look at the box, then came back in the house looking angry more than afraid.

"When I find out who did this, they will pay. That's not even a funny joke, it's a sick one," Jake said, putting his arms around Carrie. "Don't worry honey it's just some sicko out there. I'll take it into Williams and see if he can work on the postmark; however with no return address it may be rather hard to find out who sent it," he said.

"Jake, it must have been Alex. Who else could do that?" Carrie shuddered as she remembered the dead rat again. Then she thought of Alex. If he did do this, maybe he's more dangerous then she had ever thought.

"But he's still in prison I think. I'll talk to Brad and he can find out if he's out yet. His parole was this year."

"I didn't think he could leave Massachusetts." Carrie said. Jake! I can't go through this again, I tell you I think he did this, and maybe the phone calls too. Who knows?" Carrie exclaimed, getting more frantic by the minute.

Jake reached for the phone and called Brad. He filled him in on the package and the phone calls. Brad told Jake he would look into it and see where Alex Blane was at this time.

Several days passed during which Carrie seemed constantly on edge most of the time. Jo and Brad were coming out this weekend. Perhaps Brad would tell them something then. She had a funny feeling about the whole thing.

Brad and Jo arrived late Friday evening; Brad had been waiting for one phone call.

"So, do you have anything to tell us Brad?" Jake asked.

"Yes, Mr. Blane is still in prison, his parole comes up next month. They say he's a model prisoner, and was sure he would be getting out. He does have to stay in the state where he's released, so I think you can rest easy sis. Please try not to worry."

"Well! Then what about the box and the phone calls?" Carrie asked.

"I think we have all missed the point. Maybe someone else sent that box and made the calls. Jake you work with the law, do you have any enemies?" Brad asked.

"Not that I know of. Yeah, you're probably right Brad. Honey it's going to be just fine. Now how about a good game of rummy?" Jake opened a kitchen drawer and pulled out a deck of cards.

The next morning Jake saddled up both horses and he and Carrie, along with a packed lunch, rode off to the back of the farm. Since it was spring, the wild apple trees were starting to bud out. It was a nice warm spring day. As they rode out along the timberline, Jake pointed out a flock of geese flying north.

"Do you think they will stop at the pond?" Carrie sounded excited.

"Let's watch and if they circle, we can ride towards the pond and watch them." Jake turned his horse and watched.

Sure enough the birds did turn as if to be surveying the land, trying to find a proper place to rest and feed.

"I remember from year to year Bepo would put feed out by the pond, and then some of the farmers would come in to hunt. I always thought that was just awful. I could hear the gun shots from the farmhouse. "Look! There! See they are going to land in the field by the pond," she said, bringing her mare to a gallop.

They rode slowly watching the bird's circle and land in the field.

"There must be a hundred of them Jake."

"Well! Now Pop should be happy he has his birds." Jake laughed, stepping down off his horse. He helped Carrie down and took both reins in his hands and they walked quietly towards the pond, watching the geese.

"Let's have our lunch here in the gazebo and watch our new found birds," Jake said grinning at Carrie.

The two of them sat eating their lunch, watching the birds settle down. The two swans on the pond seemed to be frightened and swam close by the gazebo.

"Do you think we better pen up the swans, Jake?"

"I guess it wouldn't hurt. The geese will probably be gone by early morning," he said as he put his arm around Carrie.

"Hey! You know what Mrs. Thompson, this is the first time we've been out like this in a long time. I had hoped..."

"Well, later my dear. I think we better take care of Pop's flock."

Jake seemed a little disappointed at Carrie. She wasn't like this before she was pregnant. He felt a little put off, since she seemed cold of as late.

They unsaddled the horses and curry combed them and gave each horse some grain and then Jake penned up the swans. Carrie and Jake walked back to the house not saying a word to each other.

The days moved along. One afternoon the sky looked like it was going to burst open. The wind was picking up and the clouds were rolling in as a storm front cleared the coast range. Jake had invited Pop and Mary to have Sunday dinner with them. They sat watching the wind and the rain pour down; Oregon was well known for its spring rains and floods. The thunder let out a loud bang and both babies woke startled; Mary and Carrie disappeared to the bedroom to give comfort to two crying little infants.

Pop and Mary thought they should get back to their farms. With the rain beating down so hard and the wind howling, everyone knew that the power could go out at any moment.

"Now you give us a call when you two get home," Jake said. As they both walked out the door to Pop's truck, Jake and Carrie watched them drive down the lane and disappear out onto Roundtree Lane.

"Damn! I don't think I have ever seen a storm as bad as this one." Jake said.

"I better draw off some water in case the power fails," Carrie remarked. "Why haven't they called, Jake?"

"They will,"

Jake waited a few more minutes then he reached for the phone. The line was dead. It was getting dark and just then the lights flickered then went out

Carrie brought both babies into the living room and propped them up on the sofa, and Jake added more wood to the fire. It might be a long night.

Pop drove up into Mary's driveway and helped her into the house; he thought he better get on home to his place. Mary reached for the light switch.

"Well, I better get on home. I'll call from home and let the children know we're safe and sound. If you need me, give a call Mary," Pop turned as if to go and then looked back. Even the storm and the grey skies couldn't hide the concern he had in his eyes. "Now you stay in out of the storm, okay?" Pop said.

"Don't worry about me old man," she shot back. Since Pop had started to freely express his real feelings for Mary, it gave her a chance to be a little more guarded and to have some fun with it. "See you tomorrow," She said brightly before giving him a little peck on his cheek.

"Old man! Some day woman!" He laughed and turned and walked down the walk with the wind giving him a push.

Pop drove up his lane and parked his truck. The wind was still blowing hard. You could hear the oak limbs cracking and snapping.

Pop got out of his truck and started up the walk, at that moment he looked up to see a large oak limb falling, he tried to dodge it but he was not fast enough. He could feel a sharp pain in his lower back and left leg. Then he lost consciousness.

Jake started pacing the floor. Pop hadn't been able to call since the phone was dead but he had a gut feeling that something just wasn't right.

"Hon, I better go and check on Mary and Pop, since the phones are out. I'll see if they want to come back here, since this storm is really getting worse," Jake said giving Carrie a hug.

"Be careful Jake," Carrie said. "Will you leave Blackie here with us?"

"Sure thing," he said as he left.

He drove up to Mary's first, and found that she was fine, huddling up around her fire. Jake told her that he thought she should come back to the big house, and they would stop and get Pop on the way.

The two drove up the lane and saw Pop's truck.

"Gee! That's a big limb that fell," he told Mary.

"I think I better stay in the truck Jake. Go get your Pop."

Jake got out, walked to the steps then he saw Pop's feet showing out from under the tree limb.

"Oh my God! Pop can you hear me," he called desperately, trying to move the tree limb.

Mary saw what Jake was trying to do. She got out and pulled on the limb to help.

"Is he okay Jake, can you tell?"

"He's lying very still. I don't think we should move him. Go get some blankets, and hurry," Jake said as he felt for a pulse. It was there but weak.

"Come on old man, you hang in there. Don't you poop out on me now," Jake said rubbing his hand.

Mary returned with the blankets, and covered him up. Pop lay motionless.

"I'll go for help Mary. You stay with Pop. Try to keep him warm, and don't move him. When he wakes you tell him I've went after help. Do you understand me?" Jake said in a caring way.

"Now you watch out. That creek floods at the bridge. Go slow Jake," Mary said.

Jake drove down Roundtree Lane. As he reached the bridge, he could see all the water on the road. Mary was right – the creek was flooded. He drove slowly and he watched the water go over the running boards.

He backed the truck out and turned around, to drive back to the farmhouse. He got out and ran to the garage, took a canvas out and got back into the truck and drove back to the bridge. The water was even higher now. He took the canvas and draped it over the hood of the truck to protect the motor. Hopefully this would work and he would be able to drive through the water. He knew he had to get Doctor Reese.

Jake drove slowly with the water well up on the door of the cab. He drove across the bridge without any problems. He sped on into the village and stopped in front of Doctor

Reese's house. Jake told him about Pop. The Doctor gathered up his bag, and joined Jake in his truck.

Carrie was getting worried. It had been a good hour since Jake left. She added more logs on the fire, and got out another candle.

Ellen began to cry then Carol joined in; Blackie put his head on the sofa whining at both babies. Carrie reached for Ellen and started to feed her. Carol quieted down some, but kept on whimpering. All Carrie could think about was where Jake was.

When Jake arrived with the Doctor he could see Mary bending down by Pop, still talking to him. Doctor Reese got out his bag and checked for a heartbeat.

"We have got to get him inside if we can move him. Be very careful, Jake. He has a broken leg."

Jake picked up Pop and gently carried him into the house, then lay him down on his bed. He was moaning and trying to move.

"Hey! Pop take it easy now. You took on a tree limb outside. But the Doc is here to help you so you lay still." Jake moved back and let the Doctor step in.

Mary and Jake waited till the Doctor was through. Standing in the doorway, Jake looked at his watch, and he knew Carrie would be very worried by now as it was over two hours since he left the big house.

"I think we better move your father to a hospital as soon as this storm stops. He'll need an operation on that left leg. He took a pretty hard hit on his head too, but he is coming around. I gave him something for pain. If you can get us back to the village, I can have an ambulance waiting."

"The phones are out Doc," Jake said.

"Well, we need to get him to the clinic anyway."

"Can we put him in the back of the truck? I can put a mattress back there and then we can take him," Jake said.

"It just might work. We need something flat for him to lie on."

"Coming up Doc." Jake left the house again and came back with a sheet of plywood.

"Mary, Carrie will be out of her mind with worry. Do you think you can take Pop's truck and go to the big house and stay with her? I'll be back as soon as possible. Maybe the phones will be turned back on soon so I can call. Tell her not to worry about Pop. He's in good hands," Jake said all business like.

In times of crisis, Jake was at his best since his mind always worked in a methodical way. Then suddenly he added

"Tell her I love her okay." For a minute, Jake wondered if maybe he was the reason Carrie seemed so cold, like maybe he hadn't been paying her enough attention. His orderly mind was good for getting chores done around the farm but sometimes he forgot that his wife was his first responsibility.

Carrie fed both girls and sat thinking. What should I do? I can't take my babies out in this storm. Where is that Jake? Oh God, please let him be safe. She rubbed her hands together as she paced the floor.

Finally, Carrie saw Pop's truck driving slowly up to the big house. Carrie was worried when she saw Mary get out and rush to the door. Carrie met her there.

"Where's Jake? What's wrong? I'm out of my mind with worry!" Carrie couldn't stop bubbling over. She had tried to stay strong for the girls but she was comfortable letting it all out to Mary.

"Everything will be fine. There was an accident honey. Pop got home okay and as he was walking up the steps a huge limb broke off the big oak, and it fell on him."

"Where's Jake now?"

"He took Pop and the Doctor into the village to the clinic. They'll be taking him into the city as soon as the storm breaks. He needs surgery, honey. The Doctor said he should be just fine. Jake said he would call as soon as he could. He'd keep trying anyway."

The two women sat waiting for the phone to ring. Both babies were sleeping soundly and the storm had died down. The rain had stopped but even so the power was still out. They kept a fire built in the fireplace. Mannie and Rosa came up to the big house to see if all was okay. Carrie filled them in on the accident; it was five in the morning when the phone finally rang.

"Carrie, it's Jake."

Just hearing his voice suddenly made Carrie realize how much fear she had been holding back. She started sobbing into the phone. "Oh Honey! I've been worried sick, how is Pop?"

"He had surgery. He's going to be fine, and will be here for a couple of days. I'm leaving now and will be home in about an hour. I just wanted you to know."

"Thank God you're alright Jake. I've been so worried. Are you okay?"

"Sure, I'm okay. Just a little tired," Jake said but his voice betrayed something more. The whole incident with Pop had scared him more than he wanted to admit. He always thought of his Pop as invincible and now he realized how fragile and old the man really was.

The following Monday, Jake and Carrie drove to the city and picked up Pop. Mary insisted on going along. She wanted to take care of Pop and she offered to stay at his house. Jake rented a wheel chair so Pop could get around the house.

Back home, Jake and Carrie sat in front of the fire; the house was so quiet. The babies were sleeping soundly and Blackie was lying in front of the fire.

"I remember other nights in front of the fire like this," Jake said. He had love in his voice. "Don't you Carrie?"

"Yes. I do. I'm sorry I haven't been a loving wife of late; it's just the babies and the feedings. I do feel bad Jake." Carrie leaned over to kiss him.

"Well, sometimes it feels like I have to stand in line. Still, I know I can get distracted with all the things that need to get done around the farm myself. Maybe we both need to make a pledge to make more time for each other."

"What if we kind of make up for lost time right now, here in front of this fire?"

"Come here, little lady," Jake said tenderly, reaching for her buttons.

Chapter Twenty

Alex walked out of the prison with his head high, smiling as he walked to the taxi. He had the driver drop him off at his bank. Alex walked up to the window and showed his identification and closed out his savings account.

He thought he had made a pretty good deal on the used car; it was only five years old. The next stop would be his old apartment building; he knew his landlord had probably sold most of his things.

"Well, if it isn't Mr. Blane" the manager said.

"Sure is. In the flesh," Alex said walking into the office." So did you save any of my stuff or did you sell it all?"

"Well, I got my money for the last month's rent and there was even a box or two left over," he remarked.

Alex took the boxes and threw them in the trunk of the car. He didn't look back as he headed right for the interstate highway and headed west.

Alex opened the windows in the car and let the fresh air hit his face. The feeling of freedom was something he had been looking forward to. He was on his way to Oregon, parole officer or not. Nothing would stop him now.

His first stop was to see a man just over the state line. He was told how to get a new name and identification. No one would know where he was, and with a little dye on the hair and maybe a beard no one would recognize him. Long hair was in so he would hold up for about a month somewhere down the road, maybe in the next three states or so. He had to think all this out.

He stayed in a motel in Chicago for about a week and then moved on. His plan was to be in Oregon by the end of August, find a job in Portland on a newspaper maybe as a copy boy. No one would ever think he would take a job like that. Then he would look the farm country over, maybe Oak Valley and look up his old girlfriend Carrie Roundtree.

His new name was Allen Carpenter. He was from Reno, Nevada. Now his hair was light blond and he had a reddish beard. Alex walked with a stiff leg; he had practiced this walk for a long time, he even would wear a brace on his left leg. He had to leave Alex Blane behind in Boston. He was now Allen Carpenter.

It was easy getting a job at one of the largest newspapers in Portland. He rented a small apartment in the downtown low rent district. He fit in real well with all the hippies, his long hair and all.

One Sunday he got a map of Oregon and drove out of the city. He didn't have any trouble finding Oak Valley. It was a hot summer day and he stopped in at the café and sat down at the counter. Ida came over to him and left a menu.

"Hi stranger. What brings you to our little village?" she asked.

"Oh, I'm new in the city, just wanted to see the country. I've heard a lot about this valley," he said.

"So what can I get you?" Ida asked.

"How about a good hamburger with a large cut of onion on it?"

"Coming right up."

Alex sat there looking around. Some old men were sitting at the booth by the window and he could overhear them talking.

"It sure didn't take Jake long to make the move on that poor little girl."

"Yeah. Well they make a nice couple if you ask me. You heard they had a set of twins didn't you?" the older man said.

Alex turned at that remark and looked right at them. Carrie did get married, and even had babies, and twins no less. Damn her and that farmer, he thought.

"Here you go sir," Ida said handing him his order.

"Hey, what do they grow around here anyway?" Alex asked.

"Well, grapes and grain," she said.

"Really. I couldn't help over hearing those two men, they said someone had a set of twins."

"Yeah, a friend of mine Carrie Roundtree. I mean Thompson. I went to school with her. Why?"

"Oh, just because I'm a twin. I guess that's why I asked, you don't hear of too many," he said.

"Well, Carrie and Jake have two farms and a big new house. I guess they are doing pretty well. They even named a lane after the Roundtree's," Ida said.

"Gee, I better get going. Need to head back to the city," Alex said while looking at his watch. "Thanks for the good lunch," he said as he paid Ida and smiled at her and left. Ida stood watching the stranger leave, then thought perhaps she said too much about Carrie and Jake she frowned and went on about her work.

Alex drove around the village till he noticed the sign, Roundtree Lane. So this is where you live Carrie, maybe I better take a drive down this road and look it over.

It didn't take him long to find the big oak with the name on it. He could see the old farmhouse from the road. He drove on by, noticing the large wheat field next to another old run down house. He traveled on down the road past all the vineyards. He had never seen so many grapes. He noticed a log home beyond one vineyard. Pretty neat, he thought.

He turned the car around and headed back to the city. He had an idea and wanted to put his plan to work.

The next day at work he saw Jo. This was a real surprise. What a test. He stopped in his tracks wondering if she might know him. She looked right at him when she called for a copyboy, smiled at him and told him to take some papers to the front office. Alex was very pleased with his disguise. If anyone would recognize him it should have been Jo Hamilton.

So, Jo moved to Portland. Strange running into her here. That must be why she didn't ever come to see me. I did think she was a friend; oh well, I guess she wasn't that good of one. So now I just might have to be a little more careful or make my move sooner.

He lay on his bed; the August heat was getting to him. He had to put his plan into motion.

Chapter Twenty One

The heat was stifling for Carrie. She was happy not to be nursing the babies. The twins now being just over six months old at least now Carrie had some free time. The days on the farm seem to get longer with all the work to be done. August was one of the busiest months of the year. Jake and Mannie had all the wheat swathed and waiting to get trashed.

The vineyard was ready for picking and the weather had rushed the ripening fruit. The vines hung heavy to the ground.

Carrie would get up at four in the morning, plan her meals for the day and give the babies their bath. Then she would take both girls to the barn for a morning of work taking care of the chores now so Jake could concentrate on the farm duties.

In the late afternoon she would take the twins to the gazebo for their nap. Sometimes she would find time to read or just sit and relax watching the swans swim gracefully over the water. Jake would be dead tired when he came in at night. Farm work was very hard during the harvest. The combines had arrived and they would start working in the field next to Mary's farm first thing in the morning.

This day the twins were very cranky so Carrie walked up to the house from the pond, set them in their playpen and started to make some lemonade. The phone rang.

"Hello."

The line went dead. Well that's something, she thought. No one on the line. Could it be Alex?

Jake walked up the steps of the deck at dark, wiping his forehead from the heat. Carrie brought him a cold glass of lemonade and sat down next to him.

"Long day?" Carrie asked handing him his glass.

"Yep and a hot one at that. Tomorrow we should get half the wheat field in and then Monday Pop says we will have to start picking the grapes. Two more days and they will be ready." Jake took a big swallow of lemonade and wiped his forehead again, though this time he did it in anticipation of the work that was still to come. "So how was your day hon?" Jake said leaning towards her on his elbow.

"Those two daughters of yours kept me busy. I did get the horse stall cleaned, while they sat propped up against a grain sack. They are so cute Jake; those little outfits Mary made are so precious."

"Yeah, those little darlings are sure growing up fast. Did you notice Ellen? She's trying to talk," Jake said with a happy little giggle.

"Jake, really?"

"Okay, I know I'm rushing it a bit," he said smiling.

"Do you have something for me to eat?"

"Yes dear, come on in and wash up and I will warm it up," Carrie said getting up and opening the door.

Jake ate his dinner, and leaned back in his chair and fell asleep. Mary was about to turn off her lights when she heard her hounds barking. She looked out the window and noticed a car parked at the end of her road. Someone must be having some trouble she thought. She didn't recognize the car. What on earth is that man doing, she thought as she saw him walking around the car. It looked as if he threw something in the field.

Mary opened her door and started to walk out to the road. Her hounds were barking fiercely. Just then she saw something fly through the air. It was a torch.

"Hey! Hey you! "What do you think you are doing? Are you crazy?" She yelled.

As soon as she yelled the man turned towards her, then ran to get in his car and sped off throwing gravel everywhere.

Mary could see that he had a beard and long hair. She looked to see if she could see the license plate but couldn't make it out, but she did know what kind of car it was. A brown Volkswagen.

The fire had started and the flames were gaining. She best call for help. At first she thought she might be able to put it out but then she heard a boom. She ran back to the house and made a call.

The phone rang waking Jake.

"What! Mary slow down, what did you say?"

"Your wheat field is on fire Jake! I saw this man, and he started it. I'll call on some neighbors." She hung up quickly.

"Carrie," Jake called.

"Call Pop, we have something big here, our wheat field is on fire. I'm going to the barn to wet down some sacks." He hurried out the door.

Carrie stood there in shock, trying to comprehend what Jake had just said. She called Pop, and then the volunteer fire department in the village. She ran to the outside deck to see if she could see the fire. The flames were as tall as Mary's house and heading towards the old farmhouse. Carrie was very frightened.

She reached for her babies, holding them close to her body. The wind was blowing from the South. She didn't know what to do to help but she knew she had to stay with the babies. Just then she saw Mannie running towards her.

"The fire! It's coming our way now. If it gets to close, you leave here Miss Carrie okay," Mannie said with fear in his voice.

He ran to the barn for shovels and threw them into the back of his old truck and drove straight away through the wheat field.

Carrie could see that there were headlights coming from town and she could hear the siren from the fire truck. People were coming from all directions to help. They formed a line with wet gunnysacks and they beat at the flames.

Jake came back to the barn and started the tractor and hooked up the plow. He then made a fire line around the old farmhouse. The fire was getting away from them. He could hardly see and the smoke was choking him. Tears ran down his face from the smoke. He had to try to save the house. This fire had to be stopped.

The fire jumped the line and sparks were landing on the woodshed. Mannie and several men were working to save it, but it was too late. The woodshed and back porch were burning. They poured water on the house. They let the woodshed burn, and they kept the water on the house. Finally the house would be safe.

Carrie stood on the deck watching. If only that wind would die down, she thought. The smoke was unbearable. She closed all the windows and doors in the house and waited.

Jake finished the fire line around the old farmhouse. Just then the wind shifted and the fire was heading right for the new vineyard. He jumped on the tractor and started towards the fence row.

The fire was very hot and the smoke was so heavy, he was coughing and choking. The flames were coming over the top of the plow and then flames were on top of him. Jake jumped clear of the tractor, his shirt on fire, and he lay on the ground rolling over and over to put it out, then he made his way towards the house to have Carrie and the babies pack up.

Jake knew if the fire got past the new vineyard it might take the new house as well as the sheep barn and the timber. They had to get it under control somehow. People were coming from all corners of the county. They brought shovels and water barrels and they worked side by side.

Jake reached the deck and Carrie ran to him.

"Jake, you're hurt! Oh my God Jake! Your back! It's burned and where is your shirt?

"I had to jump off the tractor. I believe they are both gone. That is the hottest fire. Look! I think it is dying down,

Carrie. All these folks they all came out, even Mr. Temple had a shovel in his hand. I can't believe it. I have to go back." He said.

"No! Jake Thompson, you're hurt. You're back is blistered."

Just then Pop drove up, still on crutches, and made his way to the deck. "Looks like it's under control son. That could have taken everything out. These neighbors of ours, they all came to our rescue. Looks like half the wheat is gone, but your vineyard is okay Carrie," he said.

The smoldering wheat field was darkened and the men started to leave. Several stopped by the farmhouse. Jake and Carrie thanked them all and were so grateful they had such wonderful neighbors. The fire was out.

Alex looked out his mirror. He could see the night sky, lit up like the Fourth of July. He was so proud of himself, he was laughing out loud. He noticed all the headlights coming at him. The whole damn town was on it's way to Carrie's farm, so no one was looking for him. He drove right through the village, and headed towards the city.

Mary got out of her car and walked up the steps of the big house.

"Is everyone here okay?"

"My, if it hadn't been for you Mary, no telling what would have happened. And all these fine folks that helped. I'm amazed," Jake said.

"Wow! Jake your back is really blistered. Here let me help you," Carrie said, while reaching for some bandages.

Doctor Reese drove up; he had heard that Jake was hurt. He took his bag in his hand and made his way to the front door.

"Well, Jake I hear you saved the old house. You were pretty brave driving that plow through the fire like that. You're lucky to be alive," he said, looking at Carrie.

"Just do your job Doc. No need to frighten my ladies here," Jake said.

"Well, it's going to hurt for awhile Jake. Keep this medicine on your back and if the pain is too much, have Carrie put ice packs on your back. You have first degree burns, and it will be painful for a few days," the Doctor said while he closed up his bag.

Jake and Carrie watched the trucks and the fire truck leave and go back towards the village. Then Doctor Reece left. Mary and Pop stood by arm in arm.

"Well, what a night folks. What say we turn in? I think I'm very tired," Jake said.

"I thought you might like to know what I saw Jake," Mary said.

"Not tonight Mary, I can't. I have to get off my feet before I pass out." Jake walked towards the bedroom with Carrie behind him.

"Well! I saw who did it."

"What did you say woman!" Pop said.

"Well, sure. A man in one of those Volkswagen things, it was brown, he even had long hair and a beard." She said pointing her finger at him.

"Wait here." Pop entered the bedroom as Jake was trying to get comfortable. Carrie turned.

"What is it Pop?"

"Mary just told me she saw someone set the field on fire. Did you know that Jake?" He asked.

"Damn it, I remember her saying something about it, but I was so involved in the fire and getting it out...You better call Williams, Pop, and have him come out here. He won't like it because it's so late, but he better hear what ever Mary can tell him."

"Sure will, son. I will do that right now," he said as he left the room.

"Now Jake, you rest now honey. Does it hurt very badly?" Carrie asked.

"I'm just so tired," he said as he drifted off in a sound sleep.

Carrie stood there looking at her husband, then leaned over and covered him. I feel so very lucky, she thought. Tonight could have been so much worse. Thank you God in heaven for being with my Jake and all our good neighbors. She prayed. Carrie tiptoed as she left the room where Jake slept so soundly.

"So! Mary, how are you? I heard someone say that you helped too."

"You know, I was so mad that I just wanted to chase after that guy, but I knew I had to call you all and get help. Boy, if that fire would have gotten away from us the whole valley could have been at stake," she said pacing the floor.

"Did you really see what he looked like?" asked Carrie.

"Well, sorta. He was thin, had long hair and a beard. And an old beater, you know what the hippies drive, a Volkswagen. It was dark brown I think. You know he saw me too, and my boys were very upset. He looked right at me Carrie, and then he got in that thing and just sped off. I wonder why someone would do such a thing," Mary said as she sat next to Pop.

"Well, Williams will be here soon and you can tell him everything you know. Now think, Mary; did you see a license number or anything unusual?" Pop asked.

"No, I...well maybe. I think I heard a boom just as he left. And there was a dent in the driver's door. I could see it as he turned around in the light from the flames."

Carrie sat waiting for Williams with Pop and Mary. She looked at her watch. It was four in the morning. I wonder if it was Alex. Would he do this to me? And just think so many people could have been hurt. No, she thought, the man Mary saw, he had a beard and long hair. Well, he might have disguised himself. Why would he do this? I better call Brad.

Carrie called Brad and Jo and told them what had happened. Brad said he would be out as soon as he could. Carrie told Pop and Mary she wanted to go to the old house. It was starting to get daylight, so she left the twins in their care and walked down to the old house. It made her sad to see the blackened woodshed and porch. It was still smoky out and her eyes burned. Mannie and Rosa were trying to clean up, piling the burnt wood away from the house. She could have never imagined her wheat field so black and burnt to stubble.

"We can build a new porch and woodshed, Miss Carrie. I am so sorry. I tried to save it. It was bigger than I was," Mannie said.

"Yes it was Mannie, I'm very grateful to you, working so hard to save this old house. You know how much it means to me. I love it, it's part of me," Carrie said as her eyes welled up with tears.

"We saved some" Rosa said, embracing Carrie.

"Have you two have been up all night! You must get some rest now. Don't worry; things will be good again soon. Jake is resting and you should too."

"Oh, my! How is he?" Mannie asked.

"He will be all right. He collapsed from being so tired and then he had some burn blisters on his back. He said the tractor and plow were lost in the fire."

Carrie left Mannie and Rosa hoping they would get some rest. It had been a very long night for them all. As she walked, she turned to see Williams driving up the lane.

Williams asked Mary to tell what she saw. He wrote down all the information, then he told them that one of the neighbors had picked up a gas can by the edge of the burnt field. There wasn't much left of it; that must have been the bang that Mary heard.

"Whoever did this did it on purpose, and had it planned really well. It was a hot summer night with some wind. The grain field was a perfect way to start a fire. I don't think it was a firebug. This was set by someone who was holding a grudge," he said closing his tablet.

"It could have been Alex Blane. Williams, he was the man who hurt Carrie in Boston," Pop said.

"He was due to get out of prison a few months back," Carrie said wringing her hands together.

"I think I better pass this info on to the police in the City. You know if it is this Blane guy, he has broken parole and left the state. The FBI may be looking for him," Williams said.

Pop and Mary left and so did Williams. Carrie heard the twins as they were ready to start a new day. She got them up and gave them a bath and fed them. Jake heard Carrie and the twins from the bedroom; he got up and put on some pants, walked to the kitchen and poured himself some coffee.

"Good morning," Carrie said kissing Jake on the forehead.

"It's not so bad now I guess. I was really tired. Maybe a little too much smoke and all. I bet you're ready for a nap. Did you sleep any at all?"

"Nope, haven't even been to bed. I guess I just forgot how tired I was, but I am feeling it now. I went down and looked at the farmhouse. It's not too bad. Mannie said he could build a new woodshed and porch. Jake he really worked hard to save the house."

"I know he did. He is a fine man. So did Williams come out and talk to Mary?"

"Yes, he did. He's going to turn the information over to the city police. Jake do you think Alex could have done this?" Carrie asked reaching for a cup.

"I just don't know honey. Let's not cross that bridge yet. Now how about if you let me watch the twins and you take a nap?" Jake said putting his arms around her.

"I guess I am rather tired."

Brad and Jo had arrived by three. Brad had something very important to tell Jake and Carrie.

"It seems our Mr. Blane has jumped parole. The FBI is looking for him. They traced him to Chicago. He had bought a car."

"But Mary said she saw a Volkswagen," Carrie said.

"The description sure didn't fit Alex." Jake mentioned the long hair and beard. "Well, I wouldn't worry too much right now. Seems you have enough to think about. Are you going to rebuild the woodshed?"

"Yes, today we will. Pop and I need to get together and talk about the rest of the wheat. I'm not sure we can save it, and then the vineyard is coming on fast. So we have to put the work first. This fall after the harvest, we will rebuild."

Brad and Jake sat in the office talking about the fire and Alex. Jo couldn't keep her hands off the twins. She sat on the floor playing with them till they both fell asleep.

Chapter Twenty Two

Alex drove straight to his apartment, packed up his things and put them in his Volkswagen van. He figured that the parole officer had turned him in by now for not reporting in on his scheduled report date. He knew he should lay low now for some time.

Alex drove down to the Willamette Valley area and took highway twenty towards the mountains, he thought if he could get out of the city and somehow get rid of the van. He would look for work and lay low. He stopped in a small valley town at a car dealership and looked over the used cars. He found a Ford two-door coup that looked like it was in pretty good shape, the color he didn't care for but it was the best he could afford. He paid the difference and took his things and threw them in the back seat.

Alex drove up the mountain pass, thinking; *well, Carrie I hope you understood lesson number one, boy that fire was really bright, wow! I would of liked to have seen your face. I hope you were terrified and that neat farmer man of yours, I bet he had his work cut out for him.*

Now I just have to find some little hole in the wall for awhile. I need to paint this car, and change my appearance again, find a job, maybe a dishwasher, pumping gas, that would do. Then I can plan my return to Oak Valley and visit Carrie Roundtree for the last time.

Chapter Twenty Three

It took several weeks for everyone to settle down after the fire. What was left of the harvest had to be brought in, and the days were very long. Jake was right about the vineyard. It was a very good crop and Pop was moody because he wasn't doing his part in the vineyard. He could work about a half day and then he had to get off his leg. Mary had stayed with Pop while he healed from his broken leg and they were becoming closer as the days moved on.

Mary waited on Pop spoiling him and he took it all in. She was ahead in points in Gin Rummy, something for her to brag about 250 points, she could hold over his head.

October was upon them, and Mary decided to have a Halloween party for the children. She had made cute little pumpkin costumes for the twins and Buddy was invited also. She made her famous decorated cookies and home-made apple cider right from her own apple trees. Mary had become a grandmother for the very first time and loved every minute of it.

Now that the harvest was in, Jake and Mannie made plans to rebuild the woodshed and back porch of the old farmhouse. He gave instructions to Mannie to make sure to put washtubs on the back porch and to build a nice pantry for Rosa. As fall progressed, the leaves were turning their soft, gold-reddish colors and then dropping to the ground.

This was a part-time job in itself just keeping the leaves picked up.

Jake drove up to Pop's just in time for coffee. Jake could see the change in the air. It seemed crisp and cooler this morning. Jake wanted to take Pop for a walk through Carrie's vineyard. He wanted to show him something.

He and Pop stepped out of the truck and started to walk through the vineyard.

"Look here Pop. See all these plants? I do believe they will make it. They seem to have taken hold and are growing." He dug down in the dirt at one of the roots.

"Well, we might find a few, that might not make it. You know we had a very hot summer Jake, but spring will tell, and we can cut back the growth soon. The weather will change so we will be busy this winter pruning the old wood off. However Carrie's vineyard will be an easy one to work with."

While they were walking through the vineyard, Pop started to talk to Jake.

"I'm glad we came out for this here walk. I have something I want to run by you," Pop said stopping at the end of a row.

"Sure, what is it?" Jake asked, pulling his cap down.

"Well, you know that Mary and I have become pretty close. Uh, you know what I mean. It took me awhile son. She isn't one to get to know, you know it just takes time with that woman." After all I never thought I could have feelings for another woman, you know after your mother but it is so hard being alone.

"Well, I didn't want you to think I was doing something wrong, you know I loved your mother so very much and she will always be my first love," Pop said pacing through the dirt.

"Hey Pop take it easy. Carrie and I don't want you to be alone in life and if you and Mary have hit it off well, that's fine with me," Jake said patting his father on the back.

"Really? You don't mind if Mary and I carry on?"

"What do you mean carry on? Jake said looking at Pop kind of funny.

"You see we have been talking about her moving in with me. She has been there at the house most of the time anyway, and she could rent her house out," he said.

"Now Pop that's up to you and Mary. Have you thought about getting married?"

"Well, ah, maybe someday. We have kind of talked about it, but I wanted to see what you thought. I know how close you were to mom." Pop started to walk towards the big house.

"You know this is going to make my wife very happy. Carrie loves Mary like a mother and the twins adore her. She is their only grandma, you know," Jake said, reaching for the rail to the deck of the big house.

"Shall we tell Carrie then?" Pop asked.

"Sure why not?" Jake said smiling.

"Hey! Anyone home? We have company. Pop, Grandpa is here," Jake said calling out.

The twins were in their playpen and when they saw Pop they smiled big and laughed. Pop bent down and picked up Ellen and sat her on the floor and then reached for Carol. Carrie came down the stairs with linen in her arms.

"Well, so what have you two been up to?" She asked.

"We were out walking our vineyard. The plants look pretty good especially after that heat spell," Pop said.

"Carrie, Pop and I have been talking about something and he wants to tell you about it. Go ahead Pop."

"I guess I better just come out with it daughter. I was talking here with my son about Mary and me."

"Oh, I see. Yes Pop." Carrie looked at Jake smiling.

"Mary and I have become rather close and, well, I asked her to move in with me."

Carrie reached out to Pop, hugging him.

"I think that is just wonderful. Pop, I knew Mary had something on her mind. You see I can tell theses things. See we are a family." Carrie said.

Carrie reached for the phone and called Mary.

"Mary, I think you better come on over to the big house. Jake is opening a bottle of wine. I believe he wants to drink to something special," Carrie said.

"What is it girl?"

"Just come on up here, we're waiting for you!" Carrie said excitedly.

Mary's heart was pounding she was thinking perhaps Ed had told the children, Oh my I hope this goes well, she thought. A few minutes later, Mary entered the house and Pop greeted her.

"Woman, I have told the children about us."

"And," Mary said looking at him expectantly. "Mary, we think it is wonderful you and Pop being a couple. After all, you are already family," Carrie said embracing her.

"And I have told them about what you and I talked about. The moving in part," Pop said almost hesitantly.

"Well, you know I'm here most of the time cooking for this old man anyway."

"Hey! Watch who you're calling an old man," Pop remarked.

The four sat around playing with the twins. Jake even got the camera out and took several pictures.

That next week, the weather had really set in. There was early morning frost, and it was time to burn the piles of oak leaves. Mannie had the farmhouse all finished and painted before the holidays. Jake and Pop had finished some fence repairs and even had built some new ones.

Jake and Carrie bundled up the twins and took a walk to the pond. The wind was starting to blow.

"Jake, look! The ducks are back! I thought they had found a new home," Carrie said, pushing her hair out of her face.

The twins wanted to get down and play with them, and when Carrie wouldn't let them, they both started to cry. Jake spread a blanket on the floor of the gazebo and sat both the twins down.

"You know, we're going to have to build a fence around the pond soon. It won't be long and these two girls are going to be running about."

"Don't you think they better learn how to walk first," Carrie said laughing at him.

"Not my twins. I swear they will run first. Look at them Carrie. They are so beautiful, just like their mommy," Jake said taking Carol's hand. "I wanted to ask you something Carrie. Remember months ago, we talked about making the old barn into a winery?"

"Yes, I do. Are you thinking about it now this winter?" Carrie asked.

"Well, you know our harvest did very well. I do believe the farm has made good money this season," he said, standing up.

"Mannie and I will build a horse barn up on that knoll in back of the house, and we can build a split rail fence around it for the horses. Then we could start on the barn and add the tack room as we go. And within two years I believe we could start making our own wines."

"Oh, Jake do you think we could? Pop would be so happy, and I have the perfect name for our winery," Carrie said full of excitement.

"What, hon? It better be a good one."

"Let's call it BIG OAK WINERY."

"You know that's not bad. The big oak at the end of the lane. It does sound perfect."

The holidays were just a few weeks away. Jake and Carrie took the buggy and picked out a big tree. This would be a family tradition for sure, and they invited Fred and Kelly also. Brad and Jo had a trip planned to Canada for the holidays it was time Jo introduced Brad to her family. Pop and Mary announced that they were going to get married January First. They would just have the family and a very quite ceremony.

The New Year (1969) brought with it a snowstorm, along with ice; it was one of Oregon's worst winters. The power was off for several days, and this made farm life rather hard with the animals. Jake kept them in the barn locked up in their stalls, only to take them out in the barn lot for a short walk each day.

The twins were trying to stand and walk. Carrie and Jake were so very proud of their daughters.

"Well! Sure looks like the ice is melting. It's warmed up some," Pop said, as he stood looking out the window.

"It's been a cold winter so far," Mary said putting her arm in his.

"Well, as soon as it warms up some we can start on that horse barn. I think we should make sure we insulate it. You never know when we may have another one of these storms," he said.

Carrie lay in bed waiting to hear the cries of the twins. Jake cuddled close to her. "I like these cold mornings wife," he whispered, feeling her with his hand.

"My, my. What are you after husband?"

"I think we might just have time for, you know, a little loving," he said as he nibbled on her ear.

Carrie could feel the warmth coming into her face and the need to have her husband so they could be one.

"Carrie, I love you so much and you have made me so happy," Jake said as he made love to her with his gentleness.

"Oh. Mr. Thompson, you really know how to please me. We need to do this more often," Carrie said as she reached for her robe, to hurry to her children who needed her at that moment.

A black four-door car drove up Roundtree Lane stopping in front of the big house. Two men got out dressed in dark suits. They walked up on the deck looking around then knocked.

"Jake, will you get the door?" Carrie called from upstairs.

Jake made his way to the front of the house and opened the door. "Yes, what can I do for you?" he said looking at the car and noticing how these two gentlemen were dressed.

"Mr. Thompson." We are from the FBI," he said, taking his identification out of his pocket to show Jake.

"Yes, is there a problem?" Jake asked.

Carrie walked down the stairs to join Jake. "What is it Jake?" she asked.

"Mrs. Thompson, we would like to talk to you about a man by the name of Alex Blane," the agent stated.

"Yes, what about him?"

"Well, we are looking for him. We believe that he was the one that started your field on fire. His fingerprints were on a gas can. And we believe he may still be in Oregon," he said.

"Oh, no Jake," Carrie said looking at Jake.

"How can we help sir," Jake said motioning the two agents into the house.

"We want you to be on the lookout. He may come back, and we think he is laying low somewhere or he could be hiding in Canada. We really want you to be aware of this man," the agent said. Please let us know if you hear from him, like a phone call or mail. Just play it safe."

"Yes, gentlemen we will. You will be the first we call." Jake took the agents' card. The two men left and Jake and Carrie watched them drive away.

"Jake, I told you he would haunt me. What do we do now?" Carrie asked him. She shivered as she leaned against him.

"Now honey, don't worry. I'm not going to let anything happen to my family. We have protection, here come with me," he led Carrie to his office and opened a drawer to his desk. He took a key from a folder and unlocked a tin box. Inside was a gun.

"Jake I didn't know this was here."

"Well hon, it's my gun. I use it when I'm working as a Marshal. We will only leave it in a safe place and you and I will know where it is," Jake said as he took the gun and put it in the middle drawer of his desk.

Carrie was restless, thinking about Alex and living in fear. Carrie kept busy with the twins and made nice lunches and would take them out to the vineyard where Pop and Mannie were working. Jake was busy with the state getting the paper work started for the winery. They were told it could take up to a year or more for licensing. Several months passed, and the first of June the horse barn was finished. Rosa helped more and more with the twins now that they were walking. Carrie spent her free time working in her garden weeding. She loved fresh flowers for her table and she would always have plenty for Mary and Rosa too.

Jake and Pop had the plans for the winery and they were ready to start making some renovations on the barn. They had a goal set for the fall of the next year providing all the state paperwork would be in and approved. Carrie would start working on the milk- house. She wanted new paint and wallpaper, and shelving, and a new brick floor.

"Carrie, I received a letter in the mail today," Jake said as he sat at the table. "The state is having this grape association meeting and I think Pop and I better go, maybe even Mannie. Do you think you and Rosa would be here okay alone?" Jake asked.

"Yes, why not? If Alex really were around, don't you think he would have come months ago?"

"Anyway I should be home before dark. It's Monday afternoon in the city," Jake said.

Carrie and Jake sat around talking about the winery, and making plans.

Jake, Pop and Mannie left about noon the following Monday. Rosa came to the big house to stay with Carrie and the twins. It was a warm day out and stuffy. As the day progressed Carrie thought she would do the chores at the horse barn so when Jake got home it would be done. She told Rosa to stay in the house with the twins. It was getting dusk out and she really thought Jake would be home by now for some reason he was late. She made her way to the barn, closed the gate, and entered. She turned on the light in the front of the barn. The horses were very uneasy stomping around in their stalls, and she let them both out and started to clean each stall out. She thought she smelt smoke. She stood back thinking someone has been in here smoking a cigarette.

She turned just then as she heard something. She saw a glow in the corner of the barn. Someone was dragging on a cigarette.

Carrie's heart started to beat fast. She thought about Alex.

"Who is in here? Come out so I can see you?" Carrie said with fear in her voice.

"Okay, can you see me now?" Alex said as he moved out of the shadows.

"What are you doing in my barn, and who are you?"

"My, my Carrie! Can't you remember my voice?"

"Alex! Why, what are you doing here?" Carrie moved towards the door. Alex stepped in between her and the barn door. Blackie barked at Alex as he came through the door.

"Blackie stay," Carrie called at him.

"Put the dog in that room over there, NOW!" Alex ordered.

Carrie thought she better do what he said for now. She had to try to talk to him and maybe he would leave. She knew Jake would be home soon and she would have to wait it out.

Carrie took Blackie by the collar and put him in the tack room.

"Alex what are you doing here? Jake is due home at anytime. You better leave now. The FBI was here looking for you."

"I really don't care. I'm in so deep now, and I came here for a reason," he said moving towards Carrie.

"Please Alex; we can go to the house and talk? Let me help you," Carrie pleaded with him.

"No way. I came here for a reason Carrie. You sent me to prison and I don't forget easy."

"Did you set the fire Alex? And how about the phone calls?" Carrie asked.

"I thought that fire was really something. I could see the sky light up clear from the village as I drove out," Alex said.

Carrie noticed how poorly Alex looked. He had dyed his hair jet black and he had a scar on his face. She wouldn't have known him unless she had heard him talk. He moved closer to her and she moved up against the wall of the barn. Alex pinned her to the wall.

"Please Alex don't hurt me. I have two babies now and a wonderful life. You don't want to do this."

Alex took a piece of rope and tied her hands in back of her, and shoved her to the floor. Blackie was barking and carrying on like a wild animal. He couldn't get out of the tack room but all of a sudden he leaped through the window breaking the glass.

"How did you like the package I had sent to you?"

"You did that? But how?"

"I met this guy in the joint. He was coming to Seattle He mailed it for me. Boy I bet that was a ripe package." He laughed. He paced back and forth in front of Carrie.

Carrie worked her hands back and forth trying to get her hands free, but to no avail. She couldn't loosen the rope.

"I really don't want to hurt you Carrie, really. I just want to talk. Why did you have to dump me like that for all this? We could have had this too you know? I loved you Carrie, and you really hurt me."

"HURT! Alex you left me in an alley to die, you don't know what hurt is," Carrie said with hate in her voice.

"I'm sorry about that. I was drunk, you knew that. Why did you have to tell the police I was trying to kill you?"

"Because you just about did Alex. Think about it. Come on let me go. I'll help you okay," Carrie begged.

"No way. Just one more time honey," he said as he pulled at her clothes. Carrie screamed. Just then Blackie ran through the horse stall. He jumped on Alex grabbing his arm with his teeth and pulled Alex to the floor. Carrie struggled to get up and tried again to loosen the rope on her hands. Finally she slipped her hand free, reached for a pitch fork and pointed it at Alex.

"Down Blackie. Come here. Now Alex you get up slowly and stand still or I will tell my dog to go after you again."

"No please don't Carrie. This is all a joke. Honey I wouldn't hurt you, really you know that. Now give me the pitchfork."

"No way Alex," she said, pushing the fork in his ribs.

"Now I want you to move and walk to the big barn slowly Alex or Blackie will be on you, do you hear me!"

"Okay! I hear ya," he said, starting to walk towards the door.

"Now walk in front of me and go where I tell you, and remember Blackie is behind you, and I will stab you with this pitchfork if I have to so don't try anything funny."

They reached the milk house. The door was standing open. She pushed the fork in his back. He felt the pain of the fork and yelled out. He stepped into the milk house. Quickly, Carrie pulled the door shut and set the latch. She set the fork down and took a deep breath. She was trembling and a cold sweat came over her

"Let me out of here you bitch. I will kill you for this," Alex yelled, pounding on the door. Blackie barked at the sound of his voice.

There were no windows in the milk house. It was a stone block building and there was no way for Alex to get out. Carrie told Blackie to stay at the door while she went to the house to call for help.

Carrie ran to the big house out of breath. Calling for Rosa to stay with the twins, she turned to see Jake's truck.

He was home!

Carrie ran down the steps to meet Jake.

"Jake! He's here! Alex."

"What! Where? Are you all right?"

"I have him locked up in the milk house. Thanks to Blackie. Jake he saved me again." Carrie was shaking and the tears were running down her face.

"Here honey," Jake said and went right to his office. He handed her the card from the FBI agent, and told her to call them and Williams. He then walked straight to the milk house. Jake carried the gun in his hand.

Carrie made the calls. Pop was standing over Carrie giving her comfort. Mannie joined Jake at the milk house. When he arrived he heard this noise coming from inside milk house Alex was pounding on the door. Jake stood back opened the door. Alex was coming right at him. Jake grabbed him around the neck hit him hard on his jaw again and again. Jake let him go and he fell to the ground.

"No more man, I've had enough." Alex getting up unbalanced, with Jake holding on to him, his eyes were blackened and his lip was bleeding.

"Remember Mr. Blane, you fell real hard. Or the next time I will be the one coming after you. No one threatens my family," Jake said dragging him towards the house.

"Jake what did you do to him," Carrie asked.

"Oh, Mr. Blane here had a hard fall headfirst," Jake said.

"In my bottom desk drawer you will find some hand cuff. Will you get them please?" Jake asked. Jake took the handcuffs and cuffed Alex to the rail of his deck, and told him he would be staying there till someone came to get him. He kept his head down looking at the floor of the deck.

"You're not so tough now Mr. Blane. I'd say my wife and dog did a pretty good job. Wouldn't you Mr. Blane?" Jake said, smiling at Carrie.

"Jake he looks so sad. I feel sorry for him. He really is all messed up, isn't he," She said.

"Yes I'm afraid he is my dear, but I am so proud of you. Boy I hope you never get mad at me!"

"It was Blackie again Jake. He jumped through the tack room window."

"Come here boy, are you okay?" Jake checked the dog over. He had a few small cuts from the glass. Other than that he was fine and was still watching over Alex.

"You keep that dog away from me man. He ought to be shot." Alex called out.

"You're a very lucky man. Blackie could have really hurt you, Alex. You see, he's my wife's dog and he really loves my little lady." Jake put his arm around Carrie and led her into the house. He sat down with Carrie on the sofa and Rosa brought them both a glass of water. Carrie told Jake everything, and how happy she was that he was home, and now there would be an end to all this madness.

Chapter Twenty Four

Spring was in the air at the farm. Carrie could feel the cool wind upon her face as she walked towards the barn. She looked up and noticed the white fluffy clouds moving across the sky.

Carrie was lost in thought; *I am so grateful for this past winter, the snow, and cutting down the family holiday tree from our own timber. Christmas was so nice with my children and my devoted husband and Mary. Oh, I am so happy she knew Bepo, and now she is the grandma to Carol and Ellen I never dreamed she and Pop would really tie the knot. And what a nice wedding! Just the family and the pastor. To think Pop wanted to be married at the stroke of twelve on the New Year. What a romantic man! Thank you God for all my blessings and for this New Year here on the farm with my family. Dreams can be made here, I just know it. Jake will have his new winery and Pop and Mary will be happy in his home. It's so nice to have them close. I am so grateful. I knew you were with me through these past trying months, and Alex can't hurt me anymore. Jake and the girls, they fill my life with love.*

Carrie walked into the barn. "Come on Blackie let's go," she called to the dog. Blackie was on her heels; he followed her everywhere since the Alex incident in the barn.

Carrie let the horses out for a run then she cleaned out the stalls. She loved the smell of fresh straw and she leaned up against the wall looking around the inside of the barn.

She could remember the days when she helped milk the cows and she smiled as she thought of the times she would spray milk into the cat's mouths, right from the cow's teat. She laughed out loud and Blackie barked.

"Silly Blackie." Carrie fluffed his hair then bent down on one knee and drew his head to her and loved him.

"Boy! You are so special, looking after me like you do. Thank you," she said hugging the dog and then getting up and moving to the outside door of the barn. As she strolled around the barn lot, she saw the new buds on the apple trees. She walked over her garden spot. Soon Mannie could till the ground. Moving through the gate to the farmhouse she could see the crocus coming up and the leaves coming out on the lilac trees. Spring was really here she thought. She opened the door calling for Rosa.

"Hello Miss Carrie. Did you have a good walk?" Rosa said as she opened the door.

"Yes I did. To see the trees budding out! It won't be long now and Mannie and I can plant the garden." "Oh, yes and I hope I can help this year," Rosa said. "So how are my girls doing?"

"They should be waking up from their nap soon. They are so good Miss Carrie, I can't wait to have a family of my own."

"Well, maybe soon huh?" Carrie said smiling.

"Maybe." She took her hands and put them to her face.

"Rosa," Carrie said, looking at her.

"I will let you know soon. Will you go to the Doctor with me, Miss Carrie?"

"Yes, I would love to. Rosa do you think?"

"Yes I think so. Mannie does not know yet."

"I'll make an appointment for you and we can go in to see Doctor Reese together."

Carrie waited until the children woke then bundled them up and walked home to the big house. Carrie was delighted to help Rosa. They had been close friends ever since they painted and wallpapered the old house. She was truly a good friend.

Carrie watched the twins waddle along the walk, past the barn and to the house. They would stumble along wanting to pick up stones and throw them. They stood out in little overalls that matched. Mary was a great seamstress and loved to sew for the little girls. All of their clothes were identical.

Carrie helped the twins toddle up the stairs to the big house and then entered calling out.

"Daddy are you home?"

"Da, Da," called the twins, Carol bouncing into the large family room reaching for her favorite dolly. Ellen was tugging at her coat, trying to get it off. Carrie reached to help her.

Jake walked out of his office to greet his family. Smiling and picking up both twins with his strong arms, he bent down to give Carrie a kiss.

"Did you have a good walk Mommy?"

"Yes I did. And I got the stalls cleaned and let the mares out."

"That's good, I still have several hours of bookwork to do. Being president of the Wine Growers Association is more work than I thought."

As Carrie and Jake talked in the kitchen, Carol wandered to the front door. She could barely reach the doorknob standing on her tiptoes but she opened it and let the door close behind her. She toddled down the steps and walked towards the edge of the house.

Carrie made some lunch and then walked into the family room, picked up Ellen and then looked around for Carol. She went into the office and asked Jake.

"Do you have Carol in here?"

"No," he said looking up from his desk. Jake walked out from behind his desk and walked toward Carrie.

"She must be in the family room," he said calling her name.

Carrie and Jake walked through every room in the house looking for Carol; Jake took Ellen in his arms and put her in her room at the head of the stairs.

"Jake, where is Carol! She was right here when I came in. She was playing here on the floor by her toys."

"She has to be here in the house, she can't get outside," Jake said standing pushing his hair out of his face.

Carrie searched the house over again and no Carol. She was getting really worried and had an empty feeling in her stomach.

"Jake, we have to do something. She's not here. Oh my God! Do you think she might have opened the front door?"

Jake ran to the door, opened it and looked on the deck. No Carol. He then ran down the stairs calling her name, turning to Carrie. He called back; "Carrie, call Mannie and Pop. We have to find our baby. I'm going to go to the barn and look." He walked and then ran towards the barn then the pond came to mind. Could she have gone towards the pond? Oh, God in heaven please don't let my baby girl go towards the pond, he thought.

Carrie called Mannie and Pop. They were on their way because they knew they had to find Carol.

The pickup came to a stop and slid its wheels. Mannie got out and asked; "Where is Mr. Jake, Miss Carrie?"

"He went towards the barn. Please find her Mannie and hurry." Tears were running down Carrie's face as she held Ellen close to her body.

Mannie caught up with Jake and they both ran to the pond, Blackie running ahead of them sniffing around the pond just like he knew what he was looking for. But there was no Carol anywhere.

"Check the barn and I'll look in the chicken house."

"Mr. Jake do you think Carol could have gotten that far? She is so small, she must be at the house somewhere," Mannie said as she took off his hat and wiped his forehead.

Pop and Mary had arrived and were trying to calm Carrie down as she was a very worried mother Pop went outside and walked around the house. When he heard Blackie barking at the back of the house, Pop moved quickly toward the dog. Blackie was crawling under the back steps of the house and there lay little Carol all curled up sound asleep. Pop crawled under the steps, woke her and coaxed her to him. She crawled towards her grandfather and he picked her up in his arms holding her.

"Pa, Pa," Carol touched his face where big tears were running down his cheek.

"Oh baby girl, we couldn't find you, Pa Pa, loves you so," his voice broken he said as he walked towards the front of the house as Jake ran towards Pop.

"Carrie! We have her! Carrie heard those wonderful words her baby was safe, tears ran down her cheeks, reaching for her little daughter she said; "Oh baby, are you okay?" Jake took Carol from Pop and held her as he walked up the stairs and handed her to her mother.

"Thank God, oh thank you," Carrie said reaching for Carol.

"It was Blackie! He found her, under the back steps. She was taking a nap! Can you believe that dog!" Pop said appreciatively petting the dog.

"How did she get out of the house?" Mary asked.

"The front door I guess. It's time to get special locks and to build that fence around the pond," Jake said. They all sat in the family room relieved. The past hour was a nightmare no family wanted.

The weeks seemed to fly by. Spring was in full bloom and the twins couldn't get out of the house because Jake had installed gates everywhere. His two little girls would explore everything and would have to be watched for their every move.

Carrie took Rosa to see Dr. Reese and she was going to have a baby in the fall or early winter. Rosa was so happy she cried all the way home. It was time to tell Mannie that he was going to be a father.

Jake and Carrie lay in bed on a Sunday morning, the house was quiet.

"Wife, we need to talk about something," he said moving his hand over her breast.

"I'm listening husband."

"Well, I ah, the twins are about two now and I was wondering if it might be time for another baby?"

"Jake, I might as well tell you now. I was waiting till I saw the Doctor, but I think I'm already pregnant, she said smiling.

"Carrie that's wonderful! But not twins again, okay? Just a boy this time honey," Jake said laughing and pulling her on top of him, holding her so close.

At that moment two little girls came into the room and crawled up on the bed. A morning tradition. They rolled over their daddy and mommy, as Jake tickled each little child.

They got up and went into the kitchen. Jake played with the girls while Carrie stood in front of the stove making pancakes putting raisins in the batter to show a face.

The family sat eating when the phone rang.

"Hello."

"Hi Jake, it's Brad. Are you busy this weekend?"

"Not at all just the regular farm duties, really things are caught up for this time of the year, just waiting now for the harvest," Jake said as he stood up from the table.

"We thought we might come to the country for the weekend, and go riding."

"Hey that's great. Carrie and the twins will love to have you. So we will see you on Friday."

Carrie was delighted to have her brother visit. She had something she needed to talk over with Jake, and so after breakfast she joined him on the sofa.

"Jake, I would like to give Brad a parcel of land. Maybe down by the far timber on Roundtree Lane. I feel if should be his. After all Bepo was his grandfather also," Carrie said.

"Gee hon, it's your land and I do think Bepo would have liked that. It's a great idea. I believe there are about five acre's that would make a great place for a country home. I'm sure they would love it. Jo loves the farm life, and it would make a wonderful weekend getaway from the city," Jake said taking Carrie's hand in his.

"So then we can tell them this weekend. Oh Jake I'm so excited, and I feel so good about this," Carrie said getting up from the sofa.

"Let's have a family get together on Sunday. I can call Fred and Kelly too. I would love to see Buddy."

"Sounds like you have it all planned hon. I know how happy you are when you are around your friends. Let's ask Mannie and Rosa too. I feel they are family also," Jake said.

"Great, sounds like a fun weekend," Carrie said.

Jake went to the city and bought steaks and the biggest watermelon he could find. Carrie spent some time in the kitchen making fresh apple pies, then she sat the left over pie dough in front of the twins. They sat at the counter rolling out the dough, and making funny little cutouts and then Carrie would put them in the oven and bake them.

Friday was a beautiful day; Oregon was blessed with blooms from the fruit trees and sweetness filled the air.

Cool lemonade was always welcome on the front deck. Carrie would have a pitcher in the refrigerator at all times.

Brad and Jo went riding first thing on Saturday morning. They were gone several hours, returning with freshly picked wildflowers.

Pop, Mary and Fred and Kelly had arrived. Buddy loved sitting with the twins and helping them color in the books that grandma had brought. They all sat around the large table when Jake tapped a spoon on a glass.

"We are pleased and happy that we are here all together. Carrie has something she wants to say and I think so does Mannie." He motioned for Carrie.

"Well, I have something to give to somebody, and it's for my brother. Brad you didn't know our grandfather, but I think he would be very pleased for what I am about to do. Brad here is a paper. It is a deed to five acres, down by the big timber on Roundtree. I want you to have it, I hope you and Jo will be our neighbors, and that you can enjoy the country as much as we do," Carrie said handing the paper to Brad.

"Well Sis, I don't know what to say. Thank you, and yes we would love to be here in the country even if only on the weekends," he said looking at Jo.

"Carrie this is wonderful. You know I love it out here on the farm. Thank you so very much, this is really a great day," Jo said, hugging Carrie.

"Now Mannie what do you have to tell us?" Jake asked.

Rosa sat smiling and looking at Mannie, and then he got up and pushed his chair back.

"Mr. Jake and Miss Carrie I want to tell everyone that," he paused and smiled at Rosa and took her hand. "We are going to have a family soon."

Everyone clapped and got up and hugged Rosa and Mannie. He was truly family and now another baby was soon to be on the farm.

"Well, I better get my knitting needles out," Mary said, smiling at Rosa.

Fred and Jake were huddled together talking about the grape harvest; Jo was in the kitchen with Carrie.

"Carrie I feel bad I just have been so busy at work, and Brad is very busy with his practice. I miss you girlfriend," she said reaching for Carrie and embracing her.

"I know, I have to tell you about Carol and her nap under the porch," Carrie said taking a dishtowel and wiping a plate.

Carrie told Jo about Carol and how frightened they all were, and how thankful they were for Blackie, the wonder dog that always seems to come to Carrie's rescue.

"Gee Carrie, what if we had never found the letters in the attic? Things would be so different now," Jo said.

"I know, I've thought about that too, but I think my mother wanted us to find them don't you?" Carrie said handing her a plate to dry.

"Yes I do, it has to be, look what has taken place here on the farm," Jo said.

The phone rang and Jake got up to answer it. He stood there, listening. When a strange look came over his face, Brad noticed it right off and walked over to him.

"Thank you Williams, I really don't know what to say, I'll tell Carrie. I guess we won't have to worry about him anymore," Jake said. Then hung up the phone, turned around and looked at Brad.

"It's Alex Blane. He hung himself last night in his cell," Jake said.

Pop couldn't help but hear Jake. He and Mary both came into the room, as did Carrie and Jo.

"What it is Jake? You look as if someone has died," Carrie said.

Jake walked over to Carrie and put his arm around her. Then he turned to look at everyone.

"Carrie that was Williams, he had something to tell us. It seems Mr. Alex Blane has taken his own life."

Carrie put her hand over her mouth and let out a sigh.

"You mean he's dead?" Carrie replied.

"Yes hon, he is gone from our lives forever. We don't have to worry about Alex or where he is. It's over Carrie, for good." Jake took her in his arms and held her.

The farm was a very happy place to be. Two babies would soon be born, the grape harvest was in and the grain fields were plowed for the coming winter.

Fall was very colorful with the red and orange oak leaves. Carrie and Mannie's garden had produced well above what they thought it would. Rosa was busy canning green beans and Carrie made jam from the berries and grapes. Rosa was due any day with her baby, and Carrie was getting bigger and bigger, and was due December 20th. Another holiday was about to arrive; they would have the traditional ham for Thanksgiving and the big tom turkey for Christmas.

Rosa gave birth to a little boy on the twentieth of November, and Carrie had a son on Christmas day, a gift of the season that's for sure. Jake and Carrie named their baby boy Edward Bradley, after Pop and Brad.

The season's passed and the farm seemed to do nothing but prosper. The winery was in and Pop became a well-known wine maker in Oak Valley.

Carrie was truly very happy thinking back. How could I of ever sold this farm? She knew time would pass and soon her children would be going off to school.

Carrie and Jo worked weekends on the milk house making it into a gift and wine shop they picked very bright colors and special lighting with old antique's about. An old wine press stood off in a corner, and a collection of very old wine bottles and candle's. Pop had brought a few oak wine barrels for display.

Brad and Jo announced their engagement and now Jo would be a real sister. Little Eddie was Jakes shadow and followed him every where he could.

Jake and Carrie stood on the deck of the big house, with both girls standing by their side and Carrie holding little Eddie.

"This is truly our dream fulfilled Carrie. We couldn't ask for anything because we already have it all," Jake said looking down at his wife.

"Yes I know. Wouldn't it be wonderful if Bepo could know about us, our children and how his farm came back to life?"

"He does hon," Jake said.

"Sometimes when I walk to the barn I have visions that I see him in his overalls with the red hanky falling from his back pocket with that little girl calling after him; "Bepo, wait! Bepo, wait! It's me Carrie.

To my Grandmother Carrie and my Grandfather (Bepo)

Because you loved me. I have found
New joys that were not mine before:
New stars have lightened up my sky
With glories growing more and more.
Because you love me I can rise
To the heights of fame and realms of power:
Because you love me I may learn
The highest use of every hour.
Because you love me I can choose
To look through your dear eyes and see
Beyond the beauty of the Now
Far onward to Eternity.
Because you love me I can wait
With perfect patience well possessed:
Because you love me all my life
Is circled with unquestioned rest:
Yes, even Life and even Death
Is all unquestioned and all blest.

Author Unknown